*Outstanding I* **W9-DHN-254**

# THE NOVELS OF MARY JANE CLARK

### DANCING IN THE DARK

"With suspects aplenty, Clark's latest keeps readers on the edge of their seats . . . an eerie, surprising finale . . . haunting and entrancing."

*—Romantic Times BOOKclub Magazine*

"If you used to love Agatha Christie whodunits, then *Dancing in the Dark* is a book for you . . . the criminal could be anybody, and author Mary Jane Clark makes it fun to guess."

*—Pelican Press* (Sarasota, Florida)

"Clark's books are fun to read because she salts them with details about life in the fast lane at network news stations."

*—Orlando Sentinel*

"Clark pulls off a nice surprise at the close."

*—Kirkus Reviews*

"A fantastic who-done-it . . . plenty of action and lots of false leads so that readers won't guess who the real perpetrator is . . . when the audience discovers that person's identity, they will truly be shocked."

*—Midwest Book Review*

"A great summer read, one that draws you in and keeps you reading until the end."

*—Anniston Star*

### HIDE YOURSELF AWAY

"Clark has perfected the suspense novel, where in classic Christie fashion, everyone is a potential suspect."

*—Booklist*

*MORE . . .*

St. Martin's Paperbacks Titles by
**MARY JANE CLARK**

*Lights Out Tonight*

*Dancing in the Dark*

*Hide Yourself Away*

*Nowhere to Run*

*Nobody Knows*

*Close to You*

*Let Me Whisper in Your Ear*

*Do You Promise Not to Tell?*

*Do You Want to Know a Secret?*

# LIGHTS
# OUT
# TONIGHT

# MARY JANE
# CLARK

St. Martin's Paperbacks

This is a work of fiction. All of the characters, organizations, and events portrayed in this novel are either products of the author's imagination or are used fictitiously.

LIGHTS OUT TONIGHT

Copyright © 2006 by Mary Jane Clark.

Cover photo © Philip J. Brittan / Getty Images

All rights reserved.

For information address St. Martin's Press, 175 Fifth Avenue, New York, NY 10010.

Library of Congress Catalog Card Number: 2006043421

ISBN: 978-1-250-05776-1

Printed in the United States of America

St. Martin's Press hardcover edition / July 2006
St. Martin's Paperbacks edition / August 2007

St. Martin's Paperbacks are published by St. Martin's Press, 175 Fifth Avenue, New York, NY 10010.

P1

*For Elizabeth,*
*who raised the curtain on this story,*
*with much love, admiration, and joy*

# LIGHTS
# OUT
# TONIGHT

# PROLOGUE

*Sunday, July 30*

IT WAS JUST A few feet from the front door of the convenience store to the shiny, new car parked in the spot marked "handicapped." Two perfectly good legs strode to the vehicle and swung themselves inside. An able body leaned back against the car seat as two steady hands twisted the cap off a soda bottle and lifted it to a parched mouth. The first cold drink tasted good, but the second was ruined by the voice that came through the open window.

"Hey. Can't you read? The spot says 'handicapped.' " A lanky young man dressed in shorts, a black "I Love New York" T-shirt, and hiking boots stood beside the car and glared at the driver. Ignoring him didn't work.

"Hey. I'm talking to you."

"Give me a break, will you please?"

"It looks to me like you've already been given a break. All your body parts seem to be working amazingly well."

"Come on, Tommy," said a young woman in shorts and mud-caked tennis shoes who pulled at his shirtsleeve. "It's not worth it. Let's go."

"No, Amy. It's wrong, and I can't stand it when I see some lazy, inconsiderate idiot using a space meant to be there for someone who really needs it."

"Stop showing off for your girlfriend, will you, Sir Galahad? Mind your own business."

The car backed out of the parking space, leaving the indignant couple standing openmouthed. As the vehicle pulled away, the driver glanced in the rearview mirror.

Was that what it looked like? Was that stupid girl taking a picture with her cell phone? What if they were angry enough to go to the police with it? There would be a picture of the car. With the way technology was these days, they'd probably be able to enhance the image enough to make out the license plate. *Not good.*

*If the police came around now, it could ruin everything.*

TOMMY AND AMY DROVE by in their old yellow convertible, engrossed in conversation, oblivious to the fact they were being watched. Nor did either of them seem to realize they were being followed for the next few miles on the meandering country road.

The route was familiar. After the next farmhouse and barn, there would be no buildings for several miles. A long stretch of road dropped off sharply at one side. That would be the place to do it.

If they were so damned insistent on doing the right thing, why were they passing that joint back and forth? They were actually flaunting their marijuana smoking as they drove with the top down, secure in the knowledge that police cars, or any cars for that matter, on this road were few and far between. So much the better. If autopsies were done, they would show marijuana in the kids' systems, and that would be blamed for the accident.

The young man raised his arm, wrapped it around his girlfriend, and pulled her closer. Now was as good a time as any to floor the accelerator. The car sped toward the yellow convertible, catching up and ramming the already dented rear fender.

Tommy looked into his rearview mirror, and Amy twisted around to see what was happening. It took them just an instant to recognize their assailant. The young man held his middle finger up in anger and defiance as the car rammed into the yellow convertible again.

Gripping the steering wheel with both hands now, Tommy tried to maintain control, but the third collision pushed the convertible to the side of the road. The fourth sent it hurtling over the edge of the precipice.

The wheels were still spinning on the overturned convertible as the killer reached in to check Amy's and Tommy's pulses and retrieve the cell phone.

*Monday morning, July 31*

The body shop owner inspected the badly dented grill, two smashed headlights, and mangled fender.

"What did you hit?"

"Another car."

"Anybody hurt?"

The lie came easily. "No, thank goodness."

"I can have it ready for you at the end of the week."

"I need it sooner than that."

"Look around." The owner pointed to the other cars jammed into the parking lot.

"I'll pay extra. Name your price."

While the repairmen worked, there was time to go around the corner to a coffee shop and get some breakfast. Waiting for the scrambled eggs to come provided the opportunity to study the cell phone that had been in the dead girl's pocket. The last message had been sent not to a phone number but to an Internet address.

Brightlights999@hotmail.com.

It had been sent at 5:47 P.M. Had Amy managed to get off a message even as she and her boyfriend were being run off the road? Had she transmitted the picture of her attacker's car?

*Who was Brightlights?*

# WEDNESDAY

*August 2*

# CHAPTER 1

THE ALARM CLOCK SCREECHED, and Caroline squeezed her eyelids more tightly. It couldn't be time to get up already. She uttered a low groan as she turned her head to read the insistent green electronic numbers glowing from the clock on the nightstand. Four o'clock. She had to get up. In half an hour Rodney would be waiting downstairs.

Caroline willed herself to throw back the light down blanket and sit up on the edge of the queen-size bed. She sighed as she reached out to switch on the lamp, knowing she had herself to blame. If she had finished her review before she left the office yesterday, she could have had another two, or even three, hours of sleep now. Better yet, she could have taped the review in the afternoon and not have had to go in at all this morning. As it was, she was barely leaving herself enough time to compose something worthy of airing on *KEY to America*. The nation's highly rated morning news broadcast, in the person of its fanatical executive producer, Linus Nazareth, demanded her best. But a heated conversation with Linus was the reason she had bolted from the Broadcast Center yesterday before writing her review. Caroline had figured it was better to leave then than to say something she would regret.

The warm spray of the shower, usually so soothing, felt like an assault on her pale skin at this ungodly hour. Caroline braced herself as she bowed her head under the needles of water. She applied shampoo with conditioner, quickly worked it through her dark brown hair, and rinsed. Grabbing one towel and wrapping it turban-style around her head, she took another and moved it up and down her body. She didn't wipe the steam from the mirror. If her eyes and face were swollen from the crying she'd done last night, she didn't want to know, but she could thank Linus for it. She was angry with herself now for having let him get to her like that. She didn't even respect the guy. Linus Nazareth possessed none of the characteristics she valued, with the possible exception of being bright. But sometimes Caroline wondered if he really was all that smart. Perhaps his roaring directives and brash manners were his way of masking his insecurities.

*Enough time wasted on Linus Nazareth,* Caroline thought. She gathered up her toiletries and deposited them in her travel kit, which she then placed in the open suitcase lying on the bedroom floor. *Tonight I'll be with Nick.* She folded the lace nightgown, Nick's favorite, and carefully laid it on top of the pile of clothing. She was zipping the suitcase closed when she remembered the sandals Meg wanted her to bring up. Caroline walked down the hallway to her stepdaughter's bedroom and went to the double closet. She spotted the soft leather sandals she and Nick had bought for Meg when they'd been in Capri on their honeymoon. As Caroline bent down to get the sandals from the floor, she noticed a ziplock bag. She picked it up and immediately knew what she was seeing through the clear plastic.

Marijuana and rolling papers.

Her body tensed as she stared at the bag in her hands. What should she do? Confront Meg? Tell Nick? Caroline had no idea what her response should be. Either choice could blow up in her face. But this was a big problem, one that wasn't going to go away.

Conscious of the time, Caroline put the bag back where she had found it. For now, the bottom of the closet was as good a place as any to leave it. She scooped up the sandals and closed the closet door.

She walked back to the master bedroom. Dressing in the violet-colored blouse and white skirt she had laid out last night before she crawled into bed, Caroline slipped on a pair of high-heeled sandals, pulled a comb through her wet hair, grabbed her shoulder bag, and hurried out of the apartment, rolling her suitcase behind her. When the elevator doors slid open on the first floor, she looked across the lobby to the heavy glass doors. The driver was waiting at the curb outside.

"Mornin'." The man smiled as he opened the rear door of the dark blue sedan.

"Nice to see you again, Rodney. It's been a while. Thanks," said Caroline, getting into the backseat as the chauffeur took her suitcase and stashed it in the trunk. Most days—the days she was better organized and less rushed—Caroline took a taxi to work; but in the very early morning hours, it was better, safer, and more reliable to arrange for the car service. As the sedan traveled down Central Park West, Caroline heard the buzzing inside her bag and fumbled around until she found her cell phone.

"Hello?"

"Hey there, Sunshine. How's my girl?"

"Nick." Pleasure registered on Caroline's face as she leaned back against the faux leather seat. "What are you doing up?"

"I haven't gone to bed yet, my love. Remember, it's only one-thirty here."

"I couldn't forget for a second where you are, Nick, when I'm wishing you were here with me instead. But you didn't answer my question. What are you doing up?"

Caroline heard her husband sigh three thousand miles away. "The screenplay. The director wanted a change in that scene at the Laundromat, but I think I have it fixed now. It better be, anyway, because I'm not hanging around to do any more work on it. I'm determined to catch that flight out of LAX this afternoon. I can't wait to get there."

"Me, too." Caroline lowered her voice. "It seems like it's been forever."

"That's because it has been," Nick answered. "These three weeks have been an eternity. I miss you."

Caroline looked out the car window as the driver turned west on Sixty-third Street and then south on Columbus Avenue. "Well, when you've only been married for three months, three weeks is a long time. A fourth of our married life spent apart, Nick. What's wrong with that picture?"

"I know, I know," he said. "We are going to have to do something about that. But I couldn't get out of this trip, Sunshine. You said you understood."

"I do. But that doesn't mean I have to like it." Caroline watched as Lincoln Center passed by her window.

"Okay, it's settled. We both hate being apart." Nick laughed. "But it won't be long before I'm staring into those beautiful blue eyes of yours. And by the way, what are you doing up so early? I tried your cell thinking I'd leave a message before I turned in. I didn't expect you to answer."

"I've got a review in the second hour of the show, and I haven't even written it yet."

"Naughty girl. That doesn't sound like you. What happened?"

"At the last minute, Meg called from Warrenstown and asked if I could bring some things up when I came. That daughter of yours has very specific tastes, and I wanted to make sure I got her exactly what she wanted. It took some time." Caroline omitted telling Nick about the pot she'd found in his daughter's room. Nor did she mention the cutting criticism her boss had hurled her way yesterday. She knew she would tell him all about that when they were together. But she didn't want to get into a discussion about Linus over the phone.

"That was good of you, Caroline. I know how hard you're trying with Meg, and I so appreciate it, honey. She's bound to come around, sweetheart. But . . ." His voice trailed off.

"But I'm not her mother." Caroline finished the sentence for him. *And I never will be,* she thought as the sedan stopped across the street from the Broadcast Center.

Caroline knew that she could never take Meg's mother's place. She had lost her own mother at just about Meg's age from the same horrible disease. Caroline had started college with two parents and graduated an orphan. Pancreatic cancer took her mother when Caroline was a sophomore. A heart attack claimed her father eighteen months later. There still wasn't a day that went by that she didn't miss them. Caroline knew she always would.

So, in the months Caroline and Nick had dated and then married, she had understood the resentment Meg felt toward the woman who had taken her mother's place in her father's affections. She had been trying to be sensitive to Meg's emotions, excusing her moodiness and sarcasm, but she was becoming resentful herself. Dealing with a hostile stepchild was energy-sapping, and Caroline had found herself relieved when Meg left for Warrenstown for the summer. Now, having found the pot in Meg's closet, Caroline felt a new tension. It only compounded her anxiety about the possibility of losing her job.

# CHAPTER 2

NICK SCANNED THE WELL-STOCKED minibar and selected a tiny bottle of vodka from the refrigerator shelf. He poured the clear liquid over a few ice cubes and brought the glass to his lips. Walking across the hotel room, he took a seat in the comfortable armchair, kicked off his shoes, and picked up the carefully stacked pages he had placed on the coffee table. Even in the age of the computer, he made hard copies of everything he wrote. He'd learned his lesson the hard way. Hitting a key by mistake could wipe out a day's work.

Nick read through the pages again and was satisfied. He got up, walked over to the computer on the desk, and with a few clicks of the mouse, sent the reworked screenplay scene to the director. Then he returned to the minibar and took out another bottle of vodka. Going back to the armchair, Nick sat and stared at the images on the television screen.

This project had been a long, hard slog. He hoped these latest changes would be the last he'd have to make. At this point, he knew the movie that was being shot was far different from his original vision. Over the years, he'd gotten used to the reality that his screenplays could dramatically change at the whims of the director and the producers. He'd sold his screenplay and his talents, and in the end, though he tried to keep some artistic control, he had to accommodate changes if he wanted to see his work appear on the movie screen. That didn't mean he had to like it, though.

Two summers ago, when they'd had that first reading on the Warrenstown stage, he'd had such high hopes for this screenplay. The actors had read the lines just as he'd written them, without throwing in any of their own improvisations. It had been an hour and twenty minutes of pure bliss as he watched his work come to life in the voices of the skilled professionals. At the end of the reading, when he came up to take his writer's bow and answer questions from the audience, Nick had felt the deepest satisfaction. That was what he tried to remember, not all the unpleasantness and upheaval that had followed.

Swallowing the last of his drink, Nick put the glass next to the sink and went into the bedroom, unbuttoning his shirt as he walked. Emptying his pockets and tossing his wallet and some coins on the dresser, he looked at himself in the mirror that hung on the wall. *Looking good for forty-six,* he thought, though he acknowledged the last few years had taken their toll. His face was more lined, and there was much more white in his black hair now. In fact, white was predominant.

He turned to the side to get a profile view. Those trips to the gym were keeping a lot of the softness at bay, and the golf games ensured he had a tan that accentuated his blue eyes and white teeth. All in all, it was about as good as you could expect at this stage of the game.

Nick figured he was more than halfway through his life. He'd never really planned ahead, just trusted that things would work out and that he would be able to handle whatever came along. That strategy had served him nicely. He'd married well, had a child, built a successful career. Maggie had died, but within a year he'd met Caroline Enright at a movie premiere party.

He had been attracted to Caroline the moment she walked over and introduced herself. She'd been working for the newspaper then and wanted to know if she could schedule an interview with him. Nick had had no real desire to be interviewed, but he did want the chance to spend some time with the first woman who had interested him since Maggie died. He'd suggested lunch at the Four Seasons. As they sat beside the reflecting pool in the dining room, the conversation had quickly shifted from the movies to their personal lives. He'd told her about the amazingly short amount of time between Maggie's cancer diagnosis and her death. He'd shared that his college-age daughter was having a tough time of it.

Caroline had reached out across the table. "You must be having a hard time, too," she'd said, as she rested her hand on top of his. She had pulled her hand away, flustered, thinking that she might have made too forward a gesture. Nick supposed that was when he really fell for her.

Now, he had an accomplished and attractive new wife, twelve years his junior.

He got into bed, but sleep would not come.

In less than twenty-four hours, he'd be experiencing the rolling, green Berkshire Mountains with Caroline. He hadn't thought it was a good idea to return to Warrenstown last summer. There were things he didn't want to be reminded of. What had happened to Maggie after their summer there together, and what he'd done to her, weren't things Nick let himself think about.

# CHAPTER 3

AS THE STYLIST BLEW out her damp hair, Caroline held the ice pack against her swollen eyes. The makeup artist had begun to apply foundation to Caroline's face when Constance Young appeared in the doorway. Instantly, Caroline got up from the chair, deferring to the *KEY to America* host. "It's all yours, Constance," she said. "Mine can be finished later."

Wordlessly, Constance took her place in the chair. As Caroline left the room, she could feel the tension in the air. She knew the pressure was on Constance and Harry Granger. Ratings had slipped a bit lately, and while they were still strong, with millions of dollars at stake over each rating point, everybody on the *KTA* staff was feeling the heat, none more so than the hosts of the show and the executive producer.

Back in her small office, Caroline booted up her laptop and worked on the movie review. She was relieved, but not surprised, that she'd actually liked Belinda Winthrop's latest movie. It would have been uncomfortable interviewing and following the actress in the days ahead at the Warrenstown Summer Playhouse if she had just delivered a negative review. But the fact was, Caroline had enjoyed and appreciated just about every Belinda Winthrop film she had ever seen. And she had seen them all.

She felt as though she'd been following the career of

the Academy Award–winning actress forever. Fifteen years ago, when Caroline was nineteen, Belinda, at only twenty-three, had won an Oscar for her performance as Leslie Crosbie in a remake of the Bette Davis film *The Letter.* Nominated for the role in 1940, Davis had lost the Oscar to Ginger Rogers in *Kitty Foyle.* But Belinda had stunned critics and audiences alike and carried home her first gold statuette. Caroline had gone to see the movie five times. She couldn't begin to count how many hours she'd spent watching Belinda Winthrop's films since.

When other kids her age were going to the mall on Saturday afternoons, Caroline loved nothing more than enveloping herself in the darkness of a movie theater. In college, she began reviewing movies for the student newspaper, and she had parlayed her writing skills and thoughtful insights into jobs at successively larger urban newspapers until landing this spot as *KEY to America*'s film and theater critic. It had been the dream job, at least until Linus had gotten on her case.

Her mailbox was always overflowing with DVDs and, less common now, videocassettes of the latest film releases. She actually got paid for doing the thing that was her passion, watching movies. The fact that her opinion influenced the box-office habits of millions of Americans ensured her a steady stream of invitations to movie premieres, parties, and junkets as producers tried to win her over. But Caroline had stuck to the promise she'd made to herself at the beginning of her career. She was always going to tell the truth. Because of that, she had taken her fair share of irate phone calls, and even an occasional threat, from movie producers and agents angered over her reviews.

Caroline was being truthful in her review this morning, but even as she wrote it, she was aware that her boss probably wasn't going to like it. Linus would likely say it wasn't edgy enough. Translation: It wasn't smug, and it wasn't critical just for the sake of being critical.

"In this, Belinda Winthrop's thirty-second film, she

demonstrates once again why she is a superstar. She owns this role, just as she has owned almost every part she's ever been cast to play." Caroline continued reading the rest of the review out loud, knowing that how something reads silently isn't always how it sounds aloud. The tone had to be conversational, as if she were talking directly to the viewer.

"Sounds good. I'm going to try to get Mike to take me to see that this weekend if I can get a sitter for the twins." Annabelle Murphy, tall and suntanned, stood in the doorway. "I love Belinda Winthrop."

"I wish you were coming with me instead of seeing a Belinda Winthrop movie in New York," said Caroline as she tapped out a last line. "Then you could see her in person at the Warrenstown Summer Playhouse. And I would have an actual producer on this trip."

Annabelle stepped into the office. "Yeah, that would have been fun. Instead, I can hang around here and finish a two-part series on digital mammography." She frowned. "And the best part is, no one outside this building will ever know that I researched the subject, planned the shoot, screened the tapes, constructed and wrote the piece. They'll just hear and see Constance Young, and she'll get all the glory. Ah, the life of a producer."

"She may get all the glory, but she takes the heat as well, and I think it's really getting to her," Caroline observed. "I just was with her in makeup, and it doesn't look like it's going to be a good day. I know you two are good friends, so maybe I shouldn't be saying this, but I think the word *frosty* would describe the reception I got."

"May I?" Annabelle asked as she began to pull the door closed.

Caroline nodded.

Annabelle leaned with her back against the door. Her blue eyes glistened.

"Are you crying, Annabelle?"

"I guess so, but I don't know if it's out of hurt or anger. Except for Mike, Constance is my best friend. We've known each other for years. We met when I was a researcher and she was just starting as a reporter here."

Annabelle wiped away a tear that trickled down her freckled cheek before continuing. "When I left KEY News to have the twins, Constance stayed on, working her way up, volunteering for the stories none of the more seasoned correspondents wanted to do. She paid her dues until, finally, after pretty much total concentration on her career, she got the cohost spot in the morning. We've stayed friends all these years. Constance paved the way with Nazareth when I wanted to come back to work. She supported me when I was going through the tough time with Mike. She's been there for me, and now I want to be there for her when she needs help."

"That sounds right." Caroline wasn't sure what else to say.

"It *is* right," said Annabelle. "But she won't let me help. Constance keeps pushing me away. She never has time for lunch. She hasn't been returning my phone calls. When we do talk, she's irritable and has no patience. She was almost surly when I asked her to record the narration for the last piece we worked on. It's as if her whole personality has changed."

"Maybe you should find a time to pin her down so you can sit together and clear the air," said Caroline.

"Maybe. But at this point, I'm afraid that if I push things, it could damage our friendship forever," said Annabelle, shaking her head ruefully. "Constance is burning bridges with a lot of people. That's a huge mistake in this business."

# CHAPTER 4

"IN THIS, BELINDA WINTHROP'S thirty-second film, she demonstrates once again why she is a superstar. She owns this role, just as she has owned almost every part she's ever been cast to play." At least there was something to agree about with Caroline. Both of them were big Belinda Winthrop fans.

Meg listened to the rest of her stepmother's review before snapping off the portable television set. She pulled on a white T-shirt and gray yoga pants, and slid her feet into a pair of pink flip-flops. Twisting her long, jet-black hair into a bun, she secured it with a clip. Meg picked up the blue rubber mat and hurried from the tiny dorm room on the Warren College campus.

She was excused from morning warm-ups because she was assigned to run crew for *Devil in the Details*. There would be two rehearsals today—first tech and then dress—the last run-throughs before the opening. But Meg was going to exercise class anyway. It would make her feel better.

Meg hadn't slept well. She was dreading Caroline's arrival this afternoon. But even with the demands of her apprentice duties, Meg wouldn't be able to avoid her stepmother completely. She could make just so many excuses about having to be at the theater. The actual preview began at eight o'clock and would run until ten, but it was common for the cast, crew, and audience to go for a late supper afterward. If Caroline insisted that they go get something to eat, Meg was going to have to acquiesce. She had promised her father that she was going to try harder with Caroline. When she thought about it, which she tried not to, Meg supposed her real mother would want her to try harder with Caroline, too. But while Caroline may have taken her mother's place with her father, there was no way she was going to take her mother's place with Meg.

Striding across the campus lawn, Meg wished for the umpteenth time that it was her real mother who was going to be there tonight. Mom was the one who should be with Dad. Together they should be visiting their only child as she completed the Apprentice Program at the Warrenstown Summer Playhouse. They should be sharing Meg's excitement at being part of the first stage performance of the new play that so many people were talking about. They should have the thrill of watching their daughter spotlighted at the late-night cabaret this weekend. It wasn't fair that Maggie McGregor wasn't going to be here and, almost as bad, Caroline Enright McGregor was.

All through high school, mother and daughter had day-dreamed about how wonderful it would be if Meg, with her acting aspirations, could spend a summer at Warrenstown. The town and the college were named for the Revolutionary War leader James Warren, but the theater festival held on the college grounds emphasized his wife. Mercy Otis Warren was one of the most educated women of her time and wrote a number of plays.

With its prominent alumni and the proximity it provided to first-class theater professionals, the Warrenstown Summer Playhouse was one of the leading summer training programs in the country. Nearly seventy novice actors were chosen to do the least glamorous work at the festival, yet also have the opportunity to attend classes, observe the professionals at work, and audition for parts. Occasionally, an apprentice got a part in one of the Equity productions, which meant hundreds of paying customers would see him or her perform on the Main Stage. Far more likely, there might be a role in one of the skits and one-acts put on by directors in training, which mainly festival participants would see in a cafeteria or church.

After years of weekend classes at the Lee Strasberg Theatre Institute during high school and summer programs at the New York Film Academy and the Neighborhood Playhouse when Meg was on break from college, their dream was finally coming true. This was Meg's last summer before the college graduation on which her parents had insisted, and she was spending it at Warrenstown.

She stopped in the cafeteria to grab a banana and a container of orange juice before continuing on to the sports complex. She pulled open the plate-glass door and headed for the wrestling room. Why that room had been chosen for the apprentices to begin their day was a mystery to Meg. It was hot and smelly and gross.

When the apprentices had started the program in late June, they'd been informed that attendance at warm-ups was mandatory. As the summer wore on, however, attendance at the exercise classes had dwindled because the theater wannabes realized there were no consequences for missed sessions. This morning only about two dozen had shown up. Meg found a spot at the side to spread out her mat. Derek, one of the Equity actors, was standing at the front of the room, ready to lead the class.

As she got down on the floor and began to stretch, Meg wondered what her mother would think of her assignment. She decided that, once Mom had gotten over the fact that her daughter wasn't appearing onstage, she would be pleased at the idea of Meg helping Belinda Winthrop with her wardrobe each night. Mom, too, had been a big fan of the actress. Meg remembered her mother coming home after spending a week with Dad in Warrenstown two summers ago, raving about Belinda and her performance in *Treasure Trove,* a light comedy about a woman who wins the lottery, written by Daniel and Victoria Sterling.

That was before they knew that, by the time the next summer theater season rolled around, Mom would be dead. Meg often wondered how Mom would feel if she knew how quickly Dad had found someone to take her place. Though Meg was heartsick at the thought, she was glad her mother, at least, didn't know that her husband had remarried so quickly.

# CHAPTER 5

CAROLINE FINISHED DELIVERING HER review, and the broadcast went to commercial. As she unclipped her microphone and got up from the studio desk, Dr. Margo Gonzalez was waiting to take her place. Margo was the latest addition to the *KEY to America* family. A practicing psychiatrist, she had been hired to contribute her expertise on a range of stories that would interest morning viewers.

This was Margo's first week on the job, and Caroline sympathized with her. No matter how accomplished one was in her field of expertise, television had rules of its own. Caroline had keenly felt them when she came onboard six months ago. Working on newspapers, she'd been used to concentrating solely on the content of her work, the written words she used to express her opinions. But when she began at *KTA,* how she looked and how she sounded suddenly became extra important. The camera was unforgiving, picking up every stray hair, every extra pound. Caroline had learned to wear colors that would complement her on camera. She'd gotten into the habit of reviewing tapes of her reviews and critiquing her performances. She'd practiced setting her face in pleasant lines, analyzed her delivery, taken some private diction lessons.

"How's it going?" Caroline asked, passing the microphone to the slim redhead.

"I have new respect for all you guys," said Margo as

she took the mike. "You make it look so effortless. But it's not, is it?"

Caroline smiled. "Hang in there. It'll get easier, and if there's anything I can do to help, give me a call."


STANDING IN THE BACK of the studio, Caroline watched as Constance Young introduced the next segment. "Far too often, there are crime stories in the headlines which mention that the perpetrator has a mental disorder. Perhaps the most feared is the label *sociopath*. But what exactly is a sociopath, and how can we spot them? KEY News psychological expert Dr. Margo Gonzalez is here to explain."

Caroline turned to look at one of the monitors that dotted the edges of the studio to see how Margo looked on air. The camera wasn't doing her justice. She was much prettier in person.

"Good morning, Constance. Yes, sociopaths are feared, and justifiably so, because a person suffering from sociopathy has no conscience. Think about it, Constance. Not having any feeling of guilt or remorse, no concern for strangers, friends, or even family members. Imagine having no shame, no matter what kind of harmful or immoral thing you do."

"I don't think I *can* imagine that," said Constance.

Margo nodded. "Most of us can't. And that's part of the problem, too. Everyone assumes that all human beings have a conscience, so hiding the fact that you don't isn't hard. You're not confronted by others for your actions. Your cold-bloodedness is so completely out of most people's experience that almost no one even guesses at your condition . . . until it's too late."

"You mean when the crime takes place?" Constance asked.

"Sometimes. But even though we are accustomed to thinking of sociopaths as violent criminals, there's evi-

dence that about four percent of ordinary people have developed no conscience whatsoever."

"Wait a minute." Constance held up her hand. "You
mean that one in twenty-five people are secretly sociopaths? I find that very hard to believe."

"Well, it's a scary thing to wrap your mind around,
Constance. But yes, your neighbor, your boss, your
teacher, your colleague, your husband could be, and I em-
phasize *could be,* a sociopath."

"But wouldn't I be able to see that?"

"Not unless you knew what to look for, and even then,
it's difficult to be sure. But the clinical diagnosis of antiso-
cial personality disorder should be considered when
someone has three of these seven characteristics."

A graphic popped up on the television screen. Caroline
read along as Margo ticked off the list.

1. Failure to obey society's rules
2. Consistent irresponsibility
3. Impulsivity, failure to plan ahead
4. Reckless disregard for the safety of self or others
5. Irritability, aggressiveness
6. Deceitfulness, manipulativeness
7. Lack of remorse after hurting, mistreating, or stealing
   from another person

"Anything else we should be on the lookout for?" Constance asked.

"Sociopaths can be seductive, Constance. They can be
very charming and interesting. They may brag about
themselves in unrealistic terms. They'll take physical, financial, or legal risks just for the thrill of it. And they are
especially noted for their shallowness of emotion. They
have no trace of empathy and no real interest in bonding
with other human beings."

"Well, thank you, Dr. Gonzalez. You've given us a lot
to think about. But it's unnerving, to say the least, to think

that someone who's living as a seemingly normal member of the community or someone we think we're close to could, in reality, be a sociopath. Someone who can do anything at all and feel absolutely no guilt."

As the broadcast went to commercial, Caroline watched Margo Gonzalez take off her microphone and lean over to say something to Constance. The cohost barely looked up from her notes for the next segment, making no effort at congeniality.

Caroline found herself feeling sympathetic toward Margo. It was hard to be the new kid at school, and *KTA* could be a rough playground.

# CHAPTER 6

AS HE UNTANGLED THE rubber hose he had left strewn on the ground, Gus Oberon muttered to himself. A blue Mercedes convertible was sitting on the crushed stone driveway as it had every morning for the last three weeks, reminding him that Belinda Winthrop was on the property. He liked it much better when he had Curtains Up to himself. Luckily, Belinda had called to say she was coming up, giving Gus the chance to move out of the main house and back into his small apartment over the garage.

It was bad enough Belinda let that weird artist stay in the old carriage house year-round. But Remington Peters was harmless enough. The guy operated in his own little world—hardly venturing out during the day except to go into town to buy groceries or pick up his mail. And Gus had observed that lights out usually came early for Remington. He wasn't a threat, but Belinda was. She was too sharp for her own good.

The caretaker sprayed the pink coneflowers that grew along the base of the sprawling gray farmhouse. Thank goodness Belinda's busy schedule meant she had been coming up less and less frequently. She hadn't set her pedicured feet on the property since last summer, allowing him to really beef up his business over the past year. Without Belinda's prying eyes, Gus had the run of her 150-acre

Berkshire estate. The forest, the swamp, the meadow, the streams, and the spring-fed pond.

At the south end of the property, the small streams disappeared into a series of underground channels and caves carved over the millennia through the limestone bedrock. Gus had spent hours exploring those caves, and now he was putting them to productive use.

He turned the hose to the white geraniums planted in the window boxes, resenting this maintenance work. Every minute he spent pulling weeds and planting flowers and clipping shrubs and mowing grass and painting trim and sweeping dust and polishing floors and repairing fences and attending to all the other tasks required to keep up this place was time away from his far more lucrative pursuits. But keeping his job as the caretaker of Curtains Up was essential to his expanding business. He needed continued access to this property.

Squinting as the morning sun stung his eyes, Gus cupped his hand over his brow and looked up at the windows of Belinda's bedroom. The shades were still drawn, and he was sure they would stay that way for at least another hour. Those theater people went to bed late and got up even later. The longer Belinda stayed in bed, the better he liked it. When she finally did get up, he'd be anxious for her to drive over to the Playhouse again and take that playwright friend of hers with her.

Gus walked down the driveway and looked out over the meadow. Black-eyed Susans, oxeye daisies, yellow and orange hawkweed, and red clover decorated the acres of open land surrounded by pine trees, pin oaks, and giant maples. *Belinda has a gorgeous piece of property here,* thought Gus as he watched a monarch butterfly land on a daisy bush. This place sure was a far cry from the halfway house he'd lived in just before Belinda hired him. And Curtains Up was even farther from the penitentiary where he'd done three years for criminal possession of marijuana before that.

# CHAPTER 7

AFTER THEIR CONFRONTATION YESTERDAY, the absolute last thing Caroline wanted to do was talk to Linus Nazareth this morning, but she was going to make one last stab at getting a producer assigned to come to Warrenstown with her. She waited fifteen minutes after *KEY to America* went off the air for the morning, giving Linus time to get to his office from the *KTA* control room. She knocked on his open door.

The executive producer beckoned her inside. "Quite a review this morning, Caroline. Does Belinda Winthrop have you on her payroll or something?"

Caroline tried to take the remark with good humor. "Funny, Linus. That's funny."

"I'm only half joking, kiddo," said Linus, sitting behind his messy desk. "I always thought that last guy we had on the entertainment beat was in the studios' pocket. I wouldn't be surprised to hear he took kickbacks to pay for that coke habit of his."

Caroline wasn't about to get into a character assassination of her predecessor, but she was going to stand up for herself. "Look, Linus," she said. "Belinda Winthrop was terrific in the film. I'll give you the DVD, and you can see for yourself."

"Don't get all defensive on me, Caroline," said Linus, picking up the football he kept on his desk. "But see what

I mean? You could have been more provocative, more controversial. That review was a real valentine."

"You're paying me for my opinion, Linus. That's what I thought of the movie. It was good, very good. I'm supposed to say otherwise, just to be controversial?"

Linus frowned. "All I know is, I found the review too vanilla. There was nothing memorable about it. Look at the reviewers on the other nets. They get in some real zingers."

Caroline's hands clenched in the pockets of her skirt. "I'll try to spice things up next time, Linus, but there's only so much I'm comfortable doing," she said as she turned to walk out of the office. She didn't trust herself to continue the conversation. Yesterday's hurt was turning to anger.

"Hey, wait a minute," Linus called as she got to the doorway. "What did you come in to see me for?"

*Go for it,* she thought. "How about reconsidering and giving me a producer for this Warrenstown shoot?"

"Why would I want to do that?" Linus tossed the football in the air and caught it.

"Because it would contribute to a better story."

The executive producer leaned back in his chair, and the buttons on his blue oxford shirt strained against his stomach. "I would hope you'd be able to handle this assignment yourself, Caroline. You can tell the crew what to shoot and set up your own interviews, can't you?"

"Of course I can, Linus. But you know as well as I do that having a producer along will make things a lot easier. There's more to doing this story than making some appointments and figuring out shooting locations. In fact, I can get two, possibly three, stories out of this trip," she said, knowing that prospect would appeal to the ever-budget-conscious executive producer. "One on the Warrenstown Summer Playhouse, another on this new play that has all this Pulitzer buzz. *Devil in the Details* is being staged for the first time, and it will probably go on to Broadway and then to the movies. I've made arrangements to interview Belinda Winthrop about the play, and depending on what she says on tape, there might be enough to form the basis for a profile piece as well."

Linus put the football down and leaned forward, close enough for her to notice the pockmarks on his cheeks. "Look, Caroline. You haven't been in TV a long time, and you want the security of having someone along to support you, but I'm short on producers right now. It's summer. Some are on vacation, and the others are all assigned. I don't have anyone to send with you."

Caroline wondered if Linus was deliberately trying to shake her confidence by suggesting she wasn't a seasoned broadcasting veteran or if he had merely stated the blunt truth. Either way, the executive producer had effectively shut down further argument. If she kept lobbying for a producer, it could look like she wasn't confident in her ability to pull off this assignment.

As Caroline walked away from Linus's office, she was confused. If he thought she was such a neophyte, why was he letting her go to Warrenstown with no editorial backup? Did he actually have more confidence in her than she thought? Or did he really want her to fail so he could get rid of her?

# CHAPTER 8

THE LIGHT WAS BEAUTIFUL at this time of day as it streamed in through the huge picture window. Remington sighed as he looked out over the colorful meadow to the dark green mountains beyond. He loved the view from this old carriage house that Belinda had converted into a studio and loft guest quarters for him.

Remington still couldn't quite get over Belinda's generosity, though he expected guilt and pity might have had a little something to do with it. Why else would she have let him live here for the three years since the fire destroyed his studio in town? Belinda had never asked him how long he would be staying or even hinted that she wanted him to go. Remington was a dear and longtime friend, she said, and her place was his place.

*Friend.* That word was the kiss of death when you loved someone the way he loved Belinda. Remington knew with utter certainty that Belinda had no such romantic feeling for him. She had told him as much all those years ago, when they had both spent their first summer at the Playhouse—she, an extraordinarily talented young actress; he, a fledgling set designer. At summer's end, he'd poured out his heart to her. And, in return, she'd broken it.

Twenty years later, both of them had risen to prominence in their fields. The world knew well the path to glory of Belinda Winthrop. The award-winning movies she had starred in, the Broadway plays in which she'd had top billing. The tabloids had provided a steady stream of pictures over the years, documenting every change in hairstyle, every love affair. Remington had been hurt by each one. Finally, he'd stopped reading them, stopped watching television, where she would all too often appear, tracked down by shows like *Entertainment Tonight* and *The Insider.* Remington had even canceled his subscriptions to *The New York Times* and *The Berkshire Eagle,* never knowing when an article or picture of Belinda was going to turn up and upset him.

His spirit wounded by Belinda's rejection but enchanted by the serene, natural beauty of the Berkshires, Remington had decided to stay and pursue his painting after that first summer in Warrenstown. His first portrait of Belinda, done the winter after they parted, showed her in the role she had played that summer, the fiery Katharina in *The Taming of the Shrew.* The Ambrose Gallery had displayed it, though it wasn't for sale. Nor were any of the others he had painted over the years. Remington kept them for himself.

Standing before the large easel, he studied the nearly finished canvas he had been working on for so many months. He didn't need Belinda to sit for this portrait. He knew exactly how she looked now, just as he had known how she'd looked every one of the twenty years she had been coming to the Playhouse. He knew how her green eyes sparkled, how her full lips smiled, how one of her bottom teeth was just a bit crooked. He'd memorized the contours of her cheekbones and the straight line of her nose. He had studied her graceful neck and been jealous that it was only his painter's brush that had the chance to trace that neck down to Belinda's beautiful shoulders.

Remington pulled a white-bristled brush from a large wooden canister. No, he didn't need Belinda to sit for the portrait, but he did need to see her costumes for the play. Only then would he be able to do an accurate portrayal of her in her latest role. Only then would he be able to finish the latest in the Belinda Winthrop series.

# CHAPTER 9

CAROLINE WAS TRYING TO straighten up her office desk before she left for Warrenstown when the telephone rang.

"Caroline? This is Margo Gonzalez."

"Hi, Margo," she said, a bit surprised. "How are you?"

"I was wondering if you could have a cup of coffee with me."

Caroline glanced at her watch. "I'm leaving for Massachusetts in half an hour. If you think that's enough time, I can meet you in the cafeteria."

By the time Caroline took the elevator downstairs and followed the subterranean hallway that led to Station Break, Margo was waiting for her. They settled into one of the booths.

"Bet you didn't think you'd be hearing from me so soon," Margo said as she stirred the coffee in her Styrofoam cup. "Be careful about offering help to strangers."

Caroline smiled. There was something about Margo she liked right away. "Not at all. I'm glad you called. I remember when I started here. I didn't know a soul. It's stressful starting a new job, but I think trying to get a feel for all the unfamiliar people is the hardest part."

"That's why I called you, Caroline. I got the impression you'd be receptive to a novice just trying to get the lay of the land. How long have you been with KEY News anyway?"

"About six months."

"Like it?"

Caroline cocked her head to the side as she considered the question for a moment. "Well, it's different."

"Good answer," said Margo. "I've read your syndicated movie reviews for years and, when I've gone to see the films, found them to be pretty much on the money. But I'll bet writing for print is a lot different from writing for television."

Caroline nodded. "And the writing isn't the half of it. When I worked at the newspapers, I went to see the movie, I wrote the review. Period, the end. I didn't have to worry a whit about what I was going to wear or how my hair looked. The newspaper editors critiqued my reviews—not whether I was animated enough or needed more lipstick. Truth be told, I'm still not sure if this is the right fit for me. I'm hoping it will get easier in time."

"Well, it's good to hear that I'm not the only one who feels off balance," said Margo. She took a sip of her coffee. "If I were one of my own patients, I'd tell myself to relax and go with the flow, that I could be secure in knowing I have the professional credentials to handle this job. But, honestly, I had no idea how close the scrutiny would be. I can sense the eyes watching me."

Caroline laughed. "Try millions of eyes. But the ones that count the most are Linus Nazareth's. If you have him on your side, you've got it licked."

"And you've won Linus over, Caroline?"

"Hardly. He's really been on my case lately, but I guess the fact that I'm still on the show should mean something. Linus is great at keeping you on your guard. There hasn't been a day I've come to work that I've felt totally secure."

"And what about Constance Young?" asked Margo. "Is she always as friendly as she was today?"

"I noticed," said Caroline. "You can't take it personally if Constance ignores you. That's the way she is these days."

"These days?" Margo looked directly into Caroline's eyes.

Caroline nodded. "Yes. I gather she used to be a really nice person, but I haven't seen any of that since I've been here."

The talk turned to who was the most talented makeup artist and the best with hair. Caroline shared the name of the women's clothing shop on Fifty-seventh Street that, as far as she was concerned, carried the perfect suits for television. "Even my stepdaughter likes them."

"How old is she?" asked Margo.

"Twenty."

"How's that—?" Margo began to ask the question and then stopped.

"How's that going?" Caroline finished the sentence.

"Forgive me, Caroline. I'm so used to asking those types of questions, it just popped out."

"That's all right, Margo. I could actually use a sounding board." Caroline looked at the clock on the wall above the condiments counter. "Unfortunately, I don't have time now to go into detail, but let's just say Meg resents me, big-time, and last night I found some pot and rolling papers in her room. Now the question is, what do I do about it?"

# CHAPTER 10

AFTER EXERCISE CLASS, MEG walked back across campus, stopping at the theater to check the apprentices' bulletin board. Among the listings for guest speakers, daily schedules, and cabaret rehearsals, there was an announcement of a memorial service on Saturday afternoon for the two apprentices killed in the car accident. Anyone who wanted to speak at the service or help plan it was welcome.

Meg added her name to the sign-up sheet. As she walked back to her dorm, she thought about what she wanted to do for the memorial. Meg knew she had been Amy's closest friend at Warrenstown. They had liked each other right away, and in the six weeks they'd known each other, they'd found that they had much in common. Meg wanted to do something special for Amy. As for Tommy, Meg didn't know him that well, but Amy's happiness about her new boyfriend had been obvious.

Back in her room, Meg went straight to her desk and turned on her laptop. She reopened the first of the pictures Amy had sent her Sunday morning. Someone had taken a picture of Amy and Tommy standing in front of the Mt. Greylock visitors' center. The two of them were smiling, their arms around each other, oblivious to the fact that it was the last day of their lives.

Meg clicked to the next picture, sent just ten minutes after the first. It showed Tommy, baring his teeth in a mock snarl, standing beside a glass case. Meg zoomed in on the case and could see that Tommy was mimicking the expression on the stuffed bobcat on display. She recognized it from the time she had visited the center a few weeks ago. It had been fascinating to learn about the various indigenous creatures that inhabited the area.

It was over an hour before Amy had sent the next two pictures. This time, Tommy had taken them of her. In the first, Amy was sitting on top of a rock wall that surrounded a pond. In the second, she was smiling at a butterfly that had alighted on her arm. Fifteen minutes later, Amy had e-mailed a picture of a deer.

One by one, Meg looked at the other pictures, documenting the hike up the mountain, along a portion of the Appalachian Trail. The last of the series were shots from the top of Mt. Greylock. The pair had gotten another visitor to take a picture of them together in front of the Veterans War Memorial Tower, which stood at the peak. Next, there were several shots of the views from the mountaintop. Meg knew, from being up there herself, that the photos didn't do the spectacular vistas justice.

As she opened the rest of the pictures, Meg was glad, at least, that the final day of Amy's life had been spent with so much happiness amid such beauty. But she didn't understand why Amy had sent her the last blurry, blue image.

# CHAPTER 11

*NOT BAD FOR A woman in her mid-forties,* thought Victoria Sterling as she studied her reflection in the mirror over the tiger-maple dresser. Somehow, even her almost two-pack-a-day habit hadn't altered her appearance much as far as Victoria could see. She looked nothing like that defeated, wrinkled woman with the sunken, dark-circled eyes that the smoking police used in their ad campaign.

After running a comb through her dark, curly hair and pulling on a blue silk robe, Victoria grabbed a pack of cigarettes from her purse and walked out of the bedroom. She tiptoed past the closed door of Belinda's room, glad that her hostess wasn't up yet. Victoria wanted some time to herself.

The timer Belinda had set the night before ensured there was a pot of fresh coffee waiting for Victoria downstairs. She filled a mug and looked around the newly remodeled kitchen. It must have cost a small fortune. The custom cabinets, the granite countertops, the top-of-the-line professional appliances, even the antique farm table that served as an island in the center of the spacious room, all contributed to a feeling of security and well-being.

Taking a sip of the hot brew, Victoria walked over to the large bay window. It hadn't been here the last time she was a guest at Curtains Up, two years ago. She would have remembered. She and Daniel had had coffee down here every morning of their stay. They'd used the long trestle table as their desk, spreading their papers across the pine planks as they worked out the necessary changes to their play being produced that summer. While the actors were running through their rehearsals of *Treasure Trove,* she and Daniel were making adjustments to the script—right up to opening night.

Everyone said that was what had killed Daniel. The stress of that summer. He hadn't taken care of himself, and when you're a diabetic, you can't afford not to.

"Come here, kitty. Come here, Marigold." Victoria leaned down to coax the orange cat closer. But the cat walked right by on the way to her spot in the sun on the window seat.

"All right, have it your way, you little witch," Victoria said and lit up a cigarette. She turned her attention to the scene outside the window. A figure was making its way across the meadow, walking away from the house. Even from behind, Victoria knew it was Gus. She recognized those broad shoulders. That caretaker sure was a good-looking guy, in a dangerous kind of way. And she had been a widow for two long years.

# CHAPTER 12

CAROLINE STARED OUT THE back window as the crew car sped north on the New York State Thruway. The acres of farmland that lined the highway and the mountains that sat off in the distance were so soothingly green. Just a little more than an hour out of New York City, and already it was another world.

Caroline decided to try making conversation with her companions. "Boomer. How did you get that name?"

The large man in the front passenger seat turned his head and spoke over his shoulder. "Uh, they started calling me that a long time ago. Soundman. Boom mike. Get it?"

"What's your real name?"

"Michael," Boomer answered. "Hey, Lamar, let's pull in at the next rest stop. I'm hungry."

"What? Are you kidding me?" protested the driver. "We just left."

"Yeah, but I have low blood sugar," said Boomer.

"Then why don't you just bring food with you?"

"That would take too much planning."

Grudgingly, Lamar steered the car off the highway at the rest stop exit. *Mutt and Jeff,* thought Caroline, walking into the huge multi-restaurant building behind the tall, thin cameraman, Lamar Nelson, and the short, round soundman, Michael "Boomer" O'Mara. She hadn't worked with them before, and she had the distinct impression they were sizing her up.

"I'll meet you back at the car," she said as she headed for the ladies' room. It was going to be a long couple of days, she thought. The duo were well known for their bickering, which was tolerated by reporters and producers because they had no choice. In these days of budget constraints, a video crew was a hot commodity. There was always more demand than supply. When you were lucky enough to get a crew assigned to shoot your story, you grinned and got through it with them.

Caroline washed her hands and tried to dry them, rubbing them under the hot-air blower attached to the wall. When she came out of the lavatory, she stopped to buy a cup of coffee. By the time she got back to the car, Lamar and Boomer were waiting for her.

As they pulled out onto the highway again, Boomer turned his thick frame sideways in the seat. "What are we going up here to shoot anyway?" he asked as he bit into his jumbo Cinnabon.

"The Warrenstown Summer Playhouse," Caroline answered.

"Yeah, I know. What about it?" Boomer licked his lips.

"A piece on the summer theater festival, a story about this new play that everyone is talking about, and maybe, if we can get her to cooperate, a profile on Belinda Winthrop."

"Mmm. Belinda Winthrop. That is one fine woman," declared Lamar. "I fell in love with her back when I first saw her in that remake of *The Letter.* Man, I had dreams about her for months after that."

"You and millions of other suckers, Lamar," said Boomer.

"And you didn't?"

The soundman didn't answer, popping the last of the cinnamon roll into his mouth.

Lamar looked with disgust at his partner. "You got icing dripping down your chin."

"Anybody got a spare napkin?" asked Boomer as he leaned forward to check if there was one in the paper take-out tray.

"Slob. You're spilling your coffee all over the seat."

"Don't get your shorts in a knot, Lamar."

Lamar gripped the steering wheel. "You know, Boomer, when you have low blood sugar, you aren't supposed to stoke it with a sugary, zillion-calorie coffee cake."

"Oh, so you're a doctor now. I forgot."

There was silence in the car as both men figured it would better to stand down now rather than push on. They had to travel together, work together, eat together, and basically live together for the next several days. If their nudging turned into a full-scale fight, which it had been known to do, the tension would make the assignment before them sheer misery.

Changing the subject, Lamar called out to Caroline in the backseat. "So you're pretty new to television, aren't you?"

"I've been with *KTA* for about six months," she answered. "Before that, I worked for newspapers."

"Like it?"

"Still getting used to it."

Boomer crushed the paper take-out tray. "I'd read that as a no, wouldn't you, Lamar?"

"Sounds to me like a rookie trying to cope with that maniac Nazareth," said Lamar, smiling as he drove.

Boomer twisted his thick girth around toward the back-seat. "Let me tell you something, little lady. You might never get used to that crazy bastard."

*"Little lady?"* Caroline asked. "I didn't think anyone used that expression anymore. Last time I heard it was in an old John Wayne western."

"Hey, Boom." Lamar grinned. "You're busted, you chauvinist."

# CHAPTER 13

BELINDA FORCED HERSELF TO get out of bed. If she hurried, she'd have time to take a walk around the property before she had to go to the theater. What had started as a way of getting some exercise had become as essential as brushing her teeth in the morning. No matter where she was, if she didn't get that walk in, four or five times a week, Belinda found she just didn't feel good. In the final stages of rehearsal for a play, the exercise was even more important. While walking, she could go over the scenes in her head, run her lines, think about her movements.

Even though the daily maid service she'd hired wouldn't be in till noon, Belinda left her bed unmade. She went into the bathroom, brushed her teeth, and ran a comb through her ash-blond hair. Dressing in khaki shorts and a purple Warrenstown Summer Playhouse T-shirt, she laced up her walking shoes and went downstairs. The door to her study was open, but Belinda ignored the urge to check her e-mail.

"Good morning," she said when she walked into the kitchen.

Victoria turned her gaze from the window to her hostess. "Hello, sleepyhead," she said. "Have a good rest?"

"Slept like a log. I was exhausted."

"Coffee?" asked Victoria, going to the counter to get the coffeepot.

"Okay. Just a half."

"Black, right?"

Belinda nodded. She took the cup from her houseguest. "Thanks," she said. "What have you been doing so far this morning?"

"Not much. Just fantasizing a little about that caretaker of yours."

"Ah, yes. Gus." Belinda walked over to the picture window and looked out. "He's a little too handsome for his own good, don't you think?"

"Oh, I don't know about that. You can't be too rich or too thin—*or* too good looking." Victoria pulled the tie tighter on her silk robe. "A girl can dream, can't she?"

"I doubt you two would have much to talk about, Victoria. Gus is no rocket scientist—or award-winning playwright, either."

"Funny, but my fantasy had nothing to do with conversation."

Belinda chuckled and then swallowed the last bit of coffee. "I'm going out for a little exercise. When I get back, I'll take a quick shower and we can head to the theater."

"Well, that hunky caretaker got into his golf cart and headed out across the meadow." Victoria nodded toward the picture window. "If you see him on your walk, tell him I was asking for him."


STANDING IN THE DRIVEWAY, Belinda did a few stretching exercises. She inhaled the fresh morning air, crisp and without a hint of humidity. It was going to be another glorious day in the Berkshires.

She began down the driveway but then changed her mind, turning and starting across the meadow. If she could catch up with Gus, she could talk to him about the arrangements for the party she planned to have for the cast and crew after the opening tomorrow night. Gus really had to replace those pieces of flaking slate on the patio. It looked messy, and a guest could trip and fall.

She'd noticed a few things this season that Gus hadn't attended to, and she didn't like it. She hoped she wasn't going to start having problems with her caretaker because, up till now, the situation had worked out well for both of them. Gus had a steady job, was paid well, and had a cozy place to live. Belinda had great peace of mind in knowing that Curtains Up was being taken care of and wasn't deserted when she couldn't be here.

She tramped through the grass and wildflowers, heading in the direction Victoria had indicated Gus had taken. Money might not be everything, she thought as she looked out over the meadow, but she loved what her success had purchased. This serene, beautiful place was perhaps her favorite piece of real estate. As long as her career held out, she knew she would be able to maintain all the residences she kept. And even when her professional life began to flag, as it inevitably would as she aged, she could keep a few of her favorite homes, sell the others, and live more than comfortably for the rest of her life.

At the end of the meadow, Belinda stopped and called out into the woods.

There was no answer.

"Guuusss!" She tried again.

Still, no response.

She scanned the edge of the meadow, looking for a path of some kind that the golf cart might have taken into the woods, finally finding a narrow lane where the vegetation had been tamped down. Belinda hesitated for a moment. Should she just go back? She could leave a note for Gus or talk to him later.

No, she wanted to speak with him face-to-face and make sure he understood that she expected him to take care of things. She wanted him to know that the fact that she was seldom here didn't mean she wasn't paying attention to what was happening. If she waited to talk to him until she got home from the theater tonight, it would be too late. Gus would probably be in bed, and she'd be too tired.

Belinda took another deep breath of the cool mountain air and stepped into the woods.

# CHAPTER 14

KEITH FALLOWS STOOD ON the empty stage, looked out at the vacant seats, and took a deep breath. Tomorrow night the house would be packed. Every single seat had been sold or reserved. There would be four hundred sets of eyes watching, four hundred brains analyzing and judging, four hundred hearts and souls being moved—or not.

For the director, pre-opening pressure was always tough, but with all he had riding on this play, the stress was even more grueling than usual. He prayed *Devil in the Details* would be the vehicle that would propel him, finally, into producing and directing movies.

Because of their long association at Warrenstown, Victoria Sterling had given him the opportunity to option her play. He had pounced on the chance, using most of his savings to do it. All winter and spring, Keith had refused directing projects, focusing his entire energy on converting the stage play for the screen.

If this, the first stage production of *Devil in the Details*, was a hit, then Keith would be that much closer to getting the green light for a film version. But even if every reviewer raved about the show, it was far from a foregone conclusion that he could raise enough money to produce the film. For that, he needed Belinda Winthrop.

At the end of last summer, when Victoria had let them both read the play for the first time, Belinda had been mad for the role of Valerie, the wife of Davis, a man with no conscience. Keith had sat right beside Belinda and listened while she called her agent and instructed him to make sure she would be available in July for rehearsals and the first two weeks of August for the play itself. When Keith had confided his dream, to take *Devil in the Details* to Hollywood, Belinda had told him to count her in. Now she was reneging, claiming the role of Valerie was too draining and there were other projects she wanted to pursue.

Keith clenched his right hand into a fist and slammed it into the palm of his left. Belinda shouldn't have given him permission to use her name as the presumptive leading lady of the movie unless she meant it. She shouldn't have let him proceed, thinking that he could count on her. Keith had sunk his time, money, and reputation in this project, using her name as collateral to broker the financial backing for the film. Without Belinda Winthrop, the studio would pull the plug.

But Keith still held out hope that he could make her change her mind.

# CHAPTER 15

*WHO SAID GOOD THINGS never made the news? This morning's newspaper was full of happy information.*

*The autopsy reports on Amy and Tommy were in and showed marijuana in both their systems. The police were satisfied that the two Warrenstown Summer Playhouse apprentices had been under the influence of drugs when they catapulted off the road.*

*With the police satisfied, that would be the end of any investigation. The only thing that could open it again would be that damned picture Amy had e-mailed to her friend.*

*THE KILLER WENT ONLINE, set up a bogus e-mail account that couldn't be traced, and sent a carefully worded message.*

DEAR FRIENDS OF AMY,

WE ARE GETTING PHONE CALLS FROM PEOPLE WANTING TO KNOW HOW THEY CAN HELP. WE APPRECIATE THE OUTPOURING OF LOVE AND SUPPORT WE ARE RECEIVING AT THIS HEARTBREAK- ING TIME.

IT'S IMPORTANT FOR US TO KNOW WHAT AMY WAS DOING RIGHT BEFORE SHE WAS TAKEN FROM US. IF YOU HAVE ANY INFOR-

MATION TO SHARE, PLEASE LET US KNOW BY REPLY E-MAIL. AMY'S
FATHER AND I ARE JUST TOO UPSET TO TAKE PHONE CALLS AT THIS
TIME. WE KNOW YOU'LL UNDERSTAND.

> SINCERELY,
> AMY'S MOM

*The killer sent the message to only one friend. Bright-lights.*

# CHAPTER 16

WITH THE LEAVES OF the tall oaks beginning to block out the morning sun, Belinda followed the path into the woods. The deeper she went, the darker it got. She started to feel uneasy. Maybe Gus wasn't even in here. And God knew what kinds of animals or snakes were slithering around. Belinda was about to turn back when she saw the empty golf cart.

She began to call out Gus's name but thought better of it. Something didn't feel right. Belinda proceeded forward, trying not to make any noise. As she got closer to the cart, she noticed an opening in the ground. She stooped down to look inside. A ladder was propped against the wall of a hole about the width of a man's outstretched arms.

There was no way she was going down that thing alone.

AS HE REACHED THE top of the ladder and his head popped over the edge of the opening to the underground cave, Gus caught sight of Belinda's back hurrying out of the woods.

"I THINK I MIGHT have a problem with Gus," Belinda said as she steered the Mercedes out of the driveway.

"What do you mean?" Victoria asked.

Belinda told her friend about the golf cart and the ladder and the hole in the ground.

"Well, he's doing something out there, Belinda, but you can't be sure at this point that it's anything wrong. Want me to go check it out?"

Belinda considered the offer. "Maybe I should call the police," she said.

"And what if the police come and find there's a completely reasonable explanation? Then you've shown your caretaker that you don't trust him," said Victoria. "And you don't want that, do you?"

"No, I guess not."

"Look. When we get back later, pull out one of those maps of the property that Remington did and mark where the hole is. As soon as there's some free time, I'll go out there and take a look. Right now, you've got more important things to do," Victoria said. "Your focus has to be on the play."

The car traveled north along the winding two-lane road, reaching the Warrenstown traffic circle and bearing right. Belinda found a parking spot, and the two women got out and walked toward the brand-new theater building. As they reached the front steps, a pretty young blonde stood at the top holding the door open for them.

"Thanks, Langley," said Belinda. Victoria said nothing until they were out of Langley's earshot.

"I'm telling you, Belinda, that one wants to be you," said Victoria. "It's written all over her. She's so damned obsequious. It's disgusting."

Belinda smiled. "Oh, give her a break, Victoria. Langley is just a kid."

"A kid who watches your every move."

"That's because she's my understudy."

"No," Victoria insisted. "That's because she wants your life."

# CHAPTER 17

CAROLINE COULDN'T STOP STARING out the car window at the rolling farmland and majestic mountains in the distance. The view of seemingly endless, undeveloped acreage was such a welcome respite from worrying about her stepdaughter, her boss, and whether or not this crew was going to give her a hard time.

Eventually, she forced herself to pull the manila folder from her bag and began to read through the contents. She'd gotten the article from the KEY News reference library. It was a *Vanity Fair* piece on Belinda Winthrop that had run almost two years ago. It outlined Belinda's most famous roles on stage and screen. There were pictures of her beachfront home in Malibu, her chalet in Gstaad, her brownstone in Greenwich Village, and her vast country estate in Warrenstown, Massachusetts.

The article went on to describe Belinda's passion for detail. How she decorated each home herself, selecting furnishings in styles appropriate to their locations. It also told of her penchant for entertaining and described some of the parties she had given over the years. Belinda, the article said, loved to give theme parties, often coordinated with a role she was playing.

To celebrate her role in *Treasure Trove,* Belinda had given a treasure hunt. Caroline studied the artist's rendering of Belinda's Massachusetts estate that accompanied the article. The map, executed by the famed Winthrop portraitist Remington Peters, was marked with tiny stars indicating spots where Belinda's party guests had to go for clues to where the treasure was buried. $X$'s—there seemed to be a dozen or so—warned of holes leading to underground caves that the guests should be careful of.

Caroline highlighted the following passage:

> Winthrop's run of triumphs was interrupted this past summer by tragedy. Following the Treasure Trove party for the Warrenstown Summer Playhouse company and prominent locals held at Curtains Up, Winthrop's houseguest and longtime friend Daniel Sterling, widely considered the dominant half of the Victoria and Daniel Sterling playwriting team, died in a car accident. Sterling, who had diabetes, could have been suffering the effects of the disease when his car went off a deserted mountain road and overturned in a ditch in the middle of the night, but his wife said her husband had told her he fought with one of the party guests, though he wouldn't tell her who. Claiming he was too upset to sleep, he left the estate to cool off with a car ride through the Berkshire Mountains.
>
> The party guests, among them Broadway director Keith Fallows, screenwriter Nick McGregor, and acclaimed artist Remington Peters, were questioned by police, but Sterling's death was declared an accident.

Caroline re-capped the highlighter and looked out the window again.

Nick had been questioned about Daniel Sterling's death? Why hadn't he ever mentioned that? He knew she was doing a story on Belinda Winthrop. Why hadn't he volunteered that he'd been at the party at her house the night Daniel Sterling died? That wasn't something you'd forget.

"I'm hungry." Caroline's thoughts were interrupted by Boomer's voice.

"Not again, Boom." Lamar groaned.

"To tell you the truth, guys, I wouldn't mind stopping either," said Caroline. "We're almost there, so let's get some lunch. And I want to pick up a copy of the local paper."

BACK IN THE CAR after lunch, the headline on the bottom of the front page of the Albany *Times Union* caught Caroline's eye. EVIDENCE OF MARIJUANA IN PLAYHOUSE VICTIMS. She read the story about two Warrenstown Summer Playhouse apprentices who had been killed in a car accident over the weekend. Marijuana had been found in the car, and now the autopsy showed the drug in both of their systems.

*Meg must know these kids,* thought Caroline, hoping that their tragic deaths would be a cautionary tale for her stepdaughter.

# CHAPTER 18

MEG PULLED AT THE corset drawstrings.

"Tighter, Meg. You've got to pull them tighter," Belinda said. "Don't worry. I won't break."

As she stood behind the actress, Meg caught sight of her own reflection in the mirrored wall over the dressing table. Her expression was serious as she took a deep breath and pulled back on the drawstrings.

Belinda winced. "That's better," she said as her hands caressed her waistline. "That should be enough."

Meg walked over to the rack on which all the actress's costumes hung. She selected the green velvet ball gown that Belinda wore in her first and last appearances on-stage. She held the gown as Belinda stepped into it. In keeping with the style of the period, there were two dozen green velvet buttons running down the back of the gown, but a hidden zipper had been sewn in to make quick costume changes possible. There was no way twenty-four small buttons could be fastened or unfastened and Belinda still make her entrances in time.

As Meg zipped her into the dress, the star nodded approvingly. "Good," she said. "But remind me not to breathe."

Meg smiled shyly. She still was in awe of Belinda Winthrop and couldn't quite believe that not only was she in the star's dressing room but that the actress was actually talking with her. Meg was trying hard to strike the right balance between being respectful and not appearing overly impressed. But even though the Warrenstown Summer Playhouse stressed that, from apprentice to star, all of the thespians and support staff belonged here as colleagues, it was undeniable that Belinda Winthrop was in a class of her own. For Meg, it was intoxicating yet intimidating to be in such close contact with a legend.

A tinkling sound emanated from Meg's knapsack. She hesitated.

"It's all right, Meg. Go ahead and answer it," Belinda said as she pulled on her long green gloves.

Meg checked the number on the cell phone screen. "Forget it," she said, tossing the phone back in the bag. "It's not important."

CAROLINE LISTENED TO THE ring and then heard the click that meant the call was being forwarded to voice mail.

"Hi. It's Meg. Please leave a message and I'll call you back."

"Hi, Meg. It's Caroline. I just wanted to let you know I'm here. Call me when you can and we'll figure out when we can get together." She recited her cell phone number. Caroline was certain Meg already had it, but her stepdaughter wasn't above claiming she didn't. Caroline refused to give Meg any excuse not to return the call.

# CHAPTER 19

THE AUDIENCE GATHERED FOR the afternoon run-through of *Devil in the Details* was a select one. With the exception of Belinda's portrait painter, Remington Peters, who had sneaked in through a side entrance to view her in her costume, everyone was involved directly with the play. The public was decidedly unwelcome.

In the frenetic moments before the curtain would go up, actors with nonspeaking roles were called out to stand in the glare of the spotlights for a costume check. The property master hurled epithets from somewhere back-stage when he noticed that one of the glasses from a serving tray was missing. As the stage manager gave two-minute warnings over his headset to the first-scene actors, the lighting and sound engineers made final adjustments to their computers.

Keith Fallows sat in the back of the theater, where as director he could have overall perspective. Langley Tate sat closer to the front, where she could study Belinda's movements and mannerisms. Victoria Sterling positioned herself at the side, where she could make notes on her script without distracting anyone.

Finally, the lights dimmed and the curtain rose. One of the three chandeliers failed to fall from the rafters, but everyone pretended not to notice. Belinda's performance was flawless, and her presence onstage kept the other actors on their toes. Scene One introduced the play's main characters and gave the audience a sense of time and place: in turn-of-the-twentieth-century Boston, Valerie is a woman of wealth and privilege married for fourteen years to Davis, a man whom she slowly begins to suspect is a sociopath.

At the end of the first scene, Keith yelled from the back of the theater, "Hold it, everybody. This still isn't right." The director rose from his seat and walked quickly down the aisle as the actors waited.

"Belinda, darling, I think you should move more downstage when you deliver the last lines of this scene."

"Yesterday you told me to stay upstage, Keith," Belinda said.

"I know what I said yesterday, but this is today."

Belinda kept her face expressionless as she moved closer to the front of the stage. "Do you want me to run the lines again, Keith?" she asked.

"Of course I do."

*WHAT A PRO,* THOUGHT Langley as she watched the exchange between star and director. If she was in Belinda's place, she would want to wring Keith's scrawny neck. He had been constantly changing his mind about the blocking throughout the rehearsals for this production. The sets creaked, the lighting was either too bright or too dim, the costumes were uninspired, and the actors were either too animated or sleepwalking through their lines.

Langley hadn't worked with Keith Fallows before, but his reputation for exacting standards preceded him. That was what made him the successful director he was. But the understudy hadn't been prepared for Keith's sarcasm and sometimes downright anger in response to anything that displeased him. The cast and crew of *Devil in the Details* were walking on eggshells.

Except for Belinda. If Keith's behavior bothered her, she didn't let it show. No matter how many times the director changed his mind, Belinda never revealed any trace of frustration or annoyance. Langley worried about taking Belinda's place onstage and dealing with Keith's volatile temperament, but that fear wasn't enough to extinguish her appetite for the role of Valerie.

Langley Tate was a full decade younger than Belinda Winthrop and had envisioned over and over again the zest she would inject into the part. Playing Valerie at the Warrenstown Summer Playhouse could get her the attention that might lead to great things in her career. But that would never happen as long as Belinda stayed healthy.

MEG WATCHED THE FIRST two scenes on the monitor in the dressing room, paying strict attention because of the several quick costume changes she had to assist Belinda with. But with the intermission looming after the final scene of the first act, Meg grabbed the copy of the *Devil in the Details* script Belinda had left on the dressing table and went upstairs to follow along from the side of the stage.

## ACT I, SCENE 3

*The drawing room, lit only by a large fireplace, is in almost complete darkness, the light from the flickering flames dancing on the walls and furniture. The room seems empty. A few moments pass in silence.* VALERIE ENTERS *upstage and is about to turn the switch to light the lamps, but she is interrupted by a disembodied voice coming from a high-backed chair downstage.*

DAVIS: Don't touch it.

VALERIE: Oh God, Davis. You gave me a fright. (VALERIE *waits for an answer, but* DAVIS *does not speak.*) Why are you sitting here in the dark? And why would you want the lights out tonight, of all

nights? You know we have guests arriving for
the weekend.

DAVIS:      Sitting in the dark is so soothing, so calming.
The sound of your voice, though, is cutting
through me like glass, even more than usual.

VALERIE:    I will ignore that last jab, Davis. (*She walks
toward him, peeling off her gloves.*) But if you
are not feeling well, should you not be upstairs, with a cool cloth on your head?

As Meg heard Belinda deliver the line with such wifely
tenderness, she would have bet fifty dollars that Keith Fallows was going to scream "Hold." In earlier rehearsals, he
had told Belinda twice, once kindly and the second time
with his voice raised with impatience, that she was supposed to sound sarcastic when speaking about her husband's pain. Belinda had ignored that direction and spoken
the line with a lilt of genuine care and concern.

*"Hold!"* Keith jumped to his feet and bellowed the
word. Everyone onstage stood absolutely still. "Please,
Belinda," he said, gritting his teeth.

The director walked toward the stage. The actress
moved downstage, kneeling on one knee between two
footlights so that they might speak without being overheard. "What is it now?" she whispered, pretending not to
know why he'd stopped the action.

"You know damn well what's the matter," he hissed.

"Well, we're just going to have to agree to disagree,
Keith. At this point in the play, I don't think Valerie is at all
sure that Davis is the monster he turns out to be. She's still
worried she's reading too much into her husband's strange
behavior. She realizes that everything he's done in the first
two scenes has a possible and plausible explanation. If I
start playing her as bitchily as you'd like right now, I think
we spoil it for the audience. They won't have enough sym-
pathy for Valerie."

"Isn't that *my* department? Isn't the *director* supposed
to make these kinds of decisions?"

"That's the problem, Keith. I'm afraid you think that *director* and *dictator* are the same thing. Do you really think I've gotten to where I am by blindly obeying every director's whim over my own instincts?" Belinda stood up, letting him know that the conference was over.

Keith was furious, but he didn't want to have it out with Belinda with the whole cast and crew as witnesses. And he didn't want to alienate her any more than he might have already. He needed her too much; his future depended on her.

# CHAPTER 20

CAROLINE AND HER VIDEO crew arrived at the theater in time to hear the stage manager's final instruction to the cast: "All right, everyone, you have a few hours to yourselves. Seven-thirty call for an eight o'clock show."

Caroline stood at the end of the aisle and waited as Keith Fallows finished speaking to several members of the crew. When he was finally alone, she walked over and introduced herself.

The director looked at her with a blank expression on his face.

"We had an interview scheduled this afternoon, for *KEY to America*?" Caroline prompted him.

"Oh yes, that's right. How could I forget?" Keith smiled, but she detected a hint of sarcasm.

"Where would you like us to set up?" she asked. "We could do it down here in the seats, or I was thinking we might do it up on the set."

"My dear, where we do it will have to be up to you. I have no desire to direct your interview. I have enough to do."

"I was only trying to accommodate your preferences, Mr. Fallows," said Caroline evenly, determined not to show that his words had stung.

"Well, if you really want to accommodate me, would

you mind if we rescheduled? I just have too much on my mind right now."

As she and the crew left the theater, Caroline knew her pale cheeks were blushing.

"Wow. He really blew you off," said Boomer.

"Ya think?" asked Caroline with sarcasm.

"Don't need to be so touchy. I was just making an observation."

"Thanks, Boomer," said Caroline. "I don't know what I'd do without you."

# CHAPTER 21

THE LIBRARIAN LISTENED TO the request and then looked up at the clock on the wall. "We're closing in fifteen minutes."

"I know, but it's really important. I won't be able to come back tomorrow. I really need that old issue of *Vanity Fair.*"

"All right. Wait here."

Five precious minutes were eaten up waiting for the librarian to search the stacks. The elderly woman arrived back at the circulation desk with the magazine in her hand.

"There's a copy machine over against the wall if you need it," she offered.

"Thanks. I don't think that will be necessary."

The librarian turned to finish her tasks before closing as the reader walked down the row of bookshelves to a table in the corner. In seconds the article on Belinda Winthrop was folded and stashed away.

"Just what do you think you're doing?" The librarian stood over the table with books held tightly in her arms.

"What do you mean?"

"You know what I mean. I saw you."

"Saw me *what*?"

"Take those pages out of that magazine."

"You must be mistaken."

The librarian quickly considered her options. It was

her turn to lock up, and the other staffers had already gone home. She was all alone. As she stared into the unblinking eyes, she decided to avoid a conflict.

"Please leave," she said. "And do not come back here again."

*IF SHE WENT THROUGH the magazine, the nosy librarian would be able to tell which article had been taken. And if anything ever happened to Belinda Winthrop, the librarian would surely remember the stolen article and think it worthy of mentioning to the police. The librarian would be able to give a physical description.*

*The librarian had to go.*

*How?*

*There had been a metal letter opener shining at the circulation desk. That could work. It would be messy but effective.*

# CHAPTER 22

HAVING BEEN REBUFFED BY Keith Fallows, Caroline and her crew went about getting general video of the exterior of the theater and the manicured grounds that surrounded it. "Make sure you get a couple of shots at different angles of the signs," said Caroline, pointing to the huge posters that flanked the double doors to the theater lobby.

Belinda Winthrop's name appeared in large lettering over the silhouette of a masculine figure holding a pistol. Beneath the silhouette was a list, in smaller print, of the other players' names. Then, at the bottom, the print increased in size again, announcing that *Devil in the Details* was written by Victoria Sterling and directed by Keith Fallows.

"Be sure to get close-up shots on the names Winthrop, Fallows, and Sterling," said Caroline as she thought ahead to what she would need for editing purposes later. Those three were the most important interviews to get during her time in Warrenstown. Although Fallows had just blown her off, he'd promised to give her some time tomorrow. Caroline wanted to wait to get Belinda Winthrop's interview until after the play opened tomorrow night.

"Okay, let's go inside," Caroline directed. "Victoria Sterling should be here any time now."

The theater lobby had a soaring ceiling and lots of long

glass windows. The walls were lined with slotted ash panels, and the floor was cool slate. Benches were sprinkled along the sides of the spacious area.

"How about setting up over there?" Caroline suggested, indicating one of the benches.

"Fine," said Lamar.

While Lamar set up his tripod and Boomer fiddled around with his sound equipment, Caroline went over her notes. She had prepared her questions for the playwright in advance. When Victoria finally appeared, Caroline was ready.

"I'm sorry I'm late," said Victoria as Boomer clipped on her microphone. "To tell you the truth, I almost forgot we'd set up this interview. You know, last-minute preps before the opening and all."

Caroline nodded. "Of course. We just so appreciate that you are taking the time to do this."

With interviewer and subject wired up, Lamar signaled that he was ready to begin recording.

"All right," said Caroline. "I guess it goes without saying that this must be an exciting time for you."

"Exciting or nerve-racking. Take your pick," Victoria answered.

"*Devil in the Details* is your first solo effort at playwriting, isn't it?"

"Well, at least it's the first solo thing I've done in a very long time. Before I met Daniel, I had written several plays. One had even been produced off-Broadway. But once Daniel and I started to collaborate, that was it . . . until his death."

"Some say that this play, *Devil in the Details,* is better than anything you and your husband wrote together."

Victoria nodded. "I've heard that, but believe me, I take no solace in it. Daniel was a fabulously creative man, and he was taken much too soon."

"Rumor has it that *Devil in the Details* will be a contender for the Pulitzer Prize in drama. Is that true?"

"Well, the play is being submitted. As you probably

know, Caroline, the Pulitzer committee prefers that a videotape of the production itself be sent, as well as six copies of the script. That tape will be shot tomorrow night at the opening. And having Belinda Winthrop in the lead can't hurt, can it?" Victoria smiled.

"No. It certainly can't," Caroline agreed, knowing she was about to get to the part of the interview she had been dreading and Victoria Sterling probably wasn't going to like. "Would you be able to give a brief description of what the play is about?"

Victoria took a deep breath and paused a moment. "I know how you people want everything said in sound bites, so let's just say that *Devil in the Details* is the story of the marriage of a woman who is totally in love with her charismatic husband but slowly starts to realize that he isn't what she thinks he is."

"And what is he?" Caroline prompted.

"He's a man with no conscience. He's capable of doing anything to get what he wants, no matter whom he hurts."

Caroline swallowed, knowing she had to ask the next question. "Some people are speculating that the play has an autobiographical component. They say that *Devil in the Details* reflects your life with your husband. What do you say to that?"

"Not much," said Victoria.

Caroline waited for her subject to continue, but Victoria resolutely stared her down.

# CHAPTER 23

BOOMER STUDIED THE *SEE the Berkshires* tourist guide, or more specifically, he studied the restaurant ads. He settled on a place that boasted unbeatable steaks and sweet Maine lobsters. "Surf and turf. That's for me," he said, his eyes growing brighter at the prospect.

"Whatever makes you happy, Boom," said Lamar as he packed away his camera gear.

Caroline noticed that neither man extended an invitation to join them. "Thanks, guys," she said. "But I'm going to pass this time. I want to have dinner with my stepdaughter later."

Lamar looked slightly sheepish, while Boomer seemed not have picked up on her sarcasm.

"Oh, yeah? Where you going?" he asked, worried there might be someplace better than the restaurant he'd chosen.

"Not sure yet," she answered. "I'm going to leave it up to her—if I can ever reach her on the phone."

As the crew car drove away, Caroline decided to head over to Main Street. She walked past the ivy-covered brick buildings that dotted the edge of campus, aware of a sense of history. Warren College had been established just after the Revolutionary War, and many of the towered structures had been built during the 1800s. There was a feeling of permanence and serenity here. It was a privileged, protected place.

She thought of the parents of the two young apprentices who had died in the car wreck. They had sent their kids off to Warrenstown for the summer, confident that no harm would come to them here. They'd be sleeping in the Warren College dorms, eating in the Warren College cafeteria, working and learning in the theater on the Warren College campus. Instead, those parents were experiencing the worst imaginable heartbreak.

Thank God, Meg was all right. Nick would never get over it if something happened to his daughter.


CAROLINE STROLLED DOWN MAIN Street, stopping to look in the windows. She admired a gauzy, black peasant skirt displayed in a dress shop window and went inside to try it on. As she assessed herself in the long mirror, Caroline wished, as she did at least once a day, that she was taller. But the skirt looked good on her all the same, so she bought it.

She continued down the block, where a turquoise necklace at a jewelry store caught her eye, and she bought that for Meg's birthday. She wanted to get something for Nick as well. When she spotted the art gallery, she headed for the entrance. A pleasant-looking, middle-aged woman walked toward her.

"Hello. I'm Jean Ambrose," she said, extending her hand. "Welcome to the Ambrose Gallery."

Caroline looked around the spacious, open room. Carefully hung paintings graced the pale gray walls. Several precisely arranged pieces of handcrafted furniture sat on the slate-colored carpeting. A few glass display cases housed decorative artifacts. Everything in the gallery had been deliberately selected and displayed to its best advantage.

"You have a beautiful place here," said Caroline.

"Thank you," said Jean. "We're getting ready for the exhibition opening Friday night." She gestured to an empty space on a long wall. "That's where Remington Peters's new portrait of Belinda Winthrop will be displayed."

Caroline walked over to the wall and looked at the two paintings flanking the spot reserved for the new portrait. In one, the figure of a woman wearing a flowing gossamer gown swayed against a wooded background. In the other, the same woman wore a simple black dress and an especially long string of pearls around her neck. Her hair was swept up in an homage to Audrey Hepburn in *Breakfast at Tiffany's*.

"Those, of course, are Belinda Winthrop in the roles she played the last two seasons at Warrenstown. Titania, the queen of the fairies, in *A Midsummer Night's Dream* and Madison Whitehall, the main character in *Treasure Trove*," Jean explained. "We are so thrilled to be able to add Remington's newest work, with Belinda as Valerie in *Devil in the Details*."

"These are magnificent," said Caroline. "You can tell the artist cares about his subject."

Jean smiled. "That's a bit of an understatement. Remington doesn't just care about Belinda Winthrop; he adores her. He fell in love with her when they were young, and as his work attests, he's never gotten over her."

"That's a bit sad, isn't it?" Caroline stared at the portraits.

"Yes, I guess it is," Jean agreed. "But look at the fabulous product of that emotion."

"I suppose they are fabulously expensive, too."

"They aren't for sale," said Jean. "Unfortunately, Remington won't part with them. I wish he would. If he had sold the other paintings he'd done of Belinda over the years, they wouldn't have been destroyed when his studio caught fire."

"What a shame," Caroline uttered softly.

"Oh, it was truly terrible," said Jean. "The paintings were insured, of course, but no amount of money could make up for such a horrific loss."

# CHAPTER 24

THE FIRST ACT OF dress rehearsal had gone almost without a hitch. Keith Fallows had come backstage when the curtain fell, and as he delivered his notes to the cast and stage technicians, everyone felt a little more relaxed, a little more in control.

"All right, everybody," Keith said. "We'll go straight through till the end of act two, no matter what happens. We'll meet here again afterward for my final notes. Now don't forget. We'll rehearse curtain calls, too, just to see how quickly we can all get onstage."

When the curtain went up on the second act, Langley Tate stood in the wings at stage left with a copy of the script in hand, careful to stay out of the way of actors entering and exiting. The first two scenes went smoothly. As she had all night, Langley focused on only one person. The lights came up again, and Langley watched Belinda Winthop standing across the set from her stage husband. Then Langley turned her eyes down to the script.

### ACT II, SCENE 3

*The same room, some time later. The fireplace is lit and, along with a lone lamp on one of the bedside tables, it provides the room's only light.* VALERIE *and* DAVIS *are at opposite ends of the room, squared off for battle.*

VALERIE: What do you want from me, Davis?

DAVIS: I do not want anything from you. What would ever make you think I needed you at all?

VALERIE: Living with me, and making love to me, for fourteen years might have led me to suspect it.

DAVIS: (*Laughing.*) Oh, that. You have confused need with convenience, I'm afraid. (*Pause.*) You have always been a little confused. It is a part of your charm. (DAVIS *walks to the other bedside table and turns on the lamp, speaking to* VALERIE *over his shoulder.*) You have been looking a little tired lately, but you have been happy, have you not?

VALERIE: Now you are the one who is confused, Davis. Happiness and fear are not the same thing—at least, not for the rest of us.

DAVIS: Fear?

VALERIE: Yes, fear. Maybe I am the only one. The only one who knows enough about you to know that fear is the only appropriate response to you.

DAVIS: What is it you think you know, Valerie? (DAVIS *opens the drawer in his bedside table. He turns to face* VALERIE.) Tell me, damn it. What do you think you know?

VALERIE: I know that the scariest thing in the world is lying in bed next to someone who has sold his soul to the devil.

DAVIS: I am flattered you thought I had a soul to sell. (*Turning his back to* VALERIE, DAVIS *lifts a shiny pistol out of the drawer.* VALERIE *sees the pistol. She takes a step backward.* DAVIS *holds the gun loosely at his side.*)

VALERIE: Davis, I have known about the gun. You have kept it in that drawer for months so that I might lie here, night after night, afraid to close my eyes, afraid that, at any moment, you might put it to my temple and pull the trigger.

DAVIS:    Maybe I can convince you to pull the trigger *yourself*. Feel the cool steel, the smoothness. Listen to the click just before the end. Everyone would understand, you know. I would be sure to remind them, afterwards, how upset you have been lately.

(DAVIS *moves to the bedroom door, blocking* VALERIE'S *exit.* VALERIE *opens the doors to the balcony.*)

VALERIE:    Enough, Davis. This is not funny anymore. Even for you.

DAVIS:    I agree. It is not funny, but it is fun to consider the possibilities.

VALERIE:    Why not divorce me, then? Or leave me. I won't give you any trouble.

DAVIS:    But that would not work at all, dear. I have never been a failure at anything, Valerie. And I am certainly not going to let people think that I failed as a husband. (*With menace.*) Letting you go is completely out of the question.

(VALERIE *turns toward the balcony and* EXITS. DAVIS, *still carrying the gun, follows* VALERIE *offstage. Lights dim to dark.*)

# CHAPTER 25

BELINDA STEPPED OUT OF her green velvet gown, and Meg carefully hung it on the freestanding clothes rack. She folded and draped the petticoat over a wooden hanger and hung that alongside the gown.

"Oh, that feels good." Belinda sighed as Meg loosened the corset strings. "How did women in the eighteen nineties live with these things?"

Meg took the corset and put it away, then busied herself with other things as Belinda stripped down, and dressed again in jeans and a form-fitting shirt with a plunging neckline.

"Here. Let me take that," said Meg, reaching for the cotton tank top Belinda had worn under the corset. "I want to get it to the laundry."

As Meg exited the dressing room, Langley Tate was waiting in the hallway to come inside. Meg hesitated just a second before continuing on to the laundry room. She couldn't figure it out exactly, but something about Langley made Meg feel protective of Belinda. She didn't want to leave the star alone with her understudy.

Meg dropped off the undergarment and turned to go back to the dressing room when her cell phone sounded. Checking the number, she knew she had to respond this time. There was no avoiding it. She was going to have to have dinner with her stepmother. But rather than answer the phone and have to talk with her, Meg waited until Caroline left a voice-mail message and then text-messaged a reply.

BELINDA SAT BEFORE THE large mirror, wiping away her heavy stage makeup. Langley stood behind her, talking to Belinda's reflection.

"You were wonderful tonight, Belinda."

"Thanks, Langley."

"In the second act, especially, I was scared to death. The way you portray Valerie coming to the realization that her husband is going to kill her is just so incredible, Belinda. I learn so much from watching you. All those years of experience just shine through."

Removing the clips that fastened her upswept hair, Belinda shook her head, and the ash-blond locks tumbled down. "You're making me feel old, Langley." She laughed.

Langley appeared concerned. "Oh no, Belinda. That's not what I meant at all. It's just that you have such breadth of experience. Your range is staggering. It makes me feel so inadequate."

"Come on, Langley. You are very talented and you know it. You just need to give yourself more time."

"Forgive me, Belinda, but that's easy for you to say. When you were my age, you'd already won an Academy Award."

MEET U @ THAI PLACE ON MAIN. MIDDLE OF BLOCK.

Meg snapped her cell phone closed and strode back to the dressing room. As she opened the door to go inside, she heard Langley Tate's voice.

"I can only pray, when my turn comes, I'll be able to do half as good a job as you do, Belinda."

# CHAPTER 26

*AFTER THE E-MAIL ADDRESS and password were typed, and the Sign In button clicked, the fake account that the killer had set up as Amy's mother opened on the laptop screen.*

*There were no new messages.*

*No response from Brightlights. No answer from the person Amy had contacted in the moments before she died. The only person who could spoil everything.*

# CHAPTER 27

THEY BOTH ORDERED PAD Thai.

"Well, there's something we can agree on," said Caroline as she closed the menu and handed it to the waiter.

Meg smiled weakly.

"And I know there's something else we agree about."

"What's that?" Meg took a sip of water.

"We both love your father."

Meg took another drink but didn't answer.

Sensing she shouldn't push any further at the moment, Caroline shifted the conversation. "So, how's it going? Is the apprenticeship living up to your expectations?"

Meg shrugged. "I guess so."

"Do you feel your acting is improving?"

"It's hard to say," Meg responded. "I've gone to the acting classes, but I haven't gotten a part in any of the plays I've auditioned for."

"I gather it's a very rare thing for an apprentice actually to get a part in one of the Main Stage productions."

"It is," said Meg. "But I haven't even gotten a part in any of the one-acts."

The arrival of their dinner saved Caroline from having to give a lame pep talk—she was relieved to have the respite. She so wanted a good relationship with Meg, but their conversations were always so strained.

"Good, isn't it?" asked Caroline after they'd both taken a few mouthfuls of noodles.

Meg nodded as she chewed.

Caroline tried again. "It's an accomplishment that you've been picked to appear in the cabaret this weekend, Meg. I know your father is thrilled about that. He's so excited about seeing you perform."

"Well, I guess he would be after paying for all those acting and voice lessons."

"He's very proud of you, Meg. And he loves you very much."

"I know that." Meg pushed her plate away and sat back in her chair.

"That's all you're going to eat?" asked Caroline.

"I'm not that hungry."

"Don't you feel well?"

"Honestly?" Meg asked. "Honestly, if you must know, I feel pretty sad. Two of the apprentices were killed in a car accident last weekend."

"Yes, I read about that in the newspaper today," said Caroline. "Did you know them very well?"

"I didn't know the guy much, but I knew the girl. Amy and I were assigned to pick up cigarette butts and trash from the lawn in front of the theater the week we arrived, and I liked her right away. We'd been hanging out a lot together this summer."

"I'm sorry, Meg. I really am," said Caroline as she placed her fork at the side of her plate. "The paper said they had been smoking pot."

"So?" Meg looked directly at her stepmother. "Does that make it any less sad? Does that mean they had it coming because they got high?"

"Of course not, Meg. I didn't mean that at all. It was just an observation."

As Caroline listened to her own response, she realized she was forever tiptoeing around her stepdaughter. Over the months she and Nick had dated and then been married,

Caroline had tried to be patient, but she was getting tired of editing herself so as not to offend Meg in any way.

"Oh, before I forget, here's the makeup and moisturizer you wanted." Caroline pulled a paper bag from her tote. "And I got those leather sandals from your closet."

"Thanks."

As she handed the shopping bag to Meg, Caroline decided she had to say something about what she'd found. "You know, Meg," she began, "when I was in your closet, I came across something that worries me."

Meg snapped. "What were you doing snooping around my room?"

"I wasn't snooping, Meg. That bag of marijuana and rolling papers must have fallen from the closet shelf to the floor. At least I guess that's what happened. You didn't leave that stuff out where anyone could find it because you wanted to be caught, did you?"

"Of course not." Meg frowned. "But it's really not a big deal, Caroline."

"I bet those two kids who died didn't think it was a big deal either."

Meg said nothing.

"Look, Meg, at this point I'm not going to mention anything to your dad, but I'm very concerned. I want you to promise me that you'll never mix drugs with driving."

"All right," said Meg, "as long as you don't worry my father with any of this."

# CHAPTER 28

THE LIGHTS IN THE studio were on far later than usual as Remington studied his portrait of Belinda Winthrop as Valerie. After having seen the run-through of *Devil in the Details,* he was devastated that he hadn't captured on canvas what he saw onstage.

He dabbed his brush in the green paint on his palette. With expert strokes he worked on Valerie's flowing velvet gown. The dress was coming out exactly as it should. It was her expression that he'd gotten all wrong.

There was no way this portrait was going to be ready to go to the gallery in the morning.

Remington tried to imagine how he was going to explain to Zeke and Jean Ambrose when they came in the morning to pick up the painting. They had been advertising this exhibition for weeks, with the new portrait of Belinda Winthrop as Valerie billed as the most important work in the show.

Jean and Zeke had been very good to him over the years, and Remington didn't want to disappoint them. When the fire had gutted his studio, they'd swallowed the news that the Belinda Winthrop theatrical portrait collection was gone forever, and they'd focused on consoling him, urging him to continue with his work. They'd showered him with phone calls and dinners and attention. And when Belinda had offered the use of her carriage house as

a studio and apartment, the couple had helped get him settled in.

But no matter how much Remington hated to let Zeke
and Jean down, he just couldn't allow this portrait to go on
display the way it was. He would, however, do his very
best to get it right as soon as possible.

He put his paintbrush down and picked up the copy of
the *Devil in the Details* script he'd been given, which he'd
read over and over again. As he was reading through the
last scene, he heard the low roar. The sound grew stronger,
and Remington wondered, as he often did, why a plane
would be flying so low in the sky in the middle of the night
so far from the nearest airport.

Other nights he'd gotten out of bed to look into the
heavens, but he'd never been able to see anything. Still,
Remington walked out of the carriage house and looked
up. The moon was only half full, but it helped to illuminate the pollution-free, star-filled sky. When the sound of
the plane's engine was its loudest, Remington saw the
dark boxes, falling through the night sky into the meadow
below.

# THURSDAY

*August 3*

# CHAPTER 29

WHEN SHE HEARD HER Warrenstown Inn guest room door open and saw the light stream in from the hallway, Caroline stayed completely still in the king-size bed and pretended to be asleep. She listened as the door closed ever so softly while the person entering tried not to make a sound. Her heart pounded as she heard the rustle of clothing coming off, a zipper being unzipped. Caroline held her breath as she felt the weight of the body come down on the mattress.

"I thought you'd never get here," she said, rolling over and reaching out. Nick's strong arms wrapped around her, and he pulled her close.

"Me neither."


"YOU KNOW HOW LUCKY I am to have you?" Nick said afterward.

"Supremely." She reached for the glass of water on the bedside table.

"Seriously, Caroline," said Nick. "I don't know what I'd do if something happened to you."

"Nothing's going to happen to me," she said, snuggling closer. "And even if it did, you'd go on, Nick. I'd want you to."

"Yeah, but *I* wouldn't want to."

Caroline thought she heard his voice crack. "Hey," she said. "What's bringing all this on? What's the matter?"

"I don't know. I guess it's being back in Warrenstown. Last time I was here was the last trip Maggie and I ever took together. Right after we got back to New York, she got her diagnosis. The rest is history."

Caroline reached for his hand in the dark. "I know it's a painful history, but it *is* history. It's in the past now, Nick. We have so much to look forward to—our whole lives."

"I don't know, honey," he whispered. "You can be cruising along, and then, wham! Something comes out of the blue and turns your world upside down. Afterwards, nothing you can say or do will make things better."

# CHAPTER 30

THE POLICE PATROL CAR responded to the dispatcher's directions and sped to the Warrenstown Public Library. A middle-aged woman stood in the parking lot. Tears were streaming down her face.

"I got here to open up, and the doors were unlocked," she sobbed. "For a minute I was annoyed with Theresa. I thought she hadn't locked up properly last night. But then . . ." The woman covered her eyes with her hands.

"But then, what, ma'am?"

"But then, I went inside and turned on the lights and found her. Theresa was lying on the floor beside the circulation desk. I bent down to help her get up, and that's when I saw all the blood. She was so cold. I could tell she was dead." The woman wrapped her arms around herself as she shook.

"You stay right here, ma'am." The patrolman opened the double doors and went into the library. The fluorescent lighting glared on the figure lying facedown on the floor next to the front desk. The patrolman knelt on one knee, careful not to touch the dark blood, and, positioning his hands around the body, turned the dead weight over.

The patrolman couldn't be sure if the victim's face had

been stuck in an expression of surprise or terror. But there was no question at all that Theresa Templeton's eyes were wide open and her throat had been skewered by the metal letter opener that lay beside her.

# CHAPTER 31

"I ORDERED ROOM SERVICE," said Caroline as she heard the knock on the door.

"Perfect," said Nick. He got out of bed, picked up the pants he had left crumpled on the floor, and pulled money out of the pocket. He answered the door, handed the waiter a tip, and rolled the breakfast cart into the room himself.

"Shall we have breakfast in bed?" he asked. "Or do you want to eat by the window?"

"Bed," said Caroline as she sat up and propped the pillows against the headboard.

"Looks good," said Nick as he took the lids off the plates. There was enough food for a family of four: stacks of pancakes with sausage links and bacon, two plates of sliced honeydew and cantaloupe with strawberry halves, and buttered whole wheat toast cut on the diagonal. Two pitchers of hot maple syrup and a tall carafe of freshly brewed coffee sat on the corner of the starched white cloth that covered the cart.

They talked about Nick's flight from L.A. and the drive from New York to Warrenstown at night. "After you get off the highway, some of that route is mighty lonely and dark. I almost went off the road at one curve."

Caroline told Nick about the two Warrenstown apprentices who had been killed on Sunday. "But they didn't go

into that ditch because their car went off the road in the
dark," she said. "They'd been smoking pot."

Nick winced. "God help their parents."

Caroline was very tempted to tell Nick about the marijuana she'd found in Meg's closet, yet not only had she
told her stepdaughter that she wouldn't but she didn't want
to spoil their first hours together after too long a separa-
tion. The thought of the fatal car accident reminded her of
another, though.

"Nick?"

"Yes?"

"In my research, I came across an old *Vanity Fair* article
that talked about when Daniel Sterling had that car accident and was killed after Belinda Winthrop's party two
years ago."

"Uh-huh," Nick responded as he poured more coffee
into both of their cups.

"Well, it said his wife told police that Daniel said he'd
argued with someone at the party before he went for a ride
to cool off. And the article mentioned that you had been
one of the guests and had been questioned."

"Me and everyone else there, Sunshine."

"I don't understand why you never told me, Nick, especially after you knew that I was planning on doing stories
about Warrenstown and Belinda Winthrop."

Nick shrugged. "I don't know, Caroline. Maybe it's because I don't particularly like to remember that summer."

"Why not?"

"I guess, for starters, it's what I said last night. That
was the summer before Maggie died. We didn't even
know she was sick when we came up for the reading of my
screenplay. We had a good time, but I always feel guilty
that I didn't spend enough time with Maggie that summer." He paused to take another sip of coffee before continuing. "I was so engrossed in the theatrical goings-on
that I left her to wander around on her own a lot of the
time. Sure, Maggie could amuse herself, and she loved
going to the museums, especially the Clark. I know she

drove down to Stockbridge to look at Norman Rockwell's paintings and went to Lenox to tour Edith Wharton's mansion. But I've always felt I should have gone with her."

Caroline took her husband's hand. "You couldn't have known, Nick."

"I know." He exhaled deeply. "But whenever I think of that summer, I feel sad. So, male that I am, I try to avoid the subject."

Caroline leaned over and kissed her husband's cheek. "But what about Belinda Winthrop's party?" she asked. "Who do you think Daniel Sterling fought with before he drove off?"

"Sunshine, if Daniel Sterling fought with someone at Belinda's party, I have no idea who it was." Nick lifted the breakfast tray from his lap and put it on the floor. He turned to gaze at Caroline. The morning sun streaming through the window bathed her in the most enhancing light. He was enchanted by her shining blue eyes, her fine features, her pale, smooth skin. When he'd first met Caroline, she'd reminded him of what he imagined the heroines in one of the Brontë sisters' novels would look like. "Now why are we wasting our valuable time on the past?" he asked as he leaned over to kiss her. "The present interests me a lot more."

# CHAPTER 32

WHEN HE WAS FINISHED arranging the latest shipment in neat stacks, Gus sat down on the dirt floor and admired his work. He was exhausted. One night a week, every week, he had no sleep at all. He'd wait up late for the plane to come and then work until dawn, carrying the boxes from the meadow to the cave.

If he could actually trust anyone else, he could hire someone to do this lifting and hauling and storing. But he didn't want to share his profits, and he couldn't take the chance that someone might rat him out. That was what had happened the last time. That was what had sent him to jail. He wouldn't risk it again.

Gus pointed the flashlight at his watch, knowing he should be back at the house well before Belinda got up. He pulled himself to a standing position, brushed the dirt from the seat of his jeans, and climbed the ladder. He squinted as his eyes adjusted to the daylight.

He drove the golf cart out of the woods, dreading the day ahead. Belinda had that party planned for tonight, and she would no doubt have a list of things for him to do today. And he had to get down to Pittsfield this afternoon for the appointment with his parole officer. What a nuisance that was.

Gus went straight to the barn and began to take out the folding chairs that Belinda wanted arranged around the tables on the patio. He'd have that all set up by the time she came downstairs so she would be pleased. He wondered if she would bring up the hole she'd found in the woods. If she did, he still wasn't certain how he was going to explain it to her.

But Gus was pretty sure he had some more time to come up with his explanation. Belinda would be preoccupied with her new play, and the party afterward. He had at least another several hours to come up with a good lie.

# CHAPTER 33

IT NEVER CEASED TO amaze Caroline how different Meg was when she was around her father from when she was alone with Caroline. All of Meg's sullenness was gone the minute Nick showed up. Caroline was sure it had been a good idea to include Nick in the tour Meg had grudgingly agreed to give her stepmother and the camera crew.

"Thanks for putting the time aside to show us around like this, cupcake," said Nick as the group walked down the long corridor that led to the backstage area of the theater.

Meg beamed her response. But when Caroline offered her own thanks, Meg ignored her. Caroline caught the look Lamar and Boomer exchanged, signaling that they got the picture of the relationship between the two women.

"This is the greenroom," said Meg, waving her hand at a large space filled with couches, chairs, and a cot. "This is where mostly the crew waits between scenery changes. But I think there's an Actors' Equity rule. That's why there's the little bed."

Down the hallway was the laundry room, outfitted with several washing machines and dryers. It adjoined the costume shop. Long tables for spreading out and cutting yards of fabric dominated the room. Bolts of cloth stood in large canvas bins. Dress forms were stationed next to the numerous sewing machines and irons. Lamar's camera captured it all.

"Now this is where I've been spending a lot of my time, Dad," said Meg, ignoring the rest of the group as they approached the next door. "This is Belinda Winthrop's dressing room."

Lamar was still recording as Meg opened the door. The camera caught a willowy blond, dressed in a green velvet gown, standing in front of the mirror. With an annoyed look on her face, the young woman turned to face the strangers.

"Excuse me. What do you think you're . . ." Her voice trailed off and she blushed as she recognized Meg.

"Hi, Langley," said Meg.

"Oh, Meg. Hi. I was just practicing. I wanted to go over my lines and see if it felt any different wearing the costume. You know . . . just in case I ever have to fill in for Belinda."

# CHAPTER 34

ZEKE AMBROSE WHISTLED TO a tune on the radio as he turned his station wagon in to the driveway of Curtains Up. He was eager to see Remington's portrait of Belinda as Valerie in *Devil in the Details* for the first time. All the buzz about the play compounded the usual enthusiasm that Ambrose Gallery patrons expressed when they knew that a Remington Peters exhibition was scheduled. Zeke and Jean were expecting an excellent crowd for tomorrow night's opening.

Zeke wished for the umpteenth time that Remington would allow his portraits of Belinda to be sold. If he had done that, the portraits would have been in private collections and not destroyed in that horrible studio fire three years ago. Zeke tried not to think about all those fabulous works of art reduced to ash. The idea broke his heart, not only because of the tragic waste but because Remington had lost the most important pieces of his life's work.

Zeke and Jean had worried that Remington would be crushed, sinking into a depression that wouldn't allow him to paint again. They'd done all they could think of to support him, enlisting Belinda's assistance. Her offer of the carriage house as a new home for Remington and his studio had brought the first post-fire smile to the painter's face. Once Remington had moved into Belinda's place, he was able to begin working again.

Now, with the addition of the painting Zeke was picking up this morning, there would be three Remington Peters portraits of Belinda in her Warrenstown roles. Also already hanging on the wall at the Ambrose Gallery were various landscapes of the Berkshires that Remington would allow to be sold.

Pulling up to the carriage house, Zeke parked, got out, and went to the back of the car. He opened the rear hatch and lifted out the box containing the batting he would carefully wrap around the portrait before transporting it to the gallery. He carried the box to the front door, putting it down to knock.

No answer.

Zeke knocked again, then a third time. He walked around to the back of the carriage house, cupped his hands against the large window, and tried to see inside. He couldn't detect any movement. A large canvas stood on the easel, but it was positioned so the painted image Zeke was so anxious to see was obscured from view.

He went back around to the front and was about to get into the station wagon when he saw Remington walking up the driveway.

"Hello," Zeke called. "I was afraid you were standing me up."

As Remington approached, Zeke could see his shoulders were slumped and his mouth was turned down. When the two men shook hands, Zeke could feel grit on Remington's.

"What have you been doing? Gardening?" asked the gallery owner as he looked at the dirt on Remington's hands and clothes.

Remington brushed at his pants. "No. I just went for a walk in the woods."

"Oh. Well, let's get to it, man," said Zeke, his face brightening. "Let's go look at the portrait." He turned toward the front door.

"Zeke, wait."

"What is it?"

"I can't give you the portrait."

Zeke looked at Remington. "What do you mean?"

"It's not ready."

"You're too hard on yourself, Remington. I'm sure it's glorious."

"It's not. Believe me, it's not."

"Please, Remington, let's go look at it. Let me give you my opinion."

Remington looked down at the ground and spoke softly. "I respect your opinion, Zeke, you know that. But I just can't let anyone, not even you, see this portrait yet."

# CHAPTER 35

*ANOTHER CHECK OF THE computer revealed there was still no answer from Brightlights999.*

*With an e-mail address like that, odds were that the person Amy had tried to contact in the last minutes of her life was a female. But whoever it was could bring a lot of unwanted attention if he or she went to the authorities with the image captured by Amy's cell phone.*

*It had been pure luck that Amy and Tommy had been smoking weed just before they were forced off the road. With the autopsy reports showing marijuana in their systems, the police had been able to close the case.*

*But there was no way the police were going to think the death of the nosy librarian was an accident. It would be painfully obvious that the piercing of her wrinkled throat had been deliberate.*

*Law enforcement was going to be all over a murder case in charming little Warrenstown. And if Brightlights went to the cops with the digital picture of the car that Amy had sent just before she died, that could cause a suspicious detective to come knocking on the door.*

Come on, Brightlights, respond to my message. I need to know who you are.

# CHAPTER 36

VICTORIA PUTTERED AROUND THE kitchen, taking a bowl from the cupboard and some eggs and milk from the refrigerator. She cracked the eggs against the side of the bowl and emptied the contents into the milk she had already poured. After adding a bit of vanilla extract, she whisked everything together and dipped a couple of slices of sourdough bread into the mixture.

While she was waiting for the French toast to cook on the griddle, she washed and sliced some strawberries. Halving two oranges, Victoria thought of Daniel as she juiced them. It had always been their custom to have large breakfasts on the mornings their plays opened.

The usual coffee and cigarettes wouldn't do today. This was the day that *Devil in the Details* would finally be performed for the public. This was the day she'd been waiting for, ever since Daniel died.

Everyone had said that she wouldn't be able to go on without him, and Victoria understood why. Daniel had been an established, successful playwright even before they married. She had been a virtual nobody. When she'd begged Daniel to give co-writing a try, everyone had just assumed that he was the one who was really doing the work. And Victoria had to admit to herself that everyone had assumed correctly. It was only after Daniel's death that she'd actually come into her own. Now a Pulitzer Prize might actually be within her grasp.

Finding the syrup in the cabinet over the refrigerator, Victoria poured some of the thick, sticky liquid into a small pitcher and zapped it in the microwave. Cold syrup wouldn't do on her nice, warm French toast. Nothing but the best this morning, nothing but the best to begin this wonderful day.

Victoria closed her eyes as she chewed on the first bite, thinking it was good to let Belinda sleep as late as possible. Belinda had to be refreshed in order to give Valerie the energy she deserved on the stage and on the videotape for the Pulitzer committee.

# CHAPTER 37

MEG LED THE WAY through the rest of their theater tour. She showed her father, Caroline, and the crew the storage area under the stage, filled with crates of wires and scenery flats; she showed them the hydraulic lift that raised and lowered a portion of the stage; she pointed four stories up to the catwalk and explained how three chandeliers rose and fell from that height for three scenes in *Devil in the Details*.

Caroline was impressed, and she said so. "It's wonderful how you know your way around this theater, Meg."

The compliment was answered with a shrug. Caroline looked at Nick for his reaction to his daughter's response, but if he had noticed, he wasn't showing it. He was beaming at Meg. "I'm proud of you, sweetheart," he said as he put his arm around Meg and squeezed her closer.

"I've got to change tapes," said Lamar as he checked his camera.

"We've already got enough," said Caroline. "You guys can take a break, and we'll meet back here after lunch for the interview with Keith Fallows."

Caroline, Nick, and Meg left the crew as they packed up their paraphernalia. As she usually did when she was with father and daughter, Caroline found herself feeling like an outsider. "You know what? I think I'm going to leave the two of you alone for a while so I can get caught up with work," she said.

Meg's face brightened, while Nick looked at Caroline with a quizzical expression. Caroline noticed, though, that he didn't try to dissuade her. She was beginning to walk away when a young man approached Meg.

"Did you hear?" he asked. "Somebody was murdered at the town library."

# CHAPTER 38

THE SANDWICHES AT OSCAR'S Deli had names like "Julia Roberts," "Hilary Swank," "Halle Berry," and "Charlize Theron." Only Academy Award winners had the honor of having their names written, along with the lists of ingredients in their sandwiches, on the giant chalkboard that covered most of the deli wall.

Caroline stood in line and studied the menu. She was tempted by the "Tom Hanks"—corned beef, Swiss cheese, lettuce, tomato, and Russian dressing—and the "Angelina Jolie"—sautéed peppers and onions, mushrooms, melted provolone, sprouts, and tomato. But by the time it was her turn to order, Caroline had decided it might be bad luck not to order the "Belinda Winthrop"—turkey, Swiss, lettuce, tomato, mayonnaise, and cranberry sauce on rye.

"You on vacation?" the man behind the counter asked as he slathered mayonnaise on the bread.

"Actually, I'm working," said Caroline. "But it's a nice assignment."

"What do you do?"

"I'm a film and theater critic."

"Oh, yeah? For a newspaper?"

"No, television."

The man looked up from making the sandwich and

studied Caroline's face. She could tell he didn't recognize her.

"What show would I see you on?" he asked as he went back to covering the mayonnaise with sliced turkey.

*"KEY to America,"* she said.

"That explains it," said the man. "I never watch television in the morning. I have to get in here early to set up. But my wife watches it. I'm gonna tell her you were in. She'll get a real kick out of that. What's your name?"

"Caroline Enright."

"Hello, Caroline Enright. I'm Oscar Dubinsky. I'd shake your hand, but . . ." Oscar held up his hands, which were covered by thin plastic gloves.

"Don't worry about it," said Caroline.

"So, you're gonna review *Devil in the Details* when it opens tonight?" Oscar asked.

"That's the plan," said Caroline, eager now to get her sandwich and leave.

"This your first time in Warrenstown?"

"Yes."

"Too bad you have to come when all this upset is going on. Warrenstown is usually such a nice, quiet place. But between those kids killed last weekend and the cops finding the librarian murdered this morning, I don't know what our town is coming to."

"I just heard about that," said Caroline. "What a horrible thing."

"Yeah. One of our officers was just in for lunch, and he told me he never saw so much blood. Her carotid artery was completely severed." Oscar finished wrapping the sandwich and handed it across the counter. "Poor Theresa."

# CHAPTER 39

IT HADN'T BEEN SMART to cancel the interview with KEY News yesterday, thought Keith as he entered the theater. He needed all the positive press he could get, and it did no good to alienate Caroline Enright. He was determined to be much more agreeable today.

Caroline and her crew were waiting for him on the stage.

"You told me to pick the place for the interview," she said, "and I pick this."

She was right, thought Keith. Having them up on the set was much more visually interesting than just sitting out in the audience. He tried to be patient as the rotund soundman wired him. He waited as the video guy checked his white balance and made the necessary adjustments. He smiled as Caroline asked him her questions. He answered, mustering up all the charm he could. After fifteen minutes, Keith had had enough, but Caroline wasn't finished.

"Tell me about your plans for this play," she said.

"At this point, Caroline, I just want to get through opening night."

She persevered. "Of course, but if *Devil in the Details* is the success everyone expects it to be tonight, what would you like to see happen next?"

"Well, I'd like to see it please audiences for the two-week run here in Warrenstown, and after that I have little doubt that it will go on to Broadway."

"With you as director?"

"Perhaps."

"What about a screen version?"

"What about it?"

"Would you want to try your hand at directing the film version of *Devil in the Details*?"

"That's an interesting thought."

"And surely not the first time you've considered it," said Caroline.

Keith smiled a tight smile. He wasn't going to embarrass himself before a national audience by announcing he would direct his first film without knowing for certain that he had his ducks all in a row. Without Belinda in the lead, Keith's ducks were scattered. He was putting all his hopes on the performance tonight. If Belinda triumphed as Valerie, then surely he could bring her around to star in what could be another Academy Award–winning role for her.

"As I said, Caroline, at this point, I just want to get through tonight."

# CHAPTER 40

DRIVING HOME FROM PITTSFIELD, Gus smirked. It was so easy to placate his overworked, underpaid parole officer. As long as he showed up when he was supposed to, passed his drug test, demonstrated he was still holding down his job, and pretended to be a good little Boy Scout, he got a pass until the next time. No one came out to Curtains Up to check on him—not that they would necessarily discover anything even if they did. His cave was far from easy to find.

The caterer's white truck was parked at the side of the farmhouse when Gus arrived. Trays of food were being stowed in the kitchen, and crates of glassware were being carried out to the patio, where the bar was being set up. Low glass containers filled with red, yellow, and pink snapdragons sat on scarlet tablecloths spread on the round tables. Tiny red pitchforks poked out from the top of each flower arrangement.

Gus went into the kitchen, picked a deviled egg from a tray, and popped it into his mouth, ignoring the disapproving look from the caterer. Yep, he had a pretty cushy gig here, Gus thought as he eyed the devil's food cake. A good thing that could keep on going indefinitely as long as Belinda didn't stick her pretty little nose where it didn't belong.

# CHAPTER 41

BELINDA SAT IN FRONT of the makeup mirror applying her lipstick when Meg came into the dressing room carrying a glass vase filled with two dozen long-stemmed roses.

"Red. He never forgets," said Belinda as she inhaled the fragrance of the flowers.

Meg wished Belinda would volunteer who *he* was, but she wasn't about to ask what the leading lady might think was too personal a question. If she wanted Meg to know, Belinda would tell her.

On went the corset and the petticoat and the green velvet gown. As Meg zipped up the dress, there was a knock on the door.

"Come in," called Belinda.

Langley stuck her head inside. "I just wanted to say, 'Break a leg.'"

"Thanks, Langley," said Belinda.

"Oooo, you got flowers." Langley walked straight over to the dressing table. "They're beautiful. Who sent them?"

"A friend," said Belinda.

"The *friend* must be crazy about you," said Langley. "Who is it?"

Meg was embarrassed by the understudy's rudeness. But Belinda, smooth as ever, simply ignored Langley's question.

"Get me my fan, please, will you, Meg?" Belinda asked.

Meg obeyed. "You look beautiful, Belinda," she said.

"Thank you, dear. And thank you for all your help." With that, Belinda departed for the stage, leaving Meg and Langley in the dressing room.

Langley picked up the small card Belinda had left beside the flowers. "Twenty years and you grow ever more beautiful, Belinda. Valerie is very lucky tonight," Langley read aloud. "Yours forever, Remington."

# CHAPTER 42

AS THE CURTAIN LOWERED, the audience erupted in thunderous applause.

"Magnificent," Nick leaned over and yelled in Caroline's ear as the cast of *Devil in the Details* came out to take their bows. The last actor out was Belinda Winthrop, and the audience came to their feet and cheered.

Watching Belinda take her bows, Caroline was already mentally composing the review she would write, knowing that she had just witnessed a rare production. Brilliant, inspired, breathtaking—those were some of the words she wanted to include in describing not only Belinda's performance but also the content of the play. Victoria Sterling's creation deserved the Pulitzer Prize. How she had envisioned, and executed, the scenes leading to the unmasking of the sociopathic husband was amazing. Caroline couldn't help but feel that only someone who had firsthand knowledge of sociopathy could have handled the subject so expertly.

What was the old saw? *Write what you know.*

REFUSED PERMISSION TO RECORD the play, Lamar and Boomer waited in the lobby.

"I hope that dub they're giving Caroline will be of decent quality," muttered Lamar.

"Hey, it's not your problem, man," said Boomer as he munched on the giant oatmeal cookie he had purchased at the refreshment cart. "If they wouldn't let us shoot, they wouldn't let us shoot. There's nothing we can do about it."

"Yeah, but I hate depending on video shot by the audiovisual department of the Warrenstown Summer Playhouse. Who knows who's manning the camera! It could be some college kid."

The doors to the theater opened, and the audience started streaming into the lobby. Lamar studied the expressions on the theatergoers' faces. "Looks like it was a hit," he said.

Boomer grunted as he popped the last of the cookie into his mouth.

Lamar spotted Caroline and her husband. He waved to get their attention.

"Good, huh?" he asked.

"Fabulous," Caroline answered. "I'll tell you all about it later, but now let's get right downstairs to Belinda Winthrop's dressing room."

Nick let go of Caroline's hand. "I'll see you later then?" he asked.

Caroline took his hand again. "Oh no, you're coming with us. Don't you want to see Belinda?"

"HURRY UP AND WAIT," muttered Boomer as the KEY News group stood outside the dressing room door. Twenty minutes passed as Keith Fallows and Victoria Sterling each went in for a visit with the star. Finally, the dressing room door opened.

"Belinda can see you now." Meg beckoned them inside.

Belinda rose from her dressing table chair to greet the group.

"Nick McGregor! How wonderful to see you," Belinda said as she hugged him. "It's been too long."

"You were just terrific tonight, Belinda," said Nick, flashing his bright smile. "But I'm not going to stay. I know you have this interview to do, but I should also tell you how glad I am that Meg has had the experience of working with you."

Belinda's expression was puzzled as she looked from Nick to Meg.

"Meg is my daughter, Belinda."

"You're kidding. I had no idea," said Belinda. She turned to Meg. "I should have made the connection, but I just didn't. Yet now that I look at you, I can see your mother in your face. She was a lovely woman, Meg. I'm sure she'd be so proud of you."

"Thank you," said Meg.

Nick looked a bit crestfallen, thought Caroline. Did it bother him for some reason that Belinda hadn't connected Meg as his daughter, or was he upset to be reminded of Maggie?

"Well, now that I know you're here, Nick, you must come to the party at my place tonight. I insist on it."

"That's swell of you, Belinda," said Nick. "Now I won't spend another minute keeping you from your interview." He leaned over and gave Meg and Caroline pecks on the cheek. "I'll see my girls later."

"Nick, your hair has grown whiter, but don't tell me that Caroline Enright is your daughter, too," said Belinda.

Nick laughed. "No, Belinda, Caroline is my new wife. We were married a few months ago."


"I CAN'T TELL YOU how much I appreciate your taking the time tonight for this interview," said Caroline.

"My pleasure," said Belinda. "I'm especially glad I agreed, now that I know you're married to Nick. He's a wonderful guy. I'm glad he's found someone to love again."

Caroline felt uncomfortable, conscious of the fact that her stepdaughter was listening.

"I think I'll get this stuff to the laundry," said Meg, hurrying from the dressing room.

"Did I say something wrong?" asked Belinda as the door clicked shut.

Caroline shook her head. "No, you didn't. But her mother's death is still raw for Meg. It's hard for her to accept a stepmother."

"It must be hard for you, too," said Belinda. "A mother is irreplaceable. And how do you possibly fill a ghost's shoes?"

"IMAGINE BEING ASSOCIATED WITH someone who has no conscience. Victoria Sterling has given us a staggering view of the true terror it must be to be joined to a sociopath. I count myself fortunate to be able to interpret this rich and fabulous material."

Caroline felt that Belinda was forthcoming with her answers through the entire twenty-minute interview.

"Thank you for giving us your time, when I know you have a party to get to," she said. "Let me just ask you one last thing. What about taking this role to the screen? Does a *Devil in the Details* movie interest you?"

Belinda shook her head. "I'd be interested in seeing it, but I have no desire to play Valerie on film."

"That surprises me," said Caroline. "It would seem to be a natural for you."

Belinda smiled. "Let's just say there are other projects I'd rather take on."

# CHAPTER 43

THE PARTY WAS ALREADY in full swing when the hostess arrived. The guests milling around the torchlit patio broke into applause when Belinda appeared.

"Thank you, everybody, and thank you for coming to Curtains Up tonight." Belinda beamed as she looked around. "It's so wonderful to have you all here to celebrate."

"You're the best, Belinda," shouted George Essex, the actor who had played Davis.

"Brava," shouted another, and the crowd clapped again with enthusiasm.

"Well, all of you, make yourselves at home," Belinda called. "Let's eat, drink, and be merry."

WHILE THE WAITSTAFF CIRCULATED with trays of canapés, Victoria sought out her hostess and friend.

"It's a terrific party, Belinda," she said, "a fitting celebration of your triumph tonight."

"*Our* triumph tonight," said Belinda. "I only interpreted your words, my dear."

Victoria inhaled on her cigarette. As she exhaled, she smiled. "It *is* sweet, isn't it?"

"Like honey."

The two women toasted each other, softly touching

their martini glasses. Victoria speared her olive with a toothpick and slipped it in her mouth. As she chewed, she noticed Gus, beer in hand, surveying the crowd. He looked in her direction and nodded. Victoria lifted her glass.

"You're always so democratic, Belinda," Victoria whispered to her friend. "Inviting the help and all."

Belinda's eyes followed Victoria's stare. "Oh, you mean Gus. You know, I invited him the first year he came to work here just to make him feel comfortable. I guess he assumes he's always invited." Belinda took a sip of her cocktail. "It's fine, though. What's one more body?"

"Especially when it's as good looking as that one," said Victoria. "But you know, Belinda, after I saw Gus leave in his truck this afternoon, I took a little trip across the meadow. I was going to tell you tomorrow, but I don't think it should wait. What I found wasn't good."

"What is it?"

"I think he's running some sort of drug business out there in the woods."

Belinda frowned as Victoria described what she had seen. "If those boxes down there don't contain drugs, there has to be something else in them that he doesn't want anyone to know about," she finished. "Why else would he go to all the trouble of stashing them in that cave?"

"That's all I need," Belinda groaned. " 'Drug Operation at Belinda Winthrop's House.' " She made imaginary quotation marks in the air. "*Entertainment Tonight* and *Inside Edition* would be all over that."

"Don't forget *People* and the *Star*," added Victoria.

"I'm going to have to call the police," Belinda said.

"If you turn him in to the police, you risk a lot of negative publicity, Belinda."

"What else can I do?"

"Well, maybe you could just tell him you're letting him go. Then he'll have to pack up and leave."

• • •

THE BUFFET TABLE WAS laden with platters and chafing dishes filled with two summer pastas, Asian pork with a pungent wasabi, spiced ham, and chicken wings with hot sauce.

"Keith, please go ahead and get yourself a plate," said Belinda.

The director patted the empty seat next to him. "Sit down and talk to me for a minute, Belinda."

"All right." She sat at the round table. With most people in the buffet line, she and Keith had it to themselves. Belinda's eyes were drawn to Keith's waist. "I like that tie on you," she said. "Leave it to you to wear it in a way that nobody else would think of." The red silk tie that each male guest had been given as a party favor was threaded through the loops of Keith's khaki trousers.

"Nice belt, huh?" Keith smiled and, lifting the champagne flute to his lips, downed the bubbly. "You were wonderful tonight, Belinda."

"*Devil in the Details* is a team effort, Keith. We can all be proud."

"Yes, usually I'm in knots waiting to see the reviews. Tonight, I know I don't have to worry. But one thing . . ." He paused.

"What is it?" asked Belinda.

"One thing that would make the night absolutely perfect would be to hear that you will sign on for the movie version."

Belinda closed her eyes. "Oh, Keith, please, not now."

"Why? Why don't you want to do it, Belinda?"

"I just don't, that's all."

"Is it the money? I'm sure that can be arranged to your satisfaction."

"No, Keith. It's not the money."

"Well, what is it then? You said you would. What's made you change your mind?"

"Why do you insist on pursuing this, Keith? Can't you

just understand that I don't want to do the movie and leave it at that?"

The director erupted, letting his glass drop and shatter on the stone patio. "Damn it, Belinda. You owe me a better explanation than that. I've gone out on a limb, promising potential investors you'll do the movie."

Bending down to pick up the broken glass, she said in a whisper, "You shouldn't have done that, Keith, and I don't owe you anything." She stood up, with shards of glass in her hands. "Since you insist, I'm going to tell you. If you have to know the truth, it's *you*."

"What do you mean?"

"I just can't work with you again. It's too hard."

"So if someone else was directing the movie, you might play the role of Valerie for him?"

"Yes, Keith, maybe I would." Belinda turned from the table and walked away.


ON HER WAY BACK from the buffet line, Meg overheard the end of the conversation and witnessed Keith's anger. She was going to have some interesting things to write about in her journal tonight.

# CHAPTER 44

"GOD, BEING HERE BRINGS back memories," said Nick as he, Caroline, and Meg ate at one of the round tables. Nick stirred his drink with the pitchfork swizzle stick. "Belinda is famous for giving theme parties."

Caroline held out the red silk scarf each female guest had been given upon arrival and admired it. Even if it hadn't had the designer's initials featured in the flame pattern, she would have been able to tell it was expensive just by the feel of it. She draped the scarf over her shoulders.

"Tell us about the last party of Belinda's you went to," she said to Nick, changing the subject.

"She was in *Treasure Trove* that summer, playing a woman who won the lottery, so Belinda had organized a treasure hunt. All the guests were given maps and flashlights and sent out to find the treasure."

"What was the treasure, Dad?" asked Meg.

"A little chest filled with lottery tickets. But it was a lot of fun following that map. Your mother was so gung ho about it, Meg. You should have seen her scurrying through the woods, trying to be the one to finish first. She was in such a rush she didn't pay enough attention to the spots that were marked on the map to show where there were holes in the ground. She tripped over one and sprained her ankle. A group of us had to carry her out of the woods."

"They printed that treasure map in the *Vanity Fair* article I read," said Caroline as a waiter wearing horns and a devil's tail took her plate away.

"There are lots of holes out there," Nick said. "And apparently some of them lead to underground caves. But Maggie claimed the one that snagged her wasn't even on the map."

# CHAPTER 45

SLIPPING AWAY FROM THE party, Belinda walked over to the carriage house. Light streamed from the windows. Remington was still up.

The front door opened after her first knock. Remington's face registered surprise and pleasure when he saw Belinda standing in the doorway.

"I wanted to thank you for those beautiful flowers, Remington," she said. "You always remember that red roses are my favorite."

"That's something I could never forget, Belinda."

"Well, it was a lovely gesture."

"My pleasure," he said.

"Remington, won't you please come over and join us at the party?"

"Thank you, Belinda. But I'm working."

"Can't you take a break? It might be good for you. You know what they say, all work and no play . . ."

She caught a flicker of indecision on his face. "Come have a glass of wine and help yourself to the buffet," she insisted. "The caterer really outdid himself this year."

"You know it's difficult for me to be with lots of people, Belinda, but it's always been hard to say no to you."

"Well, don't start now. You've always been at my parties, and it isn't the same without you."

Remington looked down at his paint-spattered shirt. "I'll have to wash up and change," he said.

"I'll wait for you," she said. "Can I come in and see what you're working on?"

"Of course you can come in, but I'm still working on your portrait. You know I never let you see it until it's done."

"Fair enough," she said. "Go cover it. But I'm going to wait right here for you. I don't want to give you the chance to change your mind."

WHILE SHE WAITED FOR Remington to change, Belinda sat on the couch against the studio wall and stared at the cloth-covered canvas that stood in the middle of the room. She was sorely tempted to take just a peek, but if Remington caught her, Belinda knew he would be truly upset. Ever since that first summer, when she'd broken his heart, Belinda had avoided hurting Remington at all costs. She wasn't going to do it now, no matter how curious she was.

"How you doing up there?" she called to the loft.

"I'll be down in a minute."

Thinking she should be getting back to her guests, Belinda got up and paced the floor in front of the couch. A copy of the *Devil in the Details* script lying on a side table caught her eye. She picked it up and began flipping through the well-turned pages, noticing with increasing interest the passages he had marked.

"Remington," she called. "I really do have to get back. Can I trust you to hurry up and come over to the party?"

"Yes, Belinda. You can trust me."

"All right, then. I'll see you in a little bit," she said, taking the script with her as she went out the door.

# CHAPTER 46

GUS TAPPED HIS FOOT to the music and followed the blonde with his eyes, unable to place her. She was somehow familiar, but he couldn't come up with her name.

"Having a good time, Langley?" Gus heard Belinda ask the young woman.

*Langley.* Yes, that was it. She'd had dark hair when she came to the party two years ago. Gus decided he liked the blond hair better. It was much sexier.

Waiting for Belinda to move on to another guest, he walked up behind Langley. "You're even more beautiful than the last time I saw you here," he whispered into her ear.

With a smile on her face, Langley turned around. But her expression turned sour when she saw it was Gus. "I was hoping you wouldn't recognize me," she said. "Better yet, I was hoping you didn't work here anymore."

"Oh, don't be like that, Langley. We had a good time, didn't we?"

"Please," she answered with sarcasm in her voice. She turned to walk away, but Gus grabbed her arm.

"Hey, wait a minute," he said.

"Let go of my arm."

"Ah, come on. Let's take a few bong rips, for old times' sake."

"That was my mistake the last time," said Langley. "But I don't do drugs at all anymore. And I guess I can

thank you for that. The way you took advantage of me
when I was stoned was disgusting. I promised myself
never to let anything like that happen again."

"You didn't seem to mind at the time, baby. We had a
good time out there in the woods."

"You know what? You're a pig," Langley spat. "But let
me tell you something, so you'll have it straight. Two
years ago I was a different person. I was a nervous extra
at a party with the grown-ups. I thought I needed to be
stoned to relax. I don't anymore. Now I told you, let go of
my arm," she said through clenched teeth. "You're hurting me."

"Let go of her, Gus!"

Gus dropped Langley's arm and turned to see Belinda
glaring at him.

"Please, come into the study. I want to speak with you."
Belinda spun around and walked across the patio. Gus followed her into the house.

"Come on, Belinda," he began as soon as they were in
the room. "I wasn't doing any harm."

Belinda pulled the door partially closed. "Sit down,"
she said as she walked over to her desk and sat behind it.
She looked him straight in the eye. "It's not working out,
Gus. I'm letting you go."

She pulled open the desk drawer and took out her
checkbook. "I'm giving you two weeks' severance, but I
want you out, tomorrow."

He stared at her, dumbfounded. "You're kidding me."

"No, Gus. I'm not."

"Just for coming on to Langley?"

"I don't want to talk about it any further, Gus," she
said, holding out the check.

"You can't do this to me, Belinda." His face reddened
as he rose from the chair and stood, resolutely, in front of
the desk.

"I can, Gus. And I am. Please don't go back to the
party. You should go to your apartment and start packing."

# CHAPTER 47

THE MAN IN A denim shirt, a pair of wrinkled khaki pants, and worn boat shoes stood alone at the side of the patio, observing the guests. As Caroline watched him, she found herself feeling a bit sorry for him.

"Who is that?" she asked.

Nick looked in the direction of her gaze. "That's Remington Peters, the artist."

Oh, so that was the man who was so in love with Belinda Winthrop that he had devoted his adult life to her, trying to capture her essence in his paintings.

"He looks bewildered," Caroline observed.

"Remington is a strange bird," said Nick. "If you ask me, his obsession with Belinda is weird."

"Shouldn't we go over and talk with him, Nick? He's standing all by himself."

"We can if you want, but I think Remington prefers to be by himself. The only reason he's here is that it's Belinda's party. If he can't be with Belinda, he'd rather be alone."

NICK MADE THE INTRODUCTIONS. Remington shook Caroline's hand but didn't smile.

"It's a pleasure to meet you," she said. "I admired your work yesterday at the Ambrose Gallery."

"Thank you," he mumbled.

"I spoke with the gallery owner," Caroline said. "She seemed so excited about the exhibition of your new work."

Remington nodded but didn't comment.

She tried again. "After seeing Belinda's performance tonight, I'm eager myself to see how you've portrayed her as Valerie."

"You're going to have to wait a while for that," he said.

"Oh. I thought the exhibition opened tomorrow."

"Well, the portrait isn't ready." Remington stared into Caroline's eyes. She sensed he wouldn't welcome any additional questioning on the subject.

# CHAPTER 48

*DON'T PANIC. ACT LIKE* everything is just fine.

Gus stood in the busy kitchen trying to decide what to do next. Belinda had just fired him, but he wasn't sure why. He was pretty certain it couldn't be just for coming on to Langley.

Did Belinda know what he was doing out in the woods? Had she figured out the business he was running on her property? Gus had the sinking feeling that she had. And if she decided to go to the cops, he'd be going back to jail. This time, it would be a longer sentence.

But that would happen only if she went to the police.

Gus felt his chest tighten. He had to relax, remain calm. He had been in tough spots before, and he'd gotten into trouble only when he panicked.

To reassure himself, he patted the rear pocket of his jeans. Then he walked to the downstairs powder room, locked the door, and rolled himself a nice, fat joint. This was Thursday, he reasoned. He wouldn't be tested again for a full week. But that wouldn't be long enough for his urine to clear. He'd have to get some of that wretched bleachlike drink that would make him want to throw up; but it would cleanse his system for his next drug test. A nasty prospect, but a price he was willing to pay.

He ignored the knock on the door and the jiggling of

the knob as he sat on the toilet lid and inhaled. Gradually and predictably, he felt the sense of calm come over him.

The house had central air-conditioning, but Gus opened the bathroom window. He searched the cabinet over the sink for some air freshener and sprayed it around. Still, he was pretty certain that the pale brunette who was waiting to come in when he opened the door could smell what he had been doing in there. He could see it in her blue eyes.

# CHAPTER 49

SHAKEN, BELINDA SAT BEHIND the desk and tried to compose herself. Firing someone was always unpleasant. Plus, there was something about Gus that was unnerving. She couldn't be sure he would just go quietly.

Belinda picked up the script of *Devil in the Details* she had taken from Remington's place. After flipping through a few more pages, she took a large envelope from the desk drawer, slid the script into it, and got up to return to her guests.

BELINDA APPROACHED CAROLINE, NICK, and Meg. "Having a good time?" she asked.

"Almost as good as the last time I was here, Belinda," said Nick.

Caroline thought Belinda looked at Nick with a flustered expression, but then she laughed. "I'll take that as a compliment." She turned to Meg. "Would you be a darling, Meg, and take this copy of the script I just got from Remington? I'm afraid I'll forget to bring it to the dressing room tomorrow."

"No problem, Belinda," said Meg as she took the envelope from her.

# FRIDAY

*August 4*

# CHAPTER 50

WITH THE GUESTS STRAGGLING away and the catering staff packing up, Belinda sat by herself on the patio, trying to sort out what had happened in the last few hours. She'd gone from giving one of the best performances of her life to telling her director that she couldn't stand working with him and finding that he had used her name without her permission to raise financing for his movie. Worried that she could be implicated in what her caretaker was doing on her property, she'd fired him with no plan for how she was going to replace him. What she had figured out from Remington's copy of the script had to be dealt with as well. Plus, knowing that Langley was practically drooling to take over her role didn't feel great either. It was too much to deal with at one time.

It had been a marathon of a day, and Belinda was exhausted. She would get a good sleep, and in the morning, she'd be better able to cope with everything. But there was one person she had to talk to right away.

# CHAPTER 51

WHILE THE TUB WAS filling, Caroline undressed. She took the lace nightgown from her suitcase and carried it into the bathroom. She stepped into the warm water and eased herself down into the tub.

She took a deep breath and tried to relax. The excitement of the debut of *Devil in the Details,* her interview with Belinda Winthrop, and the party afterward had left her mind spinning. But beneath the enthusiasm Caroline felt about those occurrences stirred uneasiness at thoughts of the dead apprentices and the murdered librarian. Though she knew none of them, the violent ends they'd met were unnerving. She could have been that librarian, murdered while doing her job. Meg could have been one of those kids.

Caroline lifted her hand, noticed that the skin on her fingers was beginning to pucker, and realized she must have been sitting in the water for quite a while.

"Nick?" she called out.

There was no answer from the bedroom. He still hadn't returned from walking Meg to her dorm. What was taking him so long?

# CHAPTER 52

"HOW DID YOU FIND out?"

"I'm not telling you," said Belinda.

"So you know. Now what?"

"I don't know for sure," said Belinda, "but you can't expect to get away with this."

"I have so far."

Belinda shook her head in disbelief. "Don't you feel the least bit guilty?"

"Honestly? No. I'm only sorry that you found out."

Belinda turned to pick up the telephone.

"I wouldn't do that, Belinda. Put the phone down."

Ignoring the command, she began to push the numbers on the keypad, unaware of what was coming until she felt the soft silk around her neck. As it tightened, she collapsed, blacked out completely, and hit her head on the corner of the desk.

*THE KILLER DRAGGED THE dead weight of Belinda's body to the golf cart. The half-moon provided the only light for the ride to the woods. Once the cart was hidden from view, the killer turned on a flashlight to illuminate the rest of the way to the opening in the forest floor. The killer pulled Belinda out of the cart and lay her at the edge of the hole that led to the underground cave.*

*Just as with Amy, Tommy, and the sour old librarian, the killer checked Belinda's pulse and couldn't find one. Ready to push the body over the edge, the killer noticed the actress was missing one of her shoes.*

# CHAPTER 53

ROLLING OVER IN BED, Caroline opened her eyes. Nick was sleeping beside her. *So much for the lace nightgown,* she thought. She had fallen asleep and not even heard him come in.

Quietly, she got out of bed and went into the bathroom to brush her teeth. She washed and moisturized her face but didn't bother with makeup, only applying some clear lip balm. Caroline was able to dress in a pair of jeans and T-shirt and steal out of the room with her shoulder bag and laptop without waking her husband.

The downstairs coffee shop was open, and she had her pick of the empty tables. She chose one in the corner and set her computer on top.

"What can I get you?" asked the waitress.

"Just coffee right now, thanks," Caroline said.

She looked at the blank computer screen. Where should she begin with this review? Her fingers began to type.

THE WARRENSTOWN SUMMER PLAYHOUSE WAS THE SCENE OF SUSPICION, BETRAYAL, AND DEATH AS VICTORIA STERLING'S NEW PLAY, *DEVIL IN THE DETAILS*, WAS PERFORMED FOR THE FIRST TIME BEFORE A RIVETED AUDIENCE. *DEVIL IN THE DETAILS* LEAPS TO THE FRONT AS ONE OF THE MOST BITINGLY SINISTER PLAYS IN RECENT MEMORY.

PLAYING VALERIE, THE WIFE OF A MAN WHO HAS NO CON-

SCIENCE, BELINDA WINTHROP DEVELOPS A CHARACTER WHO
COMES TO REALIZE THAT THE MAN SHE HAS LOVED IS A SO-
CIOPATH. AS SHE UNCOVERS HER HUSBAND'S LIES, TREACHERY,
AND GREED, THE TENSION MOUNTS TO AN ALMOST UNBEARABLE
LEVEL.

THE TEST OF THE PLAY IS THE EFFECTIVENESS WITH WHICH IT
PORTRAYS A WOMAN GRAPPLING WITH THE DAWNING AWARENESS
THAT HER MATE IS A WICKED MAN WHO POISONS EVERYTHING HE
TOUCHES. AT FIRST, VALERIE THINKS SHE MUST BE WRONG. THEN
SHE THINKS SHE MIGHT BE CRAZY. FINALLY, NEARLY PARALYZED
WITH FEAR, SHE HAS TO FACE THE FACT THAT THE MAN WHO
SLEEPS BESIDE HER AT NIGHT IS PURE EVIL.

DIRECTOR KEITH FALLOWS HAS STAGED, PERHAPS, HIS MAS-
TERPIECE. *DEVIL IN THE DETAILS* WILL UNDOUBTEDLY GO ON TO
BROADWAY, AND PLAYWRIGHT VICTORIA STERLING COULD VERY
WELL WIN THAT PULITZER PRIZE SO MANY ARE TALKING ABOUT.
BUT AUDIENCES CAN ONLY HOPE THAT *DEVIL IN THE DETAILS*,
WITH BELINDA WINTHROP IN THE LEAD, WILL BE SUCCESSFULLY
CONVERTED TO FILM, BECAUSE THIS IS A SPELLBINDING STORY
THAT EVERYONE SHOULD HAVE THE OPPORTUNITY TO SEE.

After she clicked the button sending her review to the
KEY News Web site, Caroline took a sip of the hot coffee.
Belinda had told her in the interview that she was not going to do this film, yet Caroline still felt the last line of her
review was valid. Perhaps, if there was enough popular
demand, Belinda would change her mind. She was one of
a very few actresses who could command the stage as well
as the screen. She was meant to play Valerie.

# CHAPTER 54

*NO MATTER HOW TALENTED, exceptional, or beautiful Belinda was, she couldn't be allowed to destroy everything.*

*That Belinda was buried on her own property was somehow fitting. Everyone knew how much she cared about Curtains Up. Now, her beloved estate would be her final resting place. But there would be no headstone. No one was going to leave flowers on her grave, because no one was going to find her. The cave where Belinda now lay wasn't even on the map of the property.*

*Even if that shoe of hers was found, it wouldn't necessarily lead to Belinda. These woods were too dark, too dense.*

*Yes, Belinda was taken care of, but that damned e-mail was still hanging out there. There was still no response from Brightlights this morning.*

*Brightlights, the irritating loose end.*

# CHAPTER 55

THE EARLY-RISING BIRDS OUTSIDE Victoria's window woke her with their chirping. She opened her eyes and, for just a moment, was unsure where she was. As it dawned on her, a smile spread across her face.

Last night had been everything she had dreamed of and more. Watching *Devil in the Details* come fully to life on the stage had exceeded even her fondest hopes: the thrill of seeing her name on the playbill, the roaring applause of the audience, the praise she'd received from the people at the party. Belinda had truly done justice to the written words. No playwright could have asked for more.

Watching the play, Victoria had kept thinking that the Pulitzer might actually be within her grasp. It was all so exciting and wonderful, and she wanted to talk about it with someone. This morning it was particularly hard not to be sharing her bed with someone. He may not have been the easiest spouse, but Daniel had always been a good sounding board. She missed that.

Victoria got out of bed, went to her purse, and took out a pack of cigarettes. She walked over to the window and lit up. As she exhaled the smoke into the clean, cool air, she couldn't wait to get her hands on the videotape of the performance. She needed to see the tape to reassure herself that *Devil in the Details* was really as spectacular as she thought it had been. She wanted to be certain it was good enough to submit to the prize committee.

Victoria finished her cigarette, put on her robe, and headed downstairs to get some hot coffee. As she passed Belinda's bedroom, Victoria looked through the open doorway. The room was empty, and it was clear that no one had slept in the bed.

# CHAPTER 56

WHEN CAROLINE GOT BACK to the room, the bed was empty and she could hear the shower running. She put her laptop on the dresser beside Nick's, walked to the open bathroom door, and went in.

"Want some company?" she asked as she pulled back the shower curtain.

Nick leaned toward her and planted a clean, wet kiss on her mouth. "Nothing I'd like more, Sunshine," he said. "But unfortunately, and I mean very unfortunately, Meg just called. She thinks she lost that bracelet her mother gave her, and the last time she remembers having it on was at Belinda's last night. I promised her I would go right over there and look for it."

Caroline couldn't keep the look of disappointment from her face.

"You know how she treasures that bracelet, Caroline."

"I know she does, Nick. It's just . . ."

"Just what?" he asked as he stepped out of the shower.

"It's just that we have such a short time together."

Nick toweled himself dry. "Don't worry, Sunshine. Ride over with me now, and we can come back here later."

ALL WAS QUIET OUTSIDE the gray farmhouse.

"Looks like nobody's up yet," said Nick.

"Should we knock and let them know we're here?" Caroline asked.

"I don't think we have to do that," he answered. "I'm sure Belinda won't care if we just check ourselves."

They got out of the car and walked around to the patio. Within minutes Caroline spotted a glimmer of gold shining between two patio slates.

"I found it," she said, holding up the bracelet.

"Good girl," Nick exclaimed. "Meg will be so happy."

Caroline examined the bracelet. "She'd better get this clasp fixed," she said.

As they turned to go back around to their car, they saw Victoria standing at the French doors that led from the house to the patio. Her expression was dark.

"Hey, Victoria, why the frown?" Nick asked. "You should be on cloud nine this morning."

"When I went past Belinda's room this morning," Victoria said, "she wasn't there."

Nick shrugged. "So? Maybe she went for a walk or out to buy the newspaper or something."

"Belinda's car is in the driveway, Nick," Victoria answered. "And her bed hasn't been slept in."


CAROLINE OBSERVED THE ACTIVITY at Curtains Up with growing unease. A search of the house came up empty.

"This isn't like her," said Victoria. "She would have left a note or something. She'd know I would be wondering where she'd gone."

All three of them walked over to the barn just as Gus came ambling out.

"Have you seen Belinda this morning, Gus?" Victoria asked.

"No. I just assumed she'd be sleeping in this morning."

"Well, she's not," said Victoria. "She didn't even sleep in her bed last night."

Gus smiled. "Maybe she got lucky and slept in somebody else's."

They pretended to ignore the crude remark.

"Let's go check with Remington," said Victoria. "Maybe he's seen her. And, Gus, will you look around the grounds? Maybe Belinda's just taking her morning walk."

REMINGTON, WITH PAINTBRUSH IN hand, answered the knock on the door. When they explained they were searching for Belinda, he looked confused.

"Belinda's not here," he said. "Why would you think she'd be here?"

"We're checking everywhere," Nick answered.

"Maybe she went to the theater," he suggested.

"Her car is in the driveway," said Victoria.

"Maybe somebody came and picked her up," said Remington.

CAROLINE WALKED OUT TO the yard. She took out her cell phone and called the *KTA* office.

"Linus Nazareth, please. Caroline Enright calling."

As she waited for Linus to pick up, Caroline wondered if she was overreacting. If Belinda showed up in a little while, she could look like a jerk for having called in to report that the actress was missing. But if something had really happened to Belinda, KEY News should know about it. Caroline decided it was better to be safe than sorry.

"Nazareth." The voice was terse.

"Hi, Linus. It's Caroline."

"Yeah. What's up?"

"Belinda Winthrop may be missing," she said.

"What do you mean *may* be missing? Is she or isn't she?"

Caroline explained what had been happening.

"Ah, you know these actresses," Linus snarled. "This might be a big publicity stunt. Or maybe Winthrop just wants some attention."

"Belinda Winthrop doesn't need to whip up any attention, Linus. She already gets plenty."

She waited for a response.

"Linus?"

"Yeah. I'm thinking," he said. "Look, keep on top of it and let me know what happens. If it turns out this disappearance is legit, we'll send in the troops."

# CHAPTER 57

LINUS HUNG UP THE phone and grabbed his football. He tossed it and caught it a few times before picking up the phone again.

"It's Linus. Come see me."

ANNABELLE GROANED INWARDLY, AS she did every time she was summoned to the executive producer's office. What she'd heard people say about Linus was true. He might not *have* an ulcer, but he certainly was a carrier.

If he was calling her in, Linus had something he'd want her to do. As Annabelle walked down the hallway, she felt herself growing tense. She had promised the kids she was going to try to get out of work early and take them to the pool this afternoon. It had seemed like a promise she could keep. It was Friday. She wasn't scheduled to work this weekend. She didn't have anything that would keep her at the office late. The twins were going to be so disappointed if she didn't take them swimming.

"Hi," said Annabelle as she entered the office.

Linus dispensed with the pleasantries. "Caroline Enright just called," he said. "She thinks something might have happened to Belinda Winthrop."

"As in what? Death?" Annabelle asked.

Linus palmed his football. "Who knows?" he said. "Caroline says nobody can find her."

"How long has she been missing?" Annabelle asked.

"Apparently she had some sort of party at her house last night, and no one has seen her this morning."

Annabelle frowned. "That doesn't seem like enough to assume she's missing or something has happened to her."

"Yeah, that's what I thought, too," said Linus. "But why don't you make some calls and see what you can find out?"

# CHAPTER 58

"I DON'T TRUST THAT guy," said Caroline as she and Nick drove out the driveway.

"Who?" Nick asked. "Remington or the caretaker?"

"Remington is eccentric, but it's the caretaker I don't trust."

"Because?"

"There's just something about him," Caroline said. "I guess it could have something to do with the fact that I caught him smoking pot in the bathroom last night."

"So you're thinking he's the reason Belinda's missing?"

"I didn't say that, Nick. I just don't have a good feeling about Gus."

"I don't know, Sunshine. Smoking a little dope doesn't make the guy a criminal."

"Well, honey, actually it does. It's against the law, remember?"

"All right, yes. It's against the law. But how many people do you know who have smoked marijuana at some point?"

"A lot."

"So what I'm saying is, it's not exactly the worst thing in the world, Caroline. It doesn't mean Gus did something to Belinda. Besides, we don't even know for sure if anything *has* happened to Belinda."

Nick turned out onto the main road and steered the car

in the direction of the campus. "Let's drop the bracelet off to Meg," he said. "She'll be so relieved to get it back."

"No, Nick. Why don't you go see Meg on your own? I should touch base with the crew."

Caroline wondered if Nick would be so cavalier about the subject if he knew that his precious Meg kept her own stash of marijuana in her closet.

# CHAPTER 59

MEG LET HERSELF BACK into her dorm room and threw her yoga mat in the corner. She stripped out of her exercise clothes, put on her robe, and walked down the hall to the shared bathroom to take a shower. Standing beneath the water, she prayed that her father would find her bracelet.

When she came back to her room, she dressed in a clean T-shirt and pair of shorts before sitting down at the desk. She opened up the laptop. She hadn't checked her e-mail since the day before yesterday.

Systematically, Meg went through the entries, answering and deleting as appropriate. She continued down the list, assuming when she saw "Friends of Amy" listed as the subject of one of the e-mails, that it would contain the information about the memorial service being held Saturday afternoon. She double-clicked the mouse to open up the page.

DEAR FRIENDS OF AMY,

WE ARE GETTING PHONE CALLS FROM PEOPLE WANTING TO KNOW HOW THEY CAN HELP. WE APPRECIATE THE OUTPOURING OF LOVE AND SUPPORT WE ARE RECEIVING AT THIS HEARTBREAK-ING TIME.

IT'S IMPORTANT FOR US TO KNOW WHAT AMY WAS DOING RIGHT BEFORE SHE WAS TAKEN FROM US. IF YOU HAVE ANY INFOR-

MATION TO SHARE, PLEASE LET US KNOW BY REPLY E-MAIL. AMY'S
FATHER AND I ARE JUST TOO UPSET TO TAKE PHONE CALLS AT THIS
TIME. WE KNOW YOU'LL UNDERSTAND.

SINCERELY,
AMY'S MOM

Meg checked when the e-mail had been sent. Wednesday. Three days after Amy and Tommy crashed and died.

Meg grew angry as she reread the e-mail. What kind of
twisted joke was this?

Just like hers, Amy's mother was dead.

# CHAPTER 60

VICTORIA LIT A CIGARETTE, poured herself another cup of coffee, sat at the kitchen table, and tried to decide what to do next. If she called the police, they might think it was too early to report a missing person, but she should, at least, call Keith and let him know what was going on.

"What do you mean you can't find her?" The director's voice rose at Victoria's news.

"Just what I said, Keith. She isn't here."

"Maybe she went out for a walk or something."

"Her bed hasn't been slept in."

There was a momentary silence before Keith responded. "Damn it, Victoria. If Belinda is pulling some kind of stunt . . ."

"Belinda doesn't pull stunts, Keith. She doesn't have to. The more I think about it, the more I'm sure that something must be wrong. I'm going to call the police, and you might want to think about getting Langley Tate ready to step in for Belinda tonight. Just in case."

# CHAPTER 61

REMINGTON STARED AT THE portrait on his easel. Belinda's facial expression was so far off, he was tempted to throw out the canvas and start fresh. Instead, he picked up his brush and dabbed it on the pale pink paint on his palette. It was a shade he was expert in mixing. It was the shade of Belinda's creamy skin.

He applied a few strokes and then gave up. He couldn't concentrate. His mind was on Belinda. He tried to imagine a world without her in it, but he couldn't. She had been foremost in his thoughts for all of his adult life. No, he couldn't allow himself even to think about that unbearably bleak prospect.

Laying the brush and the palette down on his worktable, Remington went over to look out the window. He could see Belinda's car parked in front of the farmhouse, a signal that she should be safe inside. But she wasn't.

He walked to the back of the studio, pulled his key ring out of his pocket, and opened the padlock on the old wooden door that led to the dirt cellar. It was a cool, dry place to store his treasures. Remington grabbed the flashlight he kept on the small shelf at the head of the stairs and turned it on to illuminate his way down.

At the foot of the stairs, he picked up the box of matches he kept there and slowly lit the candles in seventeen ruby red glass votives before placing one in front of each of the oil paintings that lined the earthen walls.

Starting with the portrait of Belinda as Katharina in Shakespeare's *Taming of the Shrew,* her first role at the Warrenstown Summer Playhouse twenty years ago, Remington proceeded to Belinda as Cecily Cardew in Oscar Wilde's *The Importance of Being Earnest,* followed by Belinda as the scheming Abigail Williams in *The Crucible,* by Arthur Miller. Remington especially liked his rendition of Belinda in Puritan dress.

One by one, he paid his respects to Belinda in each of her portrayals in the succeeding years, coming to *The Crucible* again. Just five years ago, Belinda had agreed to interpret a different role in the same play—this time the spurned wife, Elizabeth Proctor. The following year, just before the fire, Remington had created a true masterpiece, immortalizing Belinda as the fiery Eleanor of Aquitaine in *The Lion in Winter.* This was the last painting in his cellar gallery.

Now, Remington got down on his knees before his life's greatest works and began to pray.

# CHAPTER 62

"SARGE, KEY NEWS IN New York is calling about Belinda Winthrop."

"Jeez, good news sure travels fast," said Warrenstown Police Sergeant Mo Weaver as he reached for the telephone on his desk. How did KEY News know already? He had gotten off the phone with Victoria Sterling only a few minutes ago.

"Sergeant Weaver speaking."

"Hello, Sergeant. This is Annabelle Murphy. I'm a producer with KEY News."

"What can I do for you?"

"We've had a report that Belinda Winthrop may be missing. What can you tell me about that?"

"We're looking into it."

"So she *is* missing?" asked Annabelle.

"I didn't say that."

"But you have reason to believe that she's missing?" Annabelle persisted.

"I didn't say that either."

"Well, what *can* you tell me?"

"I can tell you that we are fully aware that a person of Belinda Winthrop's stature holds enormous public interest. I understand why you are calling, Ms. Murphy, but I really have nothing else to tell you at this point."

◆ ◆ ◆

ANNABELLE WENT TO LINUS'S office to report back.

"Well, the police weren't surprised by my call."

"Oh?" said Linus, raising an eyebrow. "So Belinda Winthrop *is* missing?"

"They wouldn't confirm it, but my gut feeling . . . ?"

Linus nodded.

"Something's up." Annabelle knew as she spoke that she wouldn't be taking the twins swimming this afternoon.

# CHAPTER 63

BREAKING NEWS WASN'T HER specialty, and Caroline knew it. She wasn't sure what to do next, but she was certain her plan to walk around the campus and find some apprentices to interview for her piece on the Summer Playhouse could wait. She should be trying to find out what had happened to Belinda Winthrop.

Knowing Nick would be happy to spend the rest of the morning alone with Meg, Caroline met up with Lamar and Boomer. She told them about her visit to Belinda's estate and her conversation with Linus Nazareth.

"We have a couple of choices," said Lamar. "We can go over to the police station or drive out to Belinda Winthrop's place."

"Which do you think?" asked Caroline.

"You're the editorial person," said Lamar. "You decide."

"All right. Belinda's place," said Caroline. "That's where the most interesting video will be."

Caroline wasn't sure she was making the right decision until she saw the affirmation in Lamar's eyes.

THERE WAS A POLICE vehicle in front of the farmhouse when the KEY News team arrived. Lamar parked the crew car and hopped out, quickly gathering his gear from the trunk. He and Boomer were recording when an officer walked over to them.

Caroline identified herself and her crew.

"You'll have to leave," said the patrolman.

"What's happening, Officer?" asked Caroline.

"As I said, you have to leave. Now."


INSIDE THE FARMHOUSE, VICTORIA retold the story of not being able to find Belinda Winthrop that morning.

"Belinda usually goes for a walk in the morning, but I checked her closet, and her walking shoes are still there."

"And you're a houseguest of Ms. Winthrop's?" Sergeant Weaver asked.

"Yes."

"Anyone else on the property?"

"A caretaker and Remington Peters."

"The artist, right?"

Victoria nodded as she exhaled and ground her cigarette butt into the ashtray.

"What's the caretaker's name?" asked Weaver.

"Gus Oberon."


SERGEANT WEAVER AND A police patrolman walked across the yard to the garage. There was no one inside.

"Let's go try the artist," said Weaver.

Remington Peters answered the carriage house door on the first knock. His hair was disheveled, his mouth downturned.

"May we come in?" asked Sergeant Weaver.

"Uh, yes. Of course." Remington stood back to let the men pass.

The officers scanned the studio. Weaver's eyes fixed on the cloth-covered easel. "What are you working on?" he asked.

"A portrait," said Remington.

"Belinda Winthrop's?" asked Weaver. "I saw that you are having that exhibit over at the Ambrose Gallery." He moved closer to the easel. "Can I see?" His hand reached for the cloth.

"No." Remington positioned himself between the policeman and the canvas. "I mean, I don't let anyone see my work before it's completed."

"All right. I guess I can respect that," said Weaver, backing away. "Tell me, though, Mr. Peters. When was the last time you saw Ms. Winthrop?"

"Last night."

"Where?"

"At her party."

"How did she seem?"

"What do you mean?"

"Well, did she seem upset about anything?"

Remington paused to consider the question. He could truthfully say that Belinda, actress that she was, had been the perfect hostess. If she had been upset, she hadn't let it show. In front of her guests, Belinda had appeared as if she hadn't a care in the world.

"No, Sergeant," he answered. "Belinda didn't seem distressed at all. She had a lot to be happy about. Everyone at the party was telling her she'd just given the performance of a lifetime."


AS GUS CAME OUT of the woods, he could see the police car parked in front of the farmhouse. He crouched down, watching as two uniformed cops came out of the carriage house and walked toward the garage.

They were looking for him. Gus was sure of it.

He turned and went back into the woods. If the cops were going to be snooping around, he had to finish camouflaging the opening to his cave.

# CHAPTER 64

"YOU WERE AT HER party last night, Caroline. Did you see anything strange?" Lamar asked as they drove from Belinda's place back into town.

"Not particularly. It was a pretty happy bunch," Caroline said. "There was a lot of goodwill there. Everyone was celebrating the play."

"Lots of booze?" asked Boomer.

"Yeah, of course."

"Anybody make a scene?" asked Lamar.

"If anyone did, I didn't see it."

"Was Belinda loaded?" asked Boomer.

"I saw her with a martini glass in her hand," said Caroline, "but that doesn't mean she was drunk."

"But maybe she was," said Boomer. "I've known women to pull some pretty crazy stunts when they had a couple of drinks."

"I don't know, Boom," said Lamar. "Belinda Winthrop has her act together pretty fine. I don't see her doing something crazy."

"It's the ones who seem to have it all together who'll fool you, Lamar," Boomer said. "Those are the ones you have to watch out for."

Caroline piped up from the backseat. "Belinda

Winthrop is at the top of her game, guys. I don't think she would just up and vanish as some kind of stunt. If Belinda has disappeared, I have a feeling it's because something really has happened to her."

# CHAPTER 65

FINALLY, AN ANSWER FROM *Brightlights*.

> IF THIS IS HOW YOU GET YOUR KICKS, YOU ARE REALLY
> TWISTED. NEXT TIME, DO A LITTLE RESEARCH BEFORE YOU START
> SUCH A PATHETIC SCAM. FOR YOUR INFORMATION, YOU IMMATURE
> MORON, AMY DIDN'T HAVE A MOTHER. SHE DIED. PROUD OF
> YOURSELF?
>
> I CAN ONLY HOPE THAT YOU AREN'T ONE OF THE OTHER AP-
> PRENTICES. THAT THOUGHT MAKES ME SICK.

*The message was unsigned.*

*All right, it had been a mistake to sign the e-mail as be-
ing from Amy's mother, but how would a person know the
girl's mother was dead? The plan, to find who Amy had
sent the picture of the car to, had been a good one except
for that.*

*But now, at least, it was clear that Brightlights was a
Warrenstown Summer Playhouse apprentice. There would
have to be another way to find out who he or she was.*

# CHAPTER 66

SHAKING THE BOTTLE OF deep red nail polish, Langley was preparing to give herself a pedicure when her phone rang. It was Keith.

"You better get ready to step in for Belinda," he said.

"What do you mean? What's happened?"

"It seems nobody can find her. She'll probably turn up. But you better be prepared, just in case."

Langley was glad they were on the phone so Keith couldn't see the delighted expression on her face. She summoned up her acting skills to deliver the appropriate distressed tone. "Oh my God, Keith. That's terrible. If something has happened to Belinda, I—"

Keith cut her off by finishing her sentence. "You don't know what you'd do, right, Langley?"

The understudy caught the sarcasm but chose to ignore it. "What can I do to help?" she asked.

"Unless you know where Belinda is, the only thing you can do to help is be prepared to play Valerie tonight. We should meet at the theater this afternoon to go over some things."

"Yes, of course, Keith. That's a good idea."

"One o'clock?"

"I'll be there," said Langley. She hung up the phone and went back to polishing her toenails.

# CHAPTER 67

THE CREW CAR PULLED into the parking lot outside the Warrenstown Police Station.

If she had been some kind of hard-hitting investigative reporter, Caroline would have been more confident of her abilities to deal with the local police force. But she was a film and theater critic. With Linus expecting her to follow through on Belinda's disappearance, this wasn't a time to make mistakes because of inexperience. Lamar and Boomer were used to being out in the field, covering breaking news. The responsible thing to do was use their expertise.

She swallowed her pride and said, "I could use a little help here, guys." As the two men looked at each other, she caught Boomer rolling his eyes.

"I'll go in with you," said Lamar with a sigh.

They got out of the car and walked toward the entrance.

"They probably aren't going to tell us much, Caroline," he said. "The cops are usually pretty tight-lipped about an ongoing investigation."

"Well, we have to make the attempt," she said. "Linus will want to know what the police are saying."

The front desk stood on a raised platform. Behind it, a young uniformed officer looked down at them. "May I help you?" he asked.

Caroline introduced herself and the cameraman.

"We're with KEY News, and we're here about Belinda Winthrop."

The officer looked at them but didn't volunteer any information.

Lamar stepped up. "What can you tell us about the report we've heard that Belinda Winthrop is missing?"

"Sorry, but I don't have anything to tell you."

"Well, we already know something is up. We were just out at her place, and your guys were out there, too."

"What did they tell you?" the officer asked.

"Nothing," Caroline piped up. "They told us to get off the property." The moment the words were out of her mouth, she knew she had made a mistake. From the corner of her eye, she could see Lamar looking at her, thinking her, she imagined, a fool. The officer's answer confirmed Lamar was right.

"Well, if they didn't tell you anything and wanted you to get off the property, what would make you think that I would give you any information? My boss is out there, and if he isn't ready to talk to the press, I'm certainly not going to." The officer picked up some papers and tapped them on the desk to neaten them. "Besides, doesn't the left hand know what the right hand is doing?"

"What do you mean?" asked Caroline.

"Somebody from KEY News already called about Belinda Winthrop. We didn't give her any information either."

Caroline felt her already flushed cheeks grow hotter. Of course, Linus didn't trust her to handle this. She wasn't really surprised, but it stung a little to think he'd had someone else check up on what was going on here when she was right on scene. Still, she was glad that he was taking her trip seriously.

"Can we ask you this?" said Lamar as he pulled out his wallet and took out a business card. "If you have any news or if you will be holding a press conference or something, would you please give us a call? My cell phone number is written on the back of the card." He handed it up.

The cop took it. "No promises," he said. "But I will tell

you one thing. It's not all that uncommon for someone to
go out for a pack of cigarettes and never come back."

AS CAROLINE AND LAMAR turned away from the desk, a
call came in on the radio.

"We're doing a small search of the area to make sure
Belinda Winthrop isn't lying out there hurt. In the meantime, check with the North Adams Regional Hospital and
the Berkshire Medical Center down in Pittsfield and see if
she's shown up in the emergency room."

# CHAPTER 68

WHAT IF THE POLICE came back and wanted to search his studio? They'd want to know what was behind the padlocked door. He'd have to give them the key and let them go down to the cellar. Remington's chest tightened at the thought of it.

They'd see the portraits and know that he had lied. They'd know he'd collected the insurance money. They'd never believe his motives. They wouldn't understand that he'd set the fire as a ruse so the public would think Belinda's portraits had been destroyed. How could he explain that he just couldn't stand the thought of all those strangers gawking at his beloved?

He tried hard not to look at magazines or newspapers or reruns of her old movies on television. It pained him to think that she was so exposed. All the world could read about her and look at her and gossip about her. He hated that. Three years ago it had bothered him so much that he'd couldn't play into the public's fascination with Belinda any longer. That was when he'd come up with the idea of the fire. Over two nights, Remington had sneaked the portraits out from his old studio in town and stashed them in the back of his station wagon. He had then driven them to a storage facility in Albany. When he was through, he'd set the fire.

He hadn't counted on Belinda being so upset at the

loss. And when he'd told her that he couldn't bring himself to paint her portrait again, she hadn't realized the reason was that he didn't want to share her with anyone, didn't want to be part of the objectifying of Belinda Winthrop. She'd thought he was so destroyed by the loss of the portraits that he didn't want to be reminded of it by painting her image again.

Belinda had made it her mission to bring Remington around, to make him want to work again. He was such a great talent, she told him. It would be wrong for him to give up his art. Her fondest wish, she said, was that he paint another portrait. She would help him get back on his feet. He could come live and work at Curtains Up.

Remington had luxuriated in her attention. He'd welcomed the opportunity to be able to live so close to Belinda when she came up to Warrenstown. He couldn't say no to her, and finally, Remington had agreed to paint her again.

After she went back to New York at the end of the season, he took the paintings out of the storage facility and brought them to his new home. They were arranged in his special shrine to her in the cellar.

But now, they weren't safe.

# CHAPTER 69

CAROLINE AND LAMAR CAME out of the police station.

"Well?" asked Boomer as they climbed back into the car.

Caroline braced herself for Lamar's account of her naïve performance, but for whatever reason, he cut her a break and didn't embarrass her in front of Boomer.

"The cops plan on checking her property," Lamar answered. "And checking the hospitals."

As their car pulled out of the parking lot, Caroline's cell phone sounded. It was Linus. "What's going on up there?" he asked in his gruff tone.

She told him what she knew. "Sorry, Linus, but I really don't have much more to tell you. I think the police are stretched pretty thin up here. Somebody in town was found murdered yesterday, and two kids from the theater program died in a car accident a few days before that. This is *not* an ordinary week for them."

"I'm sending Annabelle Murphy up to help you."

"Oh?"

"Yeah. She'll be there this afternoon."

Caroline was relieved to hear that Annabelle was coming, yet somehow disappointed that Linus didn't trust her to handle things herself. But based on her less-than-stellar performance in the police station just now, Caroline suspected Linus was right to be sending up reinforcements.

She listened as the executive producer finished describing his plan. "If it turns out Belinda Winthrop is dead, we have to be in position to be all over it. I'll have Constance Young on standby, ready to get up there, too, if we need her."

# CHAPTER 70

"OH, THANK YOU, DAD," said Meg as she took the gold bracelet. "I'm so glad you found it. I don't know what I would have done if I lost it for good."

"You're welcome, sweetheart," said Nick. "You better get that clasp looked at."

"Where was it?" asked Meg, winding the bracelet around her wrist.

"Right out there on Belinda's patio, where we were sitting last night. Actually, Meg, it was Caroline who found it."

"Oh." Meg busied herself with searching through papers at her desk.

"Come on, Meg," said Nick. "Can't you please give Caroline a break?"

Meg sighed. "Look, Dad, we've been through this before. If Caroline makes you happy, I'm glad. But I can't help it. I'm not a fan."

"You've never given her a chance. You were prepared to dislike her from the first time you met her."

Meg didn't argue with her father's observation. She glanced at the radio alarm clock, suddenly eager to get away. "I'm sorry, Dad, but I have to get going. There's some stuff I have to do at the theater. I have to stitch up a seam on the sleeve of one of Belinda's gowns and then steam all of her dresses to make sure they look perfect tonight."

"I hope Belinda's there to wear them," said Nick.

"What do you mean?"

Nick described what he and Caroline had witnessed at Curtains Up.

"Oh, no, Dad," said Meg, her brow furrowed. "She's been so nice to me. She kinda reminds me of Mom. She has to be all right."

"Let's not get ahead of ourselves, sweetheart," said her father. "Belinda will turn up."

Meg shivered involuntarily. "No offense, Dad, but you said there was a good chance Mom would get better, and look how *that* turned out."

# CHAPTER 71

*WHAT WOULD JUST ABOUT every apprentice jump at the chance to do?*

*Go out to dinner with an accomplished director? Run lines with a famous star? Be an extra in an upcoming movie? Meet with a theatrical agent?*

*Any of those would work.*

*The killer tacked the notice to the bulletin board.*

**New York Theatrical Agent Will Be Holding Interviews This Weekend. If Interested, Please Print Your Name, Telephone Number, E-mail, and Where You Are Staying on Campus.**

*That should snag Brightlights.*

# CHAPTER 72

"MAYBE WE SHOULD GO over to the theater," Caroline suggested. "We can see if the word is out about Belinda's disappearance and try to get some reaction."

Lamar nodded. "That's not a bad idea."

"I'm getting hungry," said Boomer. "Maybe we should go get some lunch first."

"It's a little early for lunch, isn't it, Boomer?" asked Caroline.

"Easy for you to say. Look at you, and then look at me," said the soundman. "Now tell me, who needs to be fed on a regular basis?"

"Just think how much better everything will taste if we wait," replied Caroline, smiling.

"All right, but if we get stuck in that theater all afternoon, I'm not gonna be a happy camper."


CAROLINE WAS DISAPPOINTED WHEN they entered the lobby. It was empty. "I don't know quite what I was expecting," she said. "But I guess I was hoping that everybody would be standing around, gossiping about Belinda."

"Maybe nobody has even heard she's missing yet," said Lamar.

"I told you we should have gone for lunch," said Boomer. "Come on. Let's go."

"Not so fast, Boom. Who's that over there?" Lamar pointed in the direction of the box office.

"It's Langley Tate," said Caroline. "Belinda's understudy."

Caroline walked over.

"I guess you've heard," said Langley, her cheeks flushed.

"Yes, but I don't know much. Only that Belinda was nowhere to be found this morning at Curtains Up. Have you heard anything else?"

"No, not really. But Keith Fallows called and told me to be ready to go on tonight."

Caroline looked down at the small envelope in Langley's hand.

"I was just getting some tickets for the performance," Langley said sheepishly. "I called my parents, and they're driving up this afternoon from New Jersey."

"Of course you'd want them to see you," said Caroline. *Isn't it interesting,* she thought, *how one person's misfortune could be another's good luck?*

"Well, I better get going," said Langley. "I have to meet with Keith to go over some things."

"Let me ask you something, Langley. Would you be willing to be interviewed later?"

"You mean about Belinda?"

"Yes, and about what it feels like to be stepping into her shoes."

Langley demurred, but for only a moment. "Nobody can step into Belinda's shoes," she said. "But let me give you my cell phone number. Call me when you want to do the interview."

# CHAPTER 73

IT SEEMED INCREDIBLY SELF-SERVING at a time like this, but Victoria still wanted to make certain that the audiovisual department had successfully recorded Belinda's performance last night. Having her portrayal of Valerie on tape gave the playwright the best shot at impressing the Pulitzer committee. Belinda had been magnificent, and Victoria couldn't imagine any other actress making *Devil in the Details* more memorable than she had. Langley Tate certainly wouldn't be able to pull off the role with nearly the aplomb.

There was no one in the audiovisual office when Victoria entered. She checked the tape decks, but they all were empty. There was nothing on the desk. Finally, a scan of the shelves on the wall produced the tape.

It was the only copy, Victoria observed. She should probably leave it here and come back later when somebody was around to ask for a dub. But the tape meant too much to her. If she left it here now and something happened to it or someone else took it, she'd be screwed.

She had every right to this tape, Victoria thought as she stuffed it into her bag. She could bring it back some other time and have them make a copy for the Playhouse archives. She wasn't going to let this original out of her possession.

• • •

AS VICTORIA CAME DOWN the stairs from the office on the second level, she saw Caroline Enright and the KEY News camera crew in the lobby. Victoria really didn't want to talk to Caroline again. She just wanted to get back to Curtains Up, check on the status of the police search for Belinda, and if there was an opportunity, take her mind off things by viewing the tape.

Victoria was about to go back up and find another way out when Caroline saw her on the stairs.

"Victoria," she called out.

Caught, Victoria continued down.

"Any news on Belinda?" Caroline asked.

Victoria shook her head. "Nothing when I left Curtains Up about a half hour ago. The police asked for the master key to the buildings on the property. I hope I did the right thing in giving it to them."

"What are they saying?"

"That they still have no indication that a crime has been committed. But I have to say, I think they're giving it much more attention than they would if nobody could find you or me," said Victoria.

"What are you going to do?" asked Caroline.

"I don't think there is much else anybody can do but sit and wait."

"Maybe call the FBI?" Caroline suggested.

"The police say they're alerting them, though how much the feds will get involved at this point is anyone's guess," said Victoria. "Belinda hasn't been gone for long. We don't know if it's a kidnapping or an accident or if she is just going to come walking in with a perfectly good explanation of where she's been."

# CHAPTER 74

IT WAS PITCH-BLACK.

Her eyes were open, but she could see absolutely nothing. She lay flat on her back, feeling the packed ground beneath her body. A sharp rock was digging into her shoulder. As she tried to roll over, she cried out at the pain in her sides. Were her ribs broken?

Belinda's head throbbed as she tried to remember what had happened. But she couldn't think clearly. She did know one thing, though. It didn't really matter now how she had gotten here. All that mattered was how to get out of wherever she was, away from this terrifying darkness.

# CHAPTER 75

"THAT DOES IT," BOOMER declared. "We *have* to go to lunch. Now."

Caroline had been clued in by more than one KEY News producer that the feeding of the crew was probably the single most important ingredient for a successful shoot. If the correspondent or producer took care of the crew, the crew would take care of the correspondent or producer in the field.

"I guess this is as good a time as any. But let's just go to that deli in town," she said. "It's fast and it's close."

Ten minutes later they were staring at the menu board at Oscar's. The men placed their orders and announced they were going to use the restroom. Caroline waited at the counter for the sandwiches. Oscar was eager to strike up a conversation.

"I guess you've heard the latest," he said.

"You mean about Belinda Winthrop?"

"Yeah. I don't know what's going on with this town. My wife and I moved up here from the city to get away from crime. She's starting to wonder if we made a mistake."

Caroline watched as Oscar spread mustard on some pumpernickel bread. "I guess the police must be pretty worried," she ventured.

"You said it," chimed in Oscar. "One of them was just

in here a little while ago to pick up sandwiches for the guys at the station. The chief's called in everyone, even the guys who are supposed to be on vacation. They're freaked out about ol' Mrs. Templeton. Though, to tell you the truth, I'd have liked to smack her myself. I went into the library one day and she wouldn't give me the men's room key. She was a real pill, that one." Oscar cut a sandwich on the diagonal. "I guess she didn't deserve to die though, did she?"

Caroline shook her head.

Oscar continued working and talking. "They thought it was something a couple of years ago when that famous play writer fellow was found dead in a ditch. But what's happened this past week, with Mrs. Templeton and those Playhouse kids in that accident, and now maybe Belinda Winthrop meeting up with foul play—that's made that time back then look like a nothin'."

"I read something about that. Daniel Sterling, that was the playwright's name," said Caroline.

"That's right," said Oscar, slicing a dill pickle. "The guys on the force always thought something was fishy with the way he died, but they could never prove anything."

"He had been at one of Belinda Winthrop's parties the night before he died, right?"

"Yeah, and my friends on the force told me they thought one of those show business people did him in and made it look like an accident."

"But did any of them have a motive to kill Daniel Sterling?" asked Caroline as she took out her wallet to pay.

Oscar pushed the sandwiches across the counter. "Ah, you know those showbiz types. They act like they're all rooting for one another. I see 'em come in here, complimenting each other and acting all lovey-dovey. But if you ask me, they're all really jealous of one another, and underneath it all, a lot of them would like to wring each other's necks."

# CHAPTER 76

"NO, LANGLEY," KEITH YELLED. "You've got it all wrong."

Langley stood in the middle of the stage, biting her lower lip.

"You're supposed to be coming to the realization that the man you've loved, the man you've lived with and slept with for years, isn't what you thought and hoped he was. He's a monster, capable of doing anything, hurting anyone who gets in his way. Can you do that, Langley?"

"I'm trying, Keith."

"Well, you've got to try harder, damn it. Now again, from the top of the scene."

Three lines in, Keith stopped everything again. "No, no, no, no, no, Langley." He threw his clipboard down. "Do it more like Belinda did it."

"I'm not Belinda," said Langley, fighting back tears.

"Don't I know it!"

"Keith, please. No one else can be Belinda Winthrop, but I can be Valerie. I've worked hard to get to this point and will do anything to succeed at this. Just give me a chance."

# CHAPTER 77

AFTER THEY'D EATEN LUNCH, Caroline walked out onto the sidewalk in front of Oscar's and looked up Main Street. She saw the Ambrose Gallery and remembered that the Remington Peters exhibition was opening today.

"Why don't we go over to the gallery and see if we can get permission to shoot the new portrait of Belinda Winthrop?" she suggested.

Lamar agreed. "That would be a good element to have, no matter what our story on Belinda finally becomes."

Caroline went into the gallery while Lamar and Boomer shot video of the exterior. She immediately noted that the space left open for the portrait of Belinda as Valerie was still empty.

"Don't ask," Jean Ambrose said as she walked over and stood beside Caroline. "This is turning into such a disaster."

Caroline looked at the gallery owner and waited for her to continue.

"I suppose you've heard that nobody can find Belinda," Jean said.

Caroline nodded.

"So not only did Remington decide that his new portrait is not ready to be shown but now we have no guest of honor for our opening. I know that sounds selfish, thinking about the gallery at a time like this, but we have patrons coming from all over. They've been looking forward to this for months. So have we. Artistically and financially."

"I'm sorry," said Caroline. She looked around at the gallery walls. "But you have other Peters paintings to sell. And you told me that he wouldn't allow his portraits of Belinda to be sold anyway."

"True," said Jean. "But our clients are expecting to see the new portrait. They are going to be very disappointed, and that won't put them in any kind of mood to buy something else."

"What's wrong with the portrait, do you know?" asked Caroline.

Jean shook her head. "Zeke went over to pick it up yesterday, and Remington told him it wasn't ready. Something about not getting her expression right. But, good Lord, nobody knows every inch of Belinda Winthrop's face better than Remington Peters. I can't imagine what the big problem is."

"Would it be all right for my crew to come in and take some shots of the other paintings, specifically the other two portraits of Belinda you have?" Caroline asked.

Jean looked at the portraits of Belinda as Titania in *A Midsummer Night's Dream* and Madison Whitehall in *Treasure Trove* that flanked the space left open for Belinda as Valerie. "All right," she said. "And you might want to check back later. Zeke has gone over to Curtains Up to try again to convince Remington to give us the new portrait."

# CHAPTER 78

SEVENTEEN PORTRAITS.

Seventeen paintings to be carefully wrapped and carried upstairs. Seventeen paintings to be driven back to that storage facility in Albany, hidden from the police or anyone else.

Remington lost track of time as he readied the paintings for transport. He came up with his plan as he worked. He would be able to bundle up the paintings down here during the day. But he would have to drive them to safety when it was dark. There was no way he'd be able to get them all in the station wagon at one time, but he should be able to complete the job in two trips. With a little luck, he'd be able to be back at Curtains Up, his task completed, before sunrise.

A little luck never hurt.

Systematically, Remington wound batting around each portrait. Belinda as Katharina in *The Taming of the Shrew,* as Cecily Cardew in *The Importance of Being Earnest,* as Abigail Williams in *The Crucible,* and all the others through the years.

"Rest well, my love," he said as he kissed each version of Belinda's beautiful face.


ZEKE AMBROSE DROVE UP the driveway at Curtains Up, prepared with what he was going to say to persuade Remington to let the new portrait of Belinda be exhibited. Zeke was determined to have the painting in the rear of his station wagon when he drove back down the driveway.

He stopped to talk to the police officer stationed in front of the farmhouse.

"Hiya, Mo."

"Zeke." The officer nodded. "How are ya today?"

"Hangin' in there. Any word on Belinda?"

"So you know?"

"News travels fast, especially in *this* small town," Zeke said.

"No, nothing so far."

"Let's hope this is all a misunderstanding," said Zeke. "And that she turns up real soon. I saw her in the play last night, and she was absolutely fabulous. I can't allow myself to believe that something dreadful has happened to her."

"Were you at the party she had here afterward, Zeke?"

"Yes. Jean and I came. Belinda has been including us for years."

"See anything you thought was strange?"

"Nothing I can think of off the top of my head, Mo, but if I remember anything, I'll be sure to let you know. Actually, I'm here to talk to Remington Peters."

The police sergeant nodded toward the carriage house. "He's a weird one, isn't he?"

"Remington is an artist, Mo. He's allowed to be a little strange."

The officer waved Zeke on.

Parking at the front of the carriage house, Zeke got out, went to the front door, and knocked. He waited, then knocked again. When there was still no answer, Zeke walked around the building, cupped his hands against the glass of the giant window and looked inside. This time there was no cover draping the large canvas that sat on the easel.

Belinda stood, regally, in her sweeping green gown. She held her head high, her expression haughty, defiance in her eyes.

Zeke squinted to get a better view. He saw the pistol in Belinda's hand just as Remington came to the window and glared out at him.


ZEKE HURRIED BACK AROUND to the front door, anxious to explain what he'd been doing peeking through the window. "I'm sorry, Remington, if I frightened you," he said. "When there was no answer, I walked around to see if you were there but just didn't hear me. I wasn't trying to be nosy."

"You saw the portrait, then?" Remington glowered. Assessing the expression on the artist's face, Zeke decided not to acknowledge what he'd seen. If there was any hope of getting Remington to release the portrait to the gallery, Zeke didn't want to ruin it by angering or offending the artist.

"No, actually, I couldn't see it. There was too much glare."

Remington fixed his eyes on Zeke's face and studied it. "Good," he said. "You know how I feel about people looking at my Belindas before I'm finished with them."

"Absolutely," said Zeke, relieved that Remington seemed satisfied. "How's it coming anyway?"

"It's not ready. And with all this worry about Belinda, I'm not in any frame of mind to be working on it."

Remington's tone was such that Zeke knew better than to push any further. And after having seen the painter's interpretation of Belinda as Valerie, the gallery owner was so troubled that he was anxious to get away.

# CHAPTER 79

AS SHE CAME OUT of the Ambrose Gallery, Caroline bumped into Meg and Nick.

"We just had lunch at the Thai place," said Nick. "I didn't think you'd be able to join us."

"No need to explain. It's nice for you two to have some time together," said Caroline, but she felt a twinge of hurt just the same.

"I have to get going, Dad," said Meg. "I really have to get stuff organized back at the theater, and I have a rehearsal this afternoon for the cabaret tonight."

"All right, honey." Nick kissed his daughter on the forehead. "I guess I won't see you until the cabaret then. Break a leg."

"Thanks, Dad. See ya, Caroline."

Watching her stepdaughter walk off, Caroline was well aware of how quickly Meg wanted to get away from her. She kept trying to put herself in Meg's shoes and think how hard it would have been if someone had taken her own mother's place. Selfishly, she'd been relieved that her father hadn't found someone else. But then again, he hadn't had much time to do so before he died as well.

Caroline felt Nick's eyes on her. "Don't let it bother you," he said, reading her mind. "Eventually, Meg's got to get used to us."

Caroline tried to smile. "I hope so," she said, wishing

she didn't suspect that one of the reasons Meg felt the
need to smoke pot was to numb herself to the pain of her
father's remarriage.

MEG WENT BACK TO her room and changed into the
black slacks and top she was required to wear as a member of the play's crew. She gave her hair a good brushing
and gathered it back with a covered elastic. She was about
to leave for the theater when she remembered the envelope the actress had handed her at the party the night before. With Belinda missing, Meg wasn't sure if she should
bring it or not. Impulsively, she picked it up from the desk
and opened the thin metal clasp, taking out the copy of the
*Devil in the Details* script. It looked as though it had been
read many times. Some green paint was smudged on the
cover. Meg thought she should keep the script with her until she could give it to Belinda personally.

When she got to the theater, Meg stopped at the apprentices' bulletin board. There was a notice of a guest
speaker coming next week that Meg wanted to make sure
to hear. Another sheet announced a screening of a movie
that one of the Equity actors had appeared in; the actor
would take questions from the audience afterward. But it
was the next notice Meg read that interested her the most.

**New York Theatrical Agent Will Be Holding Inter-
views This Weekend. If Interested, Please Print Your
Name, Telephone Number, E-mail, and Where You
Are Staying on Campus.**

Meg eagerly filled in all the information that was re-
quested.

# CHAPTER 80

"WHAT DO YOU HAVE to do now?" asked Nick.

"Let me check with the crew, but I don't think there's much else we *can* do at this point," said Caroline.

After she conferred with Lamar and Boomer, they decided that they'd all keep their cell phones on in case something came up. In the meantime, the guys volunteered to ride back to the police station and see if there were any new developments there.

"Sure you don't need me to come with you?" Caroline asked, a bit surprised by their offer.

Lamar grinned. "I think we can handle it. You two lovebirds go ahead and have a good time."


"I FEEL GUILTY," SAID Caroline as she and Nick walked down the sidewalk.

"Don't worry," he said, taking her hand. "If something breaks, they'll find you."

"I suppose. All right, what do you want to do?"

"Do you have to ask? You were sleeping when I came back from dropping Meg off last night, and you were gone when I got up this morning."

"You want to go back to the hotel then?"

"Bingo. Tell the little lady what she's won."

•  •  •

AS NICK BEGAN TO kiss her neck, Caroline wondered if
Lamar and Boomer were learning anything new about Belinda from the police. As his arms wrapped around her
and he pulled her close, she tried to push thoughts of Linus Nazareth's approval from her mind. A half hour later,
she found herself imagining what it might actually be like
to be a hard news correspondent.

Caroline lay on her back, looking at the ceiling.

"You look worried, Sunshine."

"I guess I am, Nick." She told him about the tough conversations with the executive producer before she'd left
for Warrenstown. "I'm afraid my style is never going to
mesh with Linus's."

"The guy's known to be son of a bitch, Caroline. You're
not gonna change him."

"Yeah, but he rules *KTA*. What Linus says, goes." Caroline took hold of Nick's hand. "And you know, I realize I
don't want to go back to print. I really like TV. I'd hate to
leave KEY News."

Nick took her hand up to his lips and kissed it. "I have
complete confidence in you, sweetheart. Nazareth would
be a fool to let you go. And while he may be many things,
Linus is no fool."

As Caroline nuzzled her husband's neck, her thoughts
turned back to what was going on now in Warrenstown.
"Let me ask you something, Nick."

"Shoot."

"I was talking to the guy at the deli this afternoon."

"Oscar?"

"Yes," said Caroline, surprised. "You know him?"

"Anyone who's ever spent time in Warrenstown knows
Oscar, and Oscar knows them. He's the town gossip. What
was he selling today?"

"Well, he knew about Belinda, and he was talking
about all the upset in town with the two dead kids and the
murdered librarian. He said that there hadn't been as

much anxiety here since Daniel Sterling was killed two years ago."

Nick sat up and propped a pillow behind him against the headboard.

"So, what's the question?" he asked.

"Do you think Daniel Sterling was murdered?"

"I really don't know, Caroline."

"Oscar thinks he was."

"Well, that settles it then."

Caroline smiled as she jabbed her husband's arm. "I'm not kidding, Nick. Oscar said the local police thought Sterling was murdered but they just couldn't prove it."

"So?"

"So you were at the party that night before he died. What do you think?"

"I think we are wasting valuable time on something that happened a long time ago." Nick leaned over and pressed his lips against hers.

# CHAPTER 81

SAFELY BACK AT CURTAINS Up, Victoria inserted the videotape into the deck and settled in to watch *Devil in the Details*. As one scene followed another, she was entranced by Belinda's stage magic. The written words had been expertly crafted, but Belinda's delivery of them, her interpretation of Valerie, was what determined the feeling that was transmitted over the footlights. A loving spouse slowly coming to realize that her charismatic partner was pure evil left the viewer deeply shaken.

Reassured that what she had seen last night at the theater was as powerful when recorded on tape, Victoria slid the cassette out. She turned to take the tape upstairs to the safety of her bedroom and came face-to-face with Belinda's caretaker.

"Oh my God, you frightened me." Victoria held her hand against her chest. "You shouldn't sneak up on someone that way, Gus."

"Sorry," he said. "I didn't mean to scare you." He nodded toward the television screen. "That was some performance."

"How long were you standing there watching?" she asked.

"Long enough."

"She's fantastic, isn't she?"

"She's something, all right. Did she tell you she fired me?" Gus fixed his gaze directly into Victoria's eyes.

"No, she didn't," said Victoria, trying to keep her expression calm. Had Belinda told Gus that she knew of the suspicious activities going on in the cave because Victoria had told her? Somehow, Victoria didn't think so. Belinda wouldn't drag a friend into that sort of mess if she could help it.

"Well, she said she wanted me to leave," said Gus. "But now I'm wondering if I should stay for a while, at least until Belinda turns up. Maybe I should stick around and keep taking care of the place until then."

Victoria eyed the muscles that bulged beneath the sleeves of Gus's T-shirt. She knew he wasn't selling Girl Scout cookies out of that cave, but she didn't think he was a physical threat to her. In fact, he could be a physical asset if she played her cards right.

"All right, Gus," she said. "I think it *would* be a good idea for you to stay and take care of things around here, at least until Belinda shows up."

# CHAPTER 82

MEG DEPOSITED HER TOTE in the dressing room, then went to the laundry to get the undergarments she had left to be washed the night before. Bringing those back to the dressing room, she picked up Belinda's costumes and took them to be steamed. By the time she returned to arrange them on the rack in the order they were to be worn, Langley Tate was in the dressing room.

Langley sat at the makeup table, her head in her hands. She looked up, and Meg could see in the mirror that Langley had been crying.

"This isn't what I thought it was going to be at all," Langley sobbed.

Meg wasn't sure what to say, so she didn't say anything. As she hung the dresses, she listened to Langley's continued whining.

"You should have seen how mean Keith was to me this afternoon." Langley began to imitate Keith's high-pitched voice. "You don't do *this* like Belinda. You don't do *that* like Belinda. You're not going to seem mature enough to have been married for fourteen years." She spoke in her own voice again. "When I told Keith that makeup would help take care of that, he said no amount of makeup could give me the incredible acting talent that Belinda had. Way to instill confidence, Keith."

"Maybe he's just worried," Meg said.

"Well, I'm worried, too," said Langley. "And the director is supposed to reassure his actors, not tear them down and make them think they're awful. How am I supposed to go out there tonight and knock 'em dead when I know the director thinks so little of me?"

"He has to think you have talent, Langley, or he wouldn't have chosen you to be Belinda's understudy," said Meg.

"You know what, Meg? I don't think Keith ever thought that he was going to have to use me. Belinda is known for never missing a performance. She's the twenty-first century's Ethel Merman. So Keith didn't think there was a real possibility that I would ever get a chance to play Valerie." The tone of Langley's voice had changed from despair to anger.

Langley stood up, walked over to the clothing rack, and lifted off the green velvet ball gown. "Let me try on these dresses to see if the costume shop has made the alterations, Meg. And Keith Fallows can go screw himself, because I'm going to show him."

# CHAPTER 83

CAROLINE JUMPED AT THE sound of her cell phone, thinking it could be Lamar and Boomer with some news from the police about Belinda Winthrop. It wasn't.

"Hi, Caroline. It's Annabelle Murphy. I'm here."

"Where are you?"

"I just checked into my room. I'm at the Warrenstown Inn."

"So am I."

"Great. Want to meet somewhere and talk?" asked Annabelle.

"Sure." Caroline looked over at her napping husband. "How about the coffee shop downstairs?"

"Fine. See you in five minutes."

"HERE'S WHAT I KNOW," said Annabelle as she tore open a packet of Sweet'N Low and stirred the contents into her iced tea. "The police don't have a clue. They still won't even classify this as a missing-person case. But if Belinda doesn't show up, they are organizing a search of her property tomorrow morning."

"How did you find that out?" asked Caroline.

"I heard it from the guy who runs the deli in town. I stopped to get something to eat before I came to the inn. Then I called the police to confirm."

"When we went to the police station, they wouldn't tell us anything," said Caroline, shaking her head.

"Don't beat yourself up, Caroline. It's been my experience that police are pretty cagey in what they say and when they say it. When you were there, they weren't talking. Now, they aren't exactly being free with the information, but at least they confirmed something I'd already heard. And that was only because the word was out. They're looking for volunteers for the search."

"So now what?" asked Caroline.

"Wouldn't it be great if we could find her before anyone else does?" asked Annabelle with a smile. "I think we should go out to Belinda's place and snoop around."

"The police had the place blocked off when we were there this morning," said Caroline.

Annabelle shrugged. "That was hours ago, right?"

Caroline nodded.

"So, let's go out there anyway and see what we can see now."

"Should I call Lamar and Boomer to come with us?"

Annabelle twirled a strand of her long, brown hair as she considered the question. "I don't think so. That would make too large a group. We'd be too conspicuous. I brought a camcorder with me. We can use that if there's anything we need to shoot."


"I THOUGHT YOU'D BE bringing another crew with you," said Caroline as they drove toward Curtains Up.

"Are you serious? Do you really think Linus is going to spring for another human crew when he can use me and a little camcorder?" Annabelle rolled down her window and switched off the air conditioner. "You don't mind if we get some fresh air, do you? It's so clear and beautiful up here, it seems a shame to drive all cooped up."

Annabelle seemed so relaxed, so self-assured, thought Caroline. She supposed that was because Annabelle had been working in hard news for years. Whatever story broke or event came up, Annabelle was used to dealing with it. She was confident, and it showed in everything she said and did. Caroline realized she shouldn't be beating herself up because she didn't know exactly what to do to cover Belinda's disappearance. Annabelle probably wouldn't know what elements to cover in writing a review of a play or movie. Still, Caroline had to admire Annabelle and knew she could learn a lot by watching her.

"Have you been having any fun up here?" Annabelle asked as she steered the car down the curving road.

"My husband is here, so that's been nice."

"Really? You guys are newlyweds, right?"

"We've been married for three months."

"Ah," said Annabelle. "I remember those days."

Caroline felt her face grow warm, and she changed the subject. "Wednesday and yesterday were pretty good. I enjoyed doing the interviews with the director and playwright, and Belinda Winthrop, of course."

"Oooo. That's good," said Annabelle. "You might have the last interview Belinda Winthrop ever did."


ANNABELLE'S RENTAL CAR PULLED up at the entrance to Curtains Up. Caroline and Annabelle both craned their necks to get a better view. There was yellow police tape cordoning off an area around the house, but no police cars were stationed anywhere.

"I'm game. Are you?" Annabelle didn't wait for Caroline's answer before turning in to the driveway.

"Nice spread," said Annabelle, looking out across the meadow. "Have any idea how much property is hers?"

"Somebody mentioned last night that there are a hundred and fifty acres here," said Caroline.

"Last night?"

"Oh, Belinda had a party after the play opened last night."

"And you went to it?"

"Uh-huh."

"So you were among the last people to see Belinda?"

"I guess so. Yes." As Annabelle parked the car, Caroline mentally noted the similarity between last night and the party two years ago. Both had begun with an opening night party at Curtains Up and ended with unexplained events, one a death, perhaps even a murder, the other a disappearance. She remarked on it to her companion.

Annabelle's eyes grew wide. "Wouldn't it be neat if we could link the two? Linus would love that."

THERE WAS NO ANSWER when they knocked on the farmhouse door.

"Let's walk over to that carriage house and see if anyone's there," said Annabelle.

"That's where Remington Peters, the artist, lives," said Caroline.

"I guess I should know who he is, but I don't," said Annabelle.

Caroline told her about the Belinda Winthrop portraits and the stymied gallery exhibition as they walked up the hill. There was no answer to their knocks at the carriage house door, either.

"Wish we could get a look at that portrait, don't you?" Annabelle said as she started to walk around the carriage house.

"We're trespassing," whispered Caroline.

"I prefer to think we're helping with the search for Belinda Winthrop," said Annabelle. She pressed her face close to the studio window.

"I can see an easel, but there's nothing on it," she said. "It looks like there are some paintings wrapped up near the front door."

"Maybe Remington is going to let the portrait be shown after all," said Caroline. "I could check with the gallery owner to see if he changed his mind."

"Good idea," said Annabelle. "Meanwhile, let's see what else we can see."

• • •

FROM THE UPSTAIRS WINDOW of the farmhouse, Victoria peered out and saw the two brunettes walking down the hill from the carriage house. She recognized Caroline Enright but not her companion.

"What are those two doing here?" she asked under her breath. Victoria wrapped her robe around herself and stood to the side of the window so she wouldn't be seen. As Caroline and her friend walked toward the garage, Victoria turned and climbed back into her bed.

"Heads up," she whispered to the man who lay stretched out beneath the sheets. "You've got company coming."

# CHAPTER 84

THERE WERE TWO GARAGE bays. One housed a black
pickup truck; the other, a golf cart. At the side of the
garage, a staircase led to a landing and a closed door.

"Think somebody lives up there?" asked Annabelle.

"I think the caretaker does. And I think we should be
careful, Annabelle."

"All right. You wait here."

As Annabelle started up the stairs, Caroline walked
over and looked in the golf cart. The key was in the igni-
tion. There was a small tip of red material wedged between the seat and the back cushions. Caroline reached in
and pulled at it. She recognized the flame pattern. It was
one of the favors from the party. A red silk tie.

"What do you think you're doing?"

Caroline swung around to see the man standing in the
garage doorway. He had on a pair of jeans but no shirt. His
sandy hair was disheveled. It was Gus, the guy who had
come out of the powder room at the party leaving the
aroma of marijuana behind him.

Annabelle had heard the man, too. She started back
down the steps.

"Hello," she said. "I'm Annabelle Murphy, and this is
Caroline Enright. We're with KEY News."

Gus stared at her, a sullen expression on his face.
Then he turned to look at Caroline. "You were here this

morning," he said, "with your husband. He's a friend of Belinda's."

"That's right," said Caroline.

"I reckon Belinda is always happy to have friends stop by, but I know for a fact that she don't want media people swarming around here." Gus took a step forward. "She doesn't like to be hounded, especially on her own property."

"We just wanted to see if there was any news about Belinda yet," said Annabelle.

"Nothin' that I know of," said Gus.

"Do you have any thoughts about where she might be?" Caroline tried. "Or what could have happened to her?"

"I got no idea," said Gus. "Now, you ladies both better get goin'."

Caroline and Annabelle looked at each other, knowing it was time to leave. As they began to walk out of the garage, Gus looked at the red tie Caroline still held in her hand.

He reached over. "I'll take that," he said.

# CHAPTER 85

MEG FINISHED GETTING THINGS organized for Langley in the dressing room, then rushed to practice at the old church where the cabarets were held a few weekend nights each month.

As she sat through two other singers, and the same pianist who would be accompanying her, Meg felt increasingly tense. Amy's death, Belinda's disappearance, Langley's distress, her father's disappointment with her behavior toward Caroline. It was coming at her from all sides.

And she was extremely nervous about her cabaret performance. Not only would her father be coming to see her but so would the actors, directors, support staff, and other apprentices. The church would be filled to the rafters. All those people watching her, judging her.

She missed her mother, and she'd lost the only friend she'd really made in Warrenstown. Amy was the first new friend she'd made in a very long time.

Before her mother died, Meg had been outgoing and popular. Afterward, she didn't feel like doing much with her old friends. They weren't coming from the same place anymore. The things they wanted to do no longer interested Meg. Parties and the bar scene held no excitement. Neither did shopping or going out to eat. She only wanted to be left alone—and after a while, her friends did just that.

When Caroline moved in after marrying her father, Meg's loneliness only intensified. Home for school vacations, she avoided contact with Caroline as much as possible, either staying out of the apartment or holing up in her room. Sitting through meals in the dining room, watching Caroline sit where her mother used to, sickened Meg.

She just wanted the pain to go away.

Meg knew there were two more singers before it was her turn. She got up and walked outside. The fresh air felt good after the stale smell of the church. She walked around to the back of the old stone building and found a secluded, sheltered spot.

When she went back inside, fifteen minutes later, the pianist was ready for her. She took her sheet music out of her tote and handed it to him.

"Ah. 'Second Hand Rose,' " he said. "That's a good one."

Meg had chosen the song not only because she could sing it well but because she could vamp it up. She could do a little acting while displaying her voice. She climbed onto the raised platform and waited for the music to start.

She missed her cue the first time, and the pianist began again. Meg started to sing, but her voice sounded flat, and her movements were stilted and awkward. She stopped and looked at her accompanist, a dull expression on her face.

"Easy, Meg," he said. "Just try to relax and have a good time with it."

The music began again. She sang the first verse, then stopped, unable to recall the next lyrics.

"What's the matter with you, Meg?" asked the guy at the piano. "Are you stoned or something?"

# CHAPTER 86

IT FELT LIKE HER head was going to explode, and every breath she took hurt. She feared her back might be broken. If she moved, she could risk paralysis. Belinda wished she could curl into a fetal position and comfort herself. Instead, she lay on her back and stared into the darkness.

She slipped in and out of sleep. When she was awake, she had no idea what time it was or how many hours she had been there. When sleep came again, she welcomed it as an escape from her pain and fear. The cycle repeated itself; each waking moment was an opportunity to try to figure out what to do. How was anyone going to find her? How was she going to get out of this place and save herself? But then her pain and the gravity of her situation overwhelmed her and she'd fall asleep again.

Belinda awoke and listened in the darkness. She heard a low rumbling noise. At first, she thought it must be her stomach, growling in hunger. Then she realized the noise wasn't coming from her at all.

She wasn't alone.

# CHAPTER 87

"NOW WHAT?" ASKED CAROLINE as she and Annabelle drove back to town.

"I guess we should call the desk," said Annabelle, "and tell them where things stand up here. At this point, I don't see them wanting a full piece. Nothing definitive has happened."

"Belinda Winthrop is missing," said Caroline.

"Yeah, but we aren't sure if there is foul play involved or not. If she's just decided to take a powder for some reason, that isn't a national news story. She wouldn't be the first actor to want to be alone for a while."

"And skip a performance in a role that everyone is saying is one of her best?"

"Look, Caroline, I don't make the rules. But I do know what it takes to get airtime. This story doesn't have that yet. My guess is the most they'll want is some video for Eliza Blake to voice-over on the *Evening Headlines* tonight." Annabelle didn't mention the other thing, of which she was virtually certain. *Evening Headlines* was not going to have Caroline report the story. They wouldn't think a drama critic had the credentials to report hard news.

Sure enough, when Annabelle called KEY News headquarters, there was no interest in Caroline Enright doing a piece, but the anchorwoman Eliza Blake would tell the story, narrating over video of Curtains Up and general

Warrenstown B-roll. They also asked for the interview Caroline had done with Belinda the evening before. Caroline's interview would air without her getting any credit for it.

"They do want us to go over in the morning and see if we can get pictures of the police beginning the organized search of Belinda's property," reported Annabelle.

"And between now and then?" asked Caroline.

"Go have a good time with your husband tonight," said Annabelle. "I'll make sure the video gets to New York. Since we don't have a satellite truck here yet, I'll get Lamar to drive me over to the Albany affiliate, and we'll feed from there. I'll keep in touch with the police, too."

# CHAPTER 88

SLOWLY, REMINGTON FINISHED WRAPPING the last of the portraits. As he covered Belinda's lovely face with batting, Remington wondered when he would next be able to see her. He knew it could be a very long time before it would be safe to have his treasures with him again.

He snuffed out the candles that had provided his work light and lifted the canvas, carrying it up the cellar stairs. Remington propped the portrait next to the front door with the others. Now, he just had to wait for the sun to go down to load the portraits into the car and transport them to the storage facility. He would be back safe and sound, his mission accomplished, before the morning sun.

Looking at his watch, he knew he had some time, and he wanted to use it productively. Though it had been necessary, Remington felt he'd wasted his day getting ready to move the portraits. Those paintings were no longer supposed to exist. No one could see them, not only because he didn't want to share his beloved with the world but because the insurance company believed they'd been destroyed in the fire. The authorities wouldn't care that Remington had donated the payout he'd received to charity. They would care only that he'd lied and taken their money. So he'd spent his time covering his tracks instead of making any progress on the portrait on which he *should* have been working: Belinda as Valerie.

Remington went to the closet, opened it, and took out his work in progress.

"I'm sorry I had to shut you in there like that," he said. "I couldn't leave you out anymore. Everyone wants to see you, but you're not ready to be seen."

# CHAPTER 89

"I'VE MADE A RESERVATION at Pierre's," said Nick. "It's the best place in Warrenstown."

"That sounds great," said Caroline. "But do you think we could go to the Ambrose Gallery before dinner? I'd like to stop in at the exhibition opening."

While Nick went down to the bar for a drink, Caroline dressed in an off-the-shoulder blouse, the gauzy, black peasant skirt she'd purchased on Main Street, and a pair of black sandals. As she adjusted the neckline of the blouse, she remembered she wanted to pin her hair up the way Nick liked it.

Caroline was determined to have her last night with Nick be a special one. He was leaving in the morning, and she wasn't sure when he would be coming home again. She wanted both of them to enjoy themselves tonight and separate in the morning wanting more.

"You look great," Nick said when she appeared at the bar. He leaned over and kissed her. "Want a drink?"

"How about a glass of pinot grigio?"

When Caroline's wine came, Nick raised his glass. "To you, Sunshine."

"To *us*, Nick."

They gently touched glasses.

"Mmm. That tastes good," said Caroline. "It's been a long day."

As they drank, Caroline told Nick about her trip to Curtains Up with Annabelle. "That caretaker of Belinda's gives me the creeps," she said. "There's something sinister about him."

"I know, you said that this morning. Do you really think he could have something to do with Belinda's disappearance?"

Caroline took another sip of white wine as she considered the question. "I don't know. But let me ask you something."

"Shoot."

"Was Gus at Belinda's party two years ago?"

Nick grabbed some nuts from the bowl on the bar. "Yeah, as a matter of fact he *was* there. I remember being introduced to him. Belinda had just hired him, I think." He popped a couple of nuts in his mouth. "What? You're trying to tie him to Daniel Sterling's death, too?"

Caroline looked at her husband. "We don't know that Belinda is dead, Nick."

"I wasn't saying that she is, Caroline. I was asking if you were trying to tie Gus Oberon to Sterling's death as well as Belinda's disappearance."

*That's not the way it came across,* thought Caroline.

THE AMBROSE GALLERY HELD a nice-size crowd assembled for the unveiling of Remington Peters's latest portrait of Belinda Winthrop. As she and Nick walked around the room, Caroline heard snippets of conversation.

"What a disappointment. We came all this way and the portrait we most wanted to see isn't even here."

"It isn't fair that they advertised something they couldn't deliver. I'm surprised at the Ambroses. I expected more from them."

"Did you hear that Belinda Winthrop is missing?"

"Yes. When I went to pick up our tickets at the Playhouse box office, they said her understudy will be playing the role of Valerie tonight."

Caroline was standing opposite the wall with the empty space when Jean Ambrose approached her.

Caroline gave her a rueful smile. "I'm sorry Remington didn't come through for you," she said.

Jean glanced around the room. "You and everyone else here."

"Your husband couldn't convince him, huh?"

"No," said Jean, and she leaned in a little closer. "But it might be for the best. Zeke saw the painting. He said it was unrealistic and disturbing. Belinda had a maniacal look on her face, almost as if she were mentally ill."

"That doesn't sound like a description of the way Belinda looked as Valerie last night," Caroline said.

"I know it doesn't," said Jean. "Zeke and I are afraid that Remington might be losing it."

# CHAPTER 90

HIDDEN BY THE CURTAIN, Keith peeked out from the side of the stage. The house was filling up nicely. Every seat for tonight's performance was reserved. In fact, the entire run of the play was sold out.

*All these people had expected to see Belinda Winthrop when they bought their tickets,* Keith thought as he looked out at the audience. Most important, one of the potential backers for the movie version of *Devil in the Details* was sitting out there tonight. Wanting to get a better idea of what his money would be financing, he'd come all the way from Los Angeles to watch Belinda play Valerie. Instead, the backer was going to be seeing Langley Tate in the role.

Everything was unraveling. All the months of planning and working and cajoling to make *Devil in the Details* Keith Fallows's debut as a film director were coming to naught because Belinda Winthrop had failed him. It was all Belinda's fault. How dare she pull out on him?

Keith spun away from the curtain. Maybe all wasn't lost, he thought. Maybe Langley would give such a stunning performance that he could sell the idea of an ingenue in the role. It was a long shot, Keith knew, but stranger things had happened, hadn't they?

Keith's momentary optimism sank as he remembered the afternoon rehearsal. Langley had been a disappointment. When one had seen Belinda in the role, Langley's ability seemed so limited. The director had to admit to himself that he hadn't helped matters by criticizing his new leading lady when he should have been building her up.

He should have controlled his temper with Langley, just as he should have controlled his fits of anger with Belinda. If he had done that, he wouldn't be in the position he was in right now. Keith knew his temper was his weak spot, but he rationalized that, as a creative artist, it was his right, even his obligation, to feel things passionately. Let the rest of the plodders in the world play by their silly social rules. He operated by his own.

# CHAPTER 91

"AREN'T YOU GOING TO the theater?" Gus asked.

"Maybe later," said Victoria as she poured him another drink. "I don't have to see every performance now that the blocking is set."

"I'd think you'd want to see that understudy," said Gus, remembering Langley's perfect body. He'd like to watch her onstage himself. But even more than wanting to watch Langley, Gus wanted Victoria to leave so he could get out to the woods and move the cartons from the cave.

He studied the lines in Victoria's face. This was the oldest woman he'd ever been with, and she wasn't half bad in the sack. Still, she wasn't, by a long shot, his dream girl. But Victoria was Belinda's friend, and he knew he'd better suck up if he wanted to stay on the property. He needed to take care of things.

"I'd rather be here with you," said Victoria. She leaned over and kissed him.

It was clear what this middle-aged dame wanted, and he would have to give it to her yet again just to get rid of her, just to buy time to do what he needed to do.

# CHAPTER 92

THE ANNOUNCEMENT WAS MADE to the audience via the sound system.

"Good evening, and welcome to the Warrenstown Summer Playhouse. Tonight, the role of Valerie will be played by Langley Tate."

A low rumble of disappointment rippled through the auditorium.

"There will be one fifteen-minute intermission. Please make sure cell phones are turned off and refrain from taking pictures or using other electronic devices. Enjoy your evening, and thank you for supporting live theater."

When the curtains parted and Langley appeared onstage, the applause was polite but not enthusiastic.

# CHAPTER 93

THE CANDLE BURNING IN the middle of the table cast Caroline's face in a warm glow.

"You are beautiful, Sunshine."

"Thank you." She smiled. "I'm glad *you* see me that way, Nick."

"Anyone would see you that way. You're lovely, Sunshine, inside and out."

"Your daughter doesn't think so."

"Caroline, will you please stop worrying about what Meg thinks? You're my wife and I love you and that's all there is to it. Meg has to get used to our marriage. Besides, I think she seems like she's doing quite well up here, don't you?"

Caroline considered her response. She still hadn't told Nick about the marijuana she'd found in Meg's closet at home. Her main concern was why Meg felt the need to smoke pot. If she were Meg's real mother, Caroline knew for certain that she would be discussing the subject with Nick. But she was in a difficult spot. If she told Nick, Caroline suspected Meg might not ever get over what she would consider a betrayal.

"I think Meg is complicated, Nick. She's been through a lot, and it takes a long time to heal when you lose your mother. I guess you never get over it completely."

Nick leaned forward, reached across the table, and took

Caroline's hand. "I know it's hard for Meg. But she has to get on with it. Maggie is dead. There's no changing that."

"Well, I don't think it's helped Meg that her friend was killed this week. Honestly, sweetheart, I think that's set her back."

Nick dropped her hand and sat back in his chair. "I hate that Meg had to know loss so early, Caroline," he said. "It's too bad she had to learn that—*is* having to learn that—at such a young age. But there's no getting around it. We all lose people who are important in our lives. That's painful, but not fatal, for those left behind. She'll survive."

# CHAPTER 94

FINALLY, IT WAS GROWING dark.

Remington stepped away from the window, walked across the studio, and opened the front door. He looked down the hill. Lights were on in the farmhouse, but he couldn't see anyone outside.

He picked up the first wrapped portrait and loaded it into the back of his station wagon. Then he returned and repeated the process eight more times. At that point, there wasn't room for any more.

Remington realized he had calculated correctly. He'd have to make only two trips to move the seventeen paintings from the carriage house to the storage facility. But he was so tense at the thought that he might not have enough time to finish everything he had to get done tonight, he forgot to lock the front door before he drove away.

# CHAPTER 95

THE APPLAUSE AT INTERMISSION was surprisingly strong.

Langley let out a deep breath as she walked off the stage. Keith was waiting for her in the wings. "Marvelous, Langley. Marvelous," he said, hugging her.

Langley stood rigidly and accepted the director's praise, but she hadn't forgotten his venom during the rehearsal.

MEG WAS EXCITED WHEN Langley arrived in the dressing room. "I was watching on the monitor," she said. "You were great, Langley."

"Thanks, honey," Langley said, rushing by Meg. "Help me change quickly, will you? I want to have some time to go over my lines for the next act."

"You want me to run them with you?" Meg asked eagerly, knowing the copy of the script that Belinda had given her was still in her tote bag.

"Yeah, that would be perfect," said Langley.

Meg helped Langley dress in the green velvet ball gown. She pulled bobby pins from her apron pocket to secure tendrils of hair that had fallen from Langley's upsweep.

"Okay, we have about five minutes before I have to be back onstage," said Langley. "Let's go over that final scene. Let's start with, 'I know the scariest thing . . . '"

"All right," said Meg. She pulled the script out of her bag, cleared her throat, and began. "I know the scariest thing is lying in bed with someone who has sold her soul to the devil."

"No, Meg. You've got it mixed up. You're reading my lines, Valerie's lines. You're supposed to be reading Davis's."

Meg closed her eyes, hating herself. She had to stop smoking that weed. The pot was making her dumber by the day.

# CHAPTER 96

MEG HAD SECURED EXCELLENT cabaret tickets for her father and stepmother. Caroline and Nick arrived early, taking their seats at the reserved bistro table.

"This is nice," said Caroline. "We're right up front."

"How about something to drink?" asked Nick.

"Just a ginger ale, please," said Caroline. "I've already had enough wine for the night."

"You got it," said Nick.

Caroline watched her husband maneuver his way through the jumble of tables to the bar at the side of the room. She helped herself to a chocolate Kiss from the handful that had been sprinkled on their table. Then she leaned back and considered her surroundings.

She sat in what had once been a church, but all the pews had been removed and a stage stood where she supposed the altar had once been. The choir loft had been extended, forming a balcony that surrounded three sides of the room. From that elevated position, theatrical lights were trained on the stage. The room was very warm, despite the opened windows and the cool night air outside, and the smell of beer and spilled wine permeated the atmosphere.

"Here you go, sweetheart." Nick deposited her soft drink and his beer on the table as a man and woman sat at a table beside them.

"John Massey?" Nick said, leaning forward.

The man smiled, rose from his chair, and leaned over to shake hands. "Nick, my man, great to see you. This is Megan, my wife."

Nick introduced Caroline. "I didn't know you were a Warrenstown fan, John," he said. "Do you come often?"

"We've been here a few times. It's a nice break from L.A. You?"

"Yes, many times over the years, but this season my daughter is an apprentice. She'll be in the cabaret tonight. She's singing 'Second Hand Rose.' "

"So the showbiz bug has bitten her, too," said John. "Lord help her."

The couples chuckled. "We just came from seeing *Devil in the Details*," said Megan.

"We saw it last night," said Caroline. "What did you think?"

John answered the question. "I think you were the lucky ones. That understudy was actually pretty good, but how can anyone hold a candle to Belinda Winthrop? What's the story, anyway? Do you know where Belinda was tonight?"

Nick explained that no one had seen Belinda all day.

"That's weird," said John. "Nothing can happen to her. I'm about to invest a nice piece of change in a movie version of *Devil in the Details*. Keith Fallows wants to direct."

"I've been hearing rumors about that," said Nick. "And who will star?"

"Belinda Winthrop, of course," answered John. "At least, that's the only way *I'll* invest in the project. I doubt that, without Belinda playing the lead, anyone else will pony up, either."

THE AUDIENCE CLAPPED POLITELY but with none of the exuberance they'd shown for some of the other cabaret acts. Caroline winced as she watched Meg walk offstage.

She looked over at Nick. Disappointment was clearly registered on his face.

"I don't know what to say," he said.

Caroline bit her lower lip, not knowing how to respond, either. Meg simply hadn't measured up to the other, incredibly talented kids who had performed this evening. But it didn't make sense. In her college musical this past spring, Meg had been fabulous.

"This wasn't a true measure of her talent, Nick," Caroline finally responded. "Everybody has an off night once in a while."


THEY WAITED FOR MEG in the church vestibule. As the audience filed out of the building, the Masseys stopped to compliment Meg's performance politely.

"That's very kind of you," said Nick quietly. There was an awkward lull, and the couple said good-bye and moved on.

The church was nearly empty when Meg finally walked over. "What did you think?" she asked.

"I think you're capable of much better, Meg," said her father. "Honestly, I was very disappointed."

"Nick," said Caroline, reaching for his arm to stop him.

"No, Caroline. It's the truth, and Meg should hear it. If she has any real desire to work in this business, she is going to have to give a lot more than she gave tonight. Look at those other kids, will you? They were dripping with talent and energy. Meg, you were sleepwalking out there. What was the matter with you?"

Meg's gaze shifted from her father to Caroline. As the two women's eyes met, Caroline knew they both recognized this would be the perfect moment for her to reveal that her stepdaughter was smoking dope. Still, Caroline held off.

"Even the biggest stars have given performances they wish they could take back," she said. "All you can do is learn from this, Meg, and figure out what you should be doing differently." Caroline looked directly at her. "Do you know what I mean, Meg?"

"Yes," said Meg. "I get it, Caroline. I promise, I do."

# CHAPTER 97

*WELL AFTER THE LAST patron left and the theater cleared out for the night, the killer went to the bulletin board and pulled down the sign-up sheet. As expected, it looked like almost every apprentice had signed up to meet with the New York agent.*

*The killer perused the list, finding the Brightlights e-mail address, with the name, telephone number, and place where the young woman who had gotten Amy's last photo message slept at night.*

*ACROSS THE ROAD FROM the dormitory, the killer waited. The parade of students coming back to get some sleep, some of them stopping to smoke cigarettes and talk on the lawn, slowly dwindled until there was complete stillness outside the red-brick building. Each of the kids had paused at the door, using a key to get inside.*

*Trying to sneak in behind one of the students had been an option, but there would still be the problem of Meg's room being locked. And there was the even larger issue of having to deal with Meg herself. She wasn't exactly going to welcome someone into her room and hand over her computer.*

*Crossing the street, the killer approached the dormitory.*

◆  ◆  ◆

MEG TYPED HER JOURNAL entry knowing she would edit the material before she turned it in to her college theater department to get credit for her experience at Warrenstown. It wouldn't go over well if her professor read about everything that had happened today. Yet Meg wanted to write about it as a catharsis.

Her father's words after the cabaret had shaken her, as had her pathetic, stoned performance onstage. She was embarrassed, too, by the ways she had scrambled her lines with Langley, using the script Belinda had given her. But, surprisingly, Meg found herself feeling the worst about the fact that her stepmother, in spite of the resentfulness Meg made no effort to hide, had turned out to be a friend. Caroline could have told her father about the pot, but she hadn't.

What had begun as occasional recreational drug use was becoming more and more frequent. When she felt sad about losing her mother, when she felt angry at her father's remarriage, when she felt anxious about her performances or threatened by her competition—just about any situation where an emotion was involved was triggering the urge to get stoned. She wasn't giving in to every urge, but she was smoking enough that now she was worried. Of course, worrying made her want to light up a joint as well.

Meg entered all her observations and feelings in her electronic journal, including her oath to stop smoking marijuana. Somehow, seeing it in black and white made it more real. Like a contract with herself or something. When she finished, Meg closed the laptop, turned off the light, and went to bed.

THERE IT WAS. THE small metal box was attached to the wall beside the front door, the small metal box that would make entry to the dorm possible.

The killer pulled the lever and stepped back as the fire alarm pierced the air.

• • •

A SOUND THAT COULD wake the dead aroused Meg from her slumber. She was sorely tempted to ignore the alarm, but she got out of bed, peeked into the hallway, and saw her bleary-eyed floormates filing past.

"Come on, Meg," said her next-door neighbor, pulling her along.

*THERE WOULDN'T BE A lot of time. The police and fire departments were going to come running.*

*After the crowd of dorm residents came out, the killer slipped in.*

# SATURDAY
*August 5*

# CHAPTER 98

GUS STEERED THE GOLF cart into the woods, his flash-light illuminating the way. He'd gotten started later than he wanted to, in part because Victoria had kept him. She'd told him that he was the first man she'd been with since her husband died two years ago. Gus didn't know if he be-lieved that, but the woman had certainly been insatiable.

Parking the cart, he got out and walked to the opening in the ground. He stuck the flashlight in the pocket of his jeans and began to back down the ladder. At the bottom, he stopped and trained the light on the contents of the cave.

He hoisted the first carton to his shoulder and climbed up to the surface, stashing the carton in the golf cart. Then he repeated the process again, and again, and again, until he was satisfied that he'd moved everything that could be incriminating. If the police found the cave now, nothing would trace back to him.

He drove the golf cart slowly across the meadow, tak-ing care so none of the cartons would spill from the vehi-cle. Gus would have thought he still had a long night ahead of him had he not stopped by the carriage house af-ter he left Victoria. Her request that he deliver some of the party's leftovers to Remington had provided the caretaker with a windfall.

The door had been unlocked. A quick search of the premises gave him the idea. That cellar would be a better hiding place. Instead of having to unload all the cartons from the golf cart to his truck and then drive them down to Pittsfield to stow in the garage of a friend—a friend whom Gus was never really sure he could trust—he could hide the cartons in the carriage house. Even if the cops decided to search the cellar for Belinda, they probably weren't going to go opening up boxes they thought a famous artist like Remington Peters was storing there. And if, by some chance, the police did open the cartons, it would look like Remington, not Gus, was dealing.

Gus drove up to the unlit carriage house, noting that Remington's station wagon still wasn't there. Lifting the first box from the cart, Gus let himself in the front door and walked to the cellar door and down the steps.

The cellar was cool, dry, and empty except for a bunch of half-used candles sitting around on the floor. Gus carried the first carton to a nook at the rear, dropped it, and slid it into the recessed spot. He estimated that with careful arranging all the cartons would fit. Someone would really have to be looking to find them.

When he finished bringing all the cartons to their new storage spot, Gus climbed the stairs and went outside. He was just getting into the golf cart when he saw the headlights coming up the driveway. Gus pressed his foot on the accelerator and steered the cart into his garage.


REMINGTON TOOK HIS KEY and inserted it in the knob, but the door was already unlocked. His heart beat faster as he opened the door and switched on the lights. *Someone's been in here,* he thought. There was the smell of perspiration in the air.

But everything looked exactly the same as he had left it. Nothing appeared to be touched or taken. The last of the paintings were still propped up against the wall.

He turned on the light at the top of the cellar stairway, walked down, and looked around. Nothing seemed amiss in the empty space.

Maybe he was being paranoid. Remington looked at his watch. He couldn't worry about it any more right now. He had to get the next batch of portraits into the car. But this time, when he left, he made sure to lock the door.

# CHAPTER 99

BELINDA LISTENED TO THE plaintive mewing sound as she felt something soft brush against her thigh. She reached down until her fingertips touched the fur.

She gasped as she figured out what was sharing the underground cave with her. There were two kittens down here in the den their mother had lined with dried grass, leaves, and moss. Belinda decided they were probably bobcat cubs. They were hungry and, she prayed, basically harmless.

But their mother was an adult. Though bobcats didn't look for conflicts with humans, they were still carnivores. And no mother took kindly to having her babies threatened.

# CHAPTER 100

IN THE SEMIDARKNESS, CAROLINE felt for the telephone on the table beside the bed.

"Hello," she whispered, not wanting to wake up Nick.

"Sorry to disturb you, Sleeping Beauty, but the search is on at Belinda's this morning."

Caroline looked at the digital clock. 7:15.

"Annabelle?"

"Who else would be crazy enough to be setting her alarm to ring every two hours through the night so she could check the status of things with the police?" asked Annabelle.

"Whatever it is, KEY News isn't paying you enough," Caroline whispered as she walked into the bathroom and closed the door.

"Don't I know it!"

Caroline could picture Annabelle rolling her eyes. "What time will the search start?" she asked.

"Nine, but I've already called Lamar and Boomer. I want to get over there early. We're leaving the inn at eight."

"I'll meet you in the lobby in forty-five minutes then," said Caroline.

She turned on the water and pulled off her nightgown. Stepping into the shower, Caroline realized that she would be at Curtains Up when Nick had to leave. It surprised her that she didn't feel more disappointed about that. Instead, she was looking forward to following the story of Belinda's disappearance. She had covered many openings, interviewed many stars, and influenced the nation's film-going habits, but this case was exciting her in a whole different way. It was real—not the fantasy world she was used to covering—and Caroline was finding herself completely caught up in it.

"NICK. NICK," SHE WHISPERED as she sat on the edge of the bed.

Nick opened his eyes. Caroline thought he looked, for a moment, almost as though he didn't recognize her.

"I'm sorry to wake you, honey, but I wanted to say good-bye."

"What time is it?"

"Five of eight."

"Where are you going so early?" he asked, rubbing his eyes.

"They're searching Belinda's property."

"And you have to be there for that?"

"Yes. Annabelle and the crew are going. I think I should, too."

"For pity's sake, Caroline. You're a critic, not an investigative journalist."

Caroline pulled back. "Nick," she said, her tone registering her surprise at the anger in her husband's voice.

"I'm sorry, Sunshine. But I just want to have you to myself before I leave." He reached up and drew her close. Caroline kissed Nick back, but without the usual fervor.

"All right, I have to get going now," she said as she pulled away determinedly. "They're waiting for me downstairs." She stood up. "And you know what, Nick? I think you should make it a point to go over and talk with Meg before you leave. You wouldn't want what you said to her about her performance last night to be your last conversation with her, would you? That would be a lousy way to leave things between you."

# CHAPTER 101

REMINGTON HADN'T GOTTEN MUCH sleep, yet he didn't want to waste the precious early-morning light. He pulled on rumpled jeans and an old, paint-stained shirt. Slipping on a pair of moccasins, he climbed down from the loft and went to the closet. He took out the portrait and placed it on the easel.

As he looked at his work, he still didn't understand how he could have gotten it so wrong. With Belinda gone, he was determined, more than ever, to do her justice in her role of Valerie.

Hoping for inspiration, Remington walked over to the table to get his script. But the dog-eared copy wasn't there. Only the extra script that the theater department had sent him sat on the table.

That meant someone *had* been in the house when he was gone.

# CHAPTER 102

*IT HAD BEEN A damned good thing to get Meg's computer, but not for the expected reason. At first, there was relief as the killer viewed the pictures Amy had sent to Meg on the day of the fatal accident. The one that had been such a worry turned out to be just a blur of blue. It wouldn't lead the police anywhere. But, just to be thorough, the killer checked the messages in the Sent folder and was relieved to see that none had gone to the Warrenstown police.*

*Out of curiosity, the killer then clicked through some of Meg's other e-mails, chuckling upon finding the one that had been sent from "Amy's mother." Most of the other messages were a lot of nothing. But one was interesting.*

IN ORDER TO RECEIVE ACADEMIC CREDIT FOR APPRENTICING AT THE WARRENSTOWN SUMMER PLAYHOUSE PROGRAM, IT WILL BE NECESSARY TO SUBMIT A JOURNAL CHRONICLING YOUR EXPERIENCES. INSTRUCTIONS FOR JOURNALING ARE IN THE ATTACHED DOCUMENT.

*Clicking on the icon for Meg's electronic journal, the killer found the entries she had made since her arrival in town.*

# CHAPTER 103

ANNABELLE AND CAROLINE SAT in the backseat of the crew car as they drove with Lamar and Boomer to Curtains Up.

"I did a search on Gus Oberon," said Annabelle. "He spent three years in prison."

"Really?" Caroline took a breath and then exhaled deeply. "I had a feeling that guy was trouble. What was he in for?"

"Criminal possession of marijuana. There was some reference to the possibility that he was dealing, too. And if *we* know that Gus is a criminal, you can bet the police know it, too."

"I guess he hasn't learned his lesson," said Caroline, shaking her head. "The aroma he left in Belinda's powder room at the party shows he's still using. The question is, does Gus have anything to do with Belinda's disappearance?"

POLICE CHIEF HOWARD STANLEY stood in front of the crowd of law enforcement and civilian volunteers who had gathered in the driveway. Caroline estimated there were about seventy-five people there. Among them, she recognized Remington Peters, Victoria Sterling, Keith Fallows, and Langley Tate. All of them looked tired.

"We still have no actual indication that a crime has been committed," Chief Stanley told the group. "But because Ms. Winthrop hasn't turned up, not even for her theater performance last night, there is real cause for concern. Thank you for coming this morning to help in the search."

He held up a piece of paper. "There are maps of the property on the table over there. Please take one of them. Also, officers will be coming through the crowd handing out whistles."

Caroline and Annabelle, along with everyone else, took maps and whistles.

"There are one hundred fifty acres here," Stanley continued. "You'll see on the map we've drawn in search corridors. Each corridor will be traversed in two directions, at right angles to each other. In this way, the entire area will be searched.

"You'll divide into groups of four and keep to your assigned lane. When you get to the woods, stop every minute and blast your whistles, listen for a possible response, and then repeat the process.

"One last thing, the woods are full of places where the ground opens up, leading to underground caves. Some of them are on your map, some are not, so please be very careful."

"What about animals and things?" asked one of the volunteers.

"Anything out there is more afraid of you than you are of it," said Chief Stanley.

"I've heard there are bobcats in this area," another searcher called out.

"Yes, but bobcats tend to be active very early in the morning and then again from three hours or so before sunset until around midnight. So we should be clear now. Besides, bobcats are generally pretty shy, unless they're provoked. And no one is going to do that, right?"

# CHAPTER 104

THE SEARCHERS WERE DIVIDING up and moving to their positions when Caroline spotted Meg walking up the driveway.

"Dad told me about the search," she said. "He just dropped me off as he left to drive to the airport."

*Good,* thought Caroline. Nick had gone to see his daughter, just as she'd suggested.

"I'm proud of you, Meg, for getting up so early to join the search. The maps are on the table," she said. "Go get one and grab a whistle."

As Meg walked off, Caroline turned to Annabelle. "Let's have Meg join our group, all right?"

"Fine with me," said Annabelle. "But you know, I've been thinking that one of us should stay back here at the base in case one of the other groups finds anything. Why don't I stay here with my camcorder, and you and Meg go with Lamar and Boomer?"

Caroline considered the suggestion. "Maybe it would be better if you went along with the search and I stayed behind, Annabelle. I have a feeling that there will be more action out there than here, and you'd be better at covering it."

"All right, then," said Annabelle as she handed the small video camera to Caroline. "Just in case, let me give you a quick lesson in how to use this. It's really easy."

• • •

THE VOLUNTEERS SPREAD OUT across the edge of the property. Slowly, methodically, they walked the grounds, their eyes trained downward. When they got through the meadow, Caroline heard the whistles begin to sound as the search of the woods started.

# CHAPTER 105

GUS CAME OUT OF the garage and made his way to the makeshift command post. He knew he should join the search for Belinda. It would look bad if he didn't. He stopped at the table, asked where he should go, and started across the meadow.

GUS WAS WATCHED UNTIL the woods swallowed him from view.

"He worries me," Chief Stanley said. "Now that we know he's done time, I think we should take this chance to look at his place."

"What about a warrant?" asked the other cop.

"The garage is Belinda Winthrop's property."

"But it's *his* home, Chief."

Chief Stanley glared at his subordinate. "If we find something that leads us to Belinda Winthrop, nobody's gonna raise hell about a warrant. And if we hurry, we can go through the place before he gets back. He'll never even know we were there."

CAROLINE SAW THE POLICE officers walking toward the garage. She pointed the camcorder and recorded about twenty seconds of images.

# CHAPTER 106

MEG STOPPED, BLEW HER whistle, and waited. She listened for some sort of response, but only a bird's chirp answered her. Meg could hear other whistles sounding in the distance. She didn't get the feeling they were getting any replies, either.

She held up her wrist and checked the time. "I think I better get going," she said to her search companions. "I'm speaking at the memorial service this afternoon, and I haven't finished my talk yet."

"Lamar or Boomer, would one of you mind walking Meg back?" asked Annabelle.

"No," said Meg. "I'll be fine."

She started back in the direction from which they'd come, through the tall trees, along the stream that ran through the woods. Meg figured she didn't have too far to go until she would reach the end of the shadowy forest and come into the meadow when she heard what she thought was a twig snapping behind her. She turned but saw nothing except dark tree trunks standing imposingly. A gray squirrel scampered through the ferns and undergrowth that covered the ground.

Meg continued back.

• • •

*THE KILLER STOOD AGAINST the thick trunk of an oak tree, straining to hear the rustling sound of Meg's steps on the leafy forest floor.*

*This wasn't the time to grab her. There were too many people looking for Belinda, unaware that they were passing within yards of the woman for whom they were searching.*

*Smarter to take care of Meg later, when it would be less likely that anyone would see.*

# CHAPTER 107

BELINDA COULD HEAR THE whistles. As she lay on her back on the cave floor, tears of gratitude filled her eyes. People were actually looking for her. *Thank you, God. Thank you.*

She waited as the sound of the whistles grew closer. When it seemed the sound was coming from almost directly above her, she called out.

"Help. I'm here. Down here."

But though she summoned every bit of energy, Belinda's voice was only a weak rasp.

# CHAPTER 108

THE TWO POLICEMEN OPENED and looked through every closet and cabinet in Gus Oberon's garage apartment. They searched under the bed and through his dresser drawers.

"Be careful," instructed Chief Stanley. "Try not to upset things. Try to leave things just the way Oberon left them."

"These drawers are such a mess, Chief. They look like he took an eggbeater to 'em. I doubt the guy would even be able to tell we touched anything."

"When you're done with the dresser, check that bookcase," said the chief as he flipped over the mattress on the unmade bed.

The ziplock plastic bag containing marijuana was found behind stacked copies of *Penthouse*, *Playboy*, and other, even less reputable, men's magazines.

"With all we've got going on right now," said Chief Stanley, "a dime bag isn't worth bringing him in for. Put it back where he hid it."

# CHAPTER 109

CAROLINE STOOD AT A safe distance from the garage, her camera poised to take more video of the Warrenstown policemen when they came out of Gus's apartment.

"What are you doing?"

She jumped at the voice that came from behind her.

"Oh, you scared me, Meg," said Caroline as she closed her eyes for a moment.

"I didn't mean to," said Meg. "I've got to get back to campus and wanted to let you know. But what *are* you doing?"

"The police are in Gus Oberon's apartment. I'm getting pictures."

Meg's face clouded.

"What's wrong?" Caroline asked.

"I've bought pot from Gus."

"Oh, Meg. No," Caroline groaned.

"I just hope he doesn't keep any written records," said Meg.

THE POLICE CAME OUT of the garage, and Caroline watched as they headed for the carriage house. This time she could see them insert a key in the front door lock and walk right in.

Caroline recorded it all, then walked up the hill, trying to stay out of sight by keeping well to the side of the path that led to the artist's studio.

"THERE'S NOTHING SUSPICIOUS HERE, Chief."

"Except that this artist is really twisted," said Chief Stanley as he looked beneath the sheet covering the portrait on the easel. "This is one angry-looking rendering of Belinda Winthrop. He's made her look like a crazy woman."

CAROLINE SNEAKED AROUND TO the back of the carriage house and peeked in the picture window. She could see the policemen walking to the door at the rear. She watched as they started down the stairs.

When they were out of sight, Caroline struggled to get a better view of the contents of the studio. She could see Remington's easel, but a sheet covered it. She supposed that would be the portrait of Belinda Winthrop as Valerie, the painting Remington said was not ready to be exhibited.

Caroline bit her lower lip as she considered what she should do. Did she dare go inside and get a look at the portrait?

If she was going to, she had to act fast.

"THIS IS ONE CLEAN cellar, boss."

Chief Stanley grunted in agreement as he looked around. He picked up one of the votive candles from the dirt floor. "What do you suppose these are here for?" he asked.

"Beats me, Chief."

He laid down the candle and continued looking around. As Chief Stanley walked around the perimeter of the room, his eyes were drawn to a recessed area. He took the flashlight from his belt and pointed it inside the nook.

"What do we have here?" he asked.

CAROLINE HAD NEVER DONE anything like this in her life. She would never think of entering someone else's property without permission, but somehow having the video camera in hand, working on the story of Belinda's disappearance, emboldened her. Belinda was missing, two young apprentices were dead, and the town librarian had been murdered. These were not ordinary times.

She stepped over the threshold, barely pausing to listen for voices before heading to the easel. She pulled back the sheet and drew in a deep breath. Caroline knew she was looking at a killer.

Pulling the camera up to eye level, she aimed and recorded the image of Belinda as Valerie. The green velvet gown draping the erect body, the blond hair piled atop the patrician head, the piercing green eyes peering from the face with a murderous expression, the pistol gripped in one hand.

Why would Remington paint Belinda like this?

THE POLICEMEN OPENED THE first box they'd removed from the cellar nook. Chief Stanley whistled as he pulled out a plastic package and unwrapped it.

CAROLINE FINISHED RECORDING VIDEO of the painting and, knowing she was pushing it, quickly took a few shots of the studio. She was about to leave when she heard the voices coming up the steps.

There wasn't enough time to get to the front door. Even if she could, the police would surely spot her as she ran down the hill. Caroline dove forward and sunk down into the space between the couch and the wall. She held her breath and listened as the policemen entered the room.

"What should we do first, Chief? Confiscate those bundles of marijuana or bring in Remington Peters?"

"Let's get Peters. We can cordon off this place later."

Caroline could hear the footsteps grow closer and then fade as she pictured the men exiting the carriage house. After a minute, she emerged from her hiding place and cautiously looked out the doorway. Seeing the police heading toward the meadow, she made her own trip to the cellar.

The boxes were stacked in the middle of the floor. Caroline peered into one that had been left open, immediately recognizing the contents. She marveled at the thought that Remington Peters would be storing a huge stash of marijuana in his cellar. This was more in line with something Gus Oberon would do.

Realizing her time was limited, Caroline delayed further analysis. She would have time only to take some video of the boxes from various angles and get some close-up shots of the bundles of marijuana. With the search for Belinda continuing, Caroline was sure the news that the star's portraitist, a man who lived on her property, was being arrested for big-time marijuana possession at the same time Belinda was missing would pique the interest of everyone at KEY News headquarters. This had become her story, and Caroline was feeling the adrenaline rush she'd heard some of the news correspondents back at the Broadcast Center talk about: the relentless drive to follow the story, to gather all the elements, to figure things out.

The outcome of this story made a difference. It was a matter of life and death.

# CHAPTER 110

"HEY, I FOUND SOMETHING," yelled a man searching in the woods.

He bent over and picked up a woman's shoe.

# CHAPTER 111

MEG LET HERSELF INTO her dorm room and immediately went to the desk. She stared, uncomprehendingly, at the empty surface. She could have sworn she'd left the laptop right there.

As she began to look around the small room, Meg felt herself tensing. She pulled back the blanket she had left rumpled on her bed and got down on her hands and knees to check underneath. She even looked in her closet, knowing full well she hadn't put the computer there.

She tried to think back. Had she seen the laptop this morning when her father came? She couldn't remember whether it had been there when she left with him to drive to Curtains Up. The last time she could remember actually seeing the laptop was the night before, when she had made her journal entry.

Yes. She had left the laptop on the desk when she turned it off for the night, right before she'd gone to sleep. But the fire drill had awakened her. And she'd left without locking her door. She'd thought it would be fine for just that little while.

Meg felt leaden as she realized that someone had stolen her computer. The expense of replacing it didn't worry her as much as the thought that the draft of her speech for the memorial service was in that laptop, along with all her journal entries.

# CHAPTER 112

THE POLICE IN THE woods all received the same message: Remington Peters was to be escorted back to the area near the farmhouse. At the same time, Caroline called Annabelle on her cell phone and told her what she had seen and heard in the artist's place. "I think the police are in there somewhere taking Remington into custody," she said.

Annabelle scanned the wooded area from where she stood with the crew. "Somebody just found a woman's shoe," she said. "Lamar, Boomer, and I will head out. The cops will have to drag him across the meadow. But it's so dense in there, we won't necessarily be able to see the cops grab Remington. We'll be there waiting for them."

"What should I do?" asked Caroline.

"Where exactly are you?" asked Annabelle.

"I'm in the driveway. I just came from the carriage house, and I got video of the marijuana in Remington's cellar."

"You *what*?" Annabelle didn't think she could have heard Caroline correctly.

"I got video of the pot in the cellar."

"Don't tell me any more. I don't want to know right now how you did that," said Annabelle.

"All right," said Caroline. "But I've got it, along with some very disturbing shots of the portrait Remington is painting of Belinda in her latest role."

"Excellent," said Annabelle. "Look, you stay where you are and see if you can get video when the police come out with Remington as well. It won't hurt to have shots from two different angles."

"Okay," said Caroline. "And shouldn't one of us call the Broadcast Center and let them know what's going on?"

Annabelle smiled as she held the cell phone to her ear, observing her colleague's morphing from hothouse arts critic to hard-news field reporter. "God help you, Caroline."

"What do you mean?"

"You've been bitten!"

# CHAPTER 113

AFTER THEY WERE CERTAIN they had the images of Remington Peters being ushered to a police car and driven away, Annabelle called the assignment desk in New York, filling the appropriate parties in on what had been happening. She snapped her cell phone closed and reported back to her colleagues.

"*Evening Headlines* wants a piece for tonight, everybody. The satellite truck is on its way. Caroline, you will be the correspondent."

"Oh, mama," said Boomer while Lamar chuckled.

"A little baptism by fire," said Annabelle as she placed her hand on Caroline's shoulder. "But don't worry. You're going to be great."

"My reviews are always done in the studio, and I've done so few pieces out in the field, even for *KEY to America*," said Caroline. "Do I have to mention that I feel like throwing up?"

Annabelle smiled as she gestured toward Lamar and Boomer. "Well, *we* have all done *lots* of stories in the field. We're going to make sure you come out looking like Diane Sawyer."

"Promise?" asked Caroline.

"Promise."

Annabelle had failed to mention that the *Evening Headlines* producers were leery of using Caroline. They simply had no one available to send to Warrenstown this afternoon.


CAROLINE AND ANNABELLE WERE discussing the elements they already had for the *Evening Headlines* piece when Caroline's cell phone sounded. It was Meg. She quickly relayed the tale of her stolen computer.

"Now I'm trying to remember what I'd already written for the memorial service, and I know I'm forgetting things," Meg whined.

"Just write from your heart, Meg. Keep it simple, and don't make it too long. It's usually better to keep it short."

"I wish you could help me with it, Caroline."

It was the first time Meg had ever asked her stepmother to do anything with her, the first time she had ever asked for any sort of help. Caroline didn't want to refuse Meg, yet she felt the pressure of knowing she had to use the next hours to work on the *Evening Headlines* piece.

"Tell you what," she said. "You keep writing and I'll try to go over it with you before the memorial service."

# CHAPTER 114

THE KEY NEWS TEAM left Curtains Up and headed for the Warrenstown Inn. In the coffee shop, they ordered sandwiches and iced tea and put their heads together on what needed to be done for the *Evening Headlines* piece.

"It's absolutely fabulous that Caroline got that video of the marijuana in Remington's cellar," said Annabelle. "Even if the other networks show up here this afternoon, none of them will have that."

"What you did, Caroline, was pretty damned ballsy," said Boomer with grudging admiration.

Lamar winked at Caroline. "Yeah, Boom, not bad for a *little lady,* huh?"

"And let's not forget, we also have an exclusive on Remington's latest portrait of Belinda," said Caroline. "It's disturbing stuff."

"I'd like to see that," said Annabelle.

Caroline handed the camcorder to Lamar, who looked at the tiny viewing screen, scrolling the video back until he came to the pictures of the portrait. He handed the camera over to Annabelle.

"This'll shake our audience up," said Annabelle as she viewed the images. "From the looks of this, our artist isn't so fond of Belinda Winthrop after all. He's made her look like a monster."

"And she's supposed to be the character in *Devil in the*

*Details* in this painting, right?" Lamar said. "Why don't we get the copy of the tape the theater's audiovisual department recorded on opening night? We could show the difference between the artist's interpretation and reality."

"Good idea," said Annabelle. "Let's do that right after lunch."

Caroline sipped her tea and thought about the elements to be covered in the script she'd be writing later. There was the search at Curtains Up this morning, the police going into Gus Oberon's garage and Remington's carriage house, Remington being taken into custody after the police search. And she had the interview she'd done with Belinda in her dressing room right after the opening. That was almost certainly the last video in which Belinda appeared. Though the *Evening Headlines* may have used a clip of it last night, the interview definitely belonged in tonight's piece.

"We should find out what's going on with Remington," said Caroline. "How long will they be able to hold him? What are the charges going to be? Does he have an attorney yet? Do the police think he's guilty of more than stashing marijuana in his cellar? Do they think he has something to do with Belinda's disappearance?"

"You're right, Caroline." Annabelle reached out and put her hand on her colleague's forearm. "We'll have to get to all of that in the piece tonight, but all in good time, my dear."

"Better watch out, Annabelle," Lamar said, smiling. "Caroline is thinking of all the things *you're* supposed to think of."

"I've been noticing that, Lamar," answered Annabelle. "I think Caroline's coming over to the dark side."


AS THEY WERE WAITING for the server to bring the check, Annabelle's cell phone sounded. All three of her companions could hear Linus Nazareth's voice barking into Annabelle's ear.

"I don't have to tell you, do I, how annoyed I am that all this great stuff I hear you've gotten is going to appear first on *Evening Headlines*? *KEY to America* sent you up there, Annabelle. Did you forget that?"

"Of course I didn't forget, Linus," said Annabelle. "But most of the material we have was shot *after* our show this morning. *Evening Headlines* is the next broadcast up."

"Save it," said Linus. "By tomorrow morning all the other networks will be up there and the KEY News exclusive footage will have already aired on *Evening Headlines*. My show will be out of luck. I don't like being out of luck, Annabelle."

"I know you don't, Linus."

"Well, I'm sending Constance Young to host from there tomorrow morning. She's not too happy about working on the weekend."

"All right," said Annabelle. "If that's what you want."

"Yeah, that's what I want. So tell Caroline that Constance will be taking over on this story. If Caroline has decided to play 'girl reporter,' tell her to get used to this. She's being bigfooted."

# CHAPTER 115

IN A CONFERENCE ROOM at the Warrenstown Police Station, Remington sat, with his head in his hands, across the table from his attorney.

"First of all, the search will be determined to be illegal," said the lawyer.

"I don't know," said Remington. "The carriage house is Belinda's property, not mine."

"Yeah, but you're living there. It's your domain. They had no right to go in there and snoop around without a warrant."

"I have no idea how that marijuana got there," said Remington.

The attorney looked skeptically at his client.

"I *don't,*" Remington insisted.

"Of course you don't," said the attorney as he got up. "You're an upstanding member of the community. Now I'm going to see about getting you released, either on bail or on your own recognizance."

# CHAPTER 116

"WE'LL NEED SOME REACTION from townspeople for the piece," said Annabelle as they walked out of the Warrenstown Inn. "Why don't we go to the memorial service for those kids? We can get general shots of the population in mourning and grab a few interviews."

"Oh, I almost forgot," said Caroline. "I told Meg I would look over her speech."

Annabelle didn't say anything, but Caroline got the feeling the producer didn't appreciate the thought of her being distracted from the task at hand.

"It won't take long," she said. "I promise. I'll meet you at the theater at two o'clock."


"THANKS FOR COMING, CAROLINE." Meg's face brightened as she opened the door of her dorm room.

"I said I would, didn't I?"

"I know you did, but I still wasn't sure you'd be able to make it."

"How're you doing on your speech?" Caroline asked.

"Better than I thought I would," said Meg. "But it's a pain having to write in longhand. I hope I'll be able to read my own writing."

"Want me to take a look?" asked Caroline.

"Better yet, why don't I read it to you?"

Caroline pushed the button on the timer portion of her watch and listened for the next six minutes as Meg talked about Amy and how their friendship had developed over their weeks as apprentices. She explained the bond the two had instantly felt when they learned they'd each lost their mothers. She listed Amy's qualities and talents, and spoke of Amy's happiness over her budding relationship with Tommy. She described the pleasure of receiving the e-mails from Amy that documented the fun the young couple had had on the last day of their lives.

"Except for one that wasn't worth using, I've had all the e-mail photos printed on leaflets that will be distributed at the memorial service," explained Meg. "Everyone will be able to see what Amy and Tommy were doing right before they died."


"ALL RIGHT, MEG. GOOD luck and relax. I know you'll do a wonderful job." Impulsively, Caroline leaned over to kiss her stepdaughter on the cheek. To her surprise, Meg didn't pull away.

"What are you going to do about your computer?" asked Caroline.

"Well, it was a couple of years old, and I was going to ask Dad for a new laptop for my birthday anyway. Until then, I can use the ones in the computer lab when I go back to school in the fall," said Meg as she picked up some pages from her desk. "But I wish I'd been printing out my journal entries all along. It's going to be a big pain trying to re-create those so I can get credit for this apprenticeship."

# CHAPTER 117

THERE WASN'T AN EMPTY seat in the theater, and people stood crowded at the rear and a third of the way down the side aisles. All of the Warrenstown Summer Playhouse community and many of the local citizenry came to pay their respects to the deceased apprentices. Each mourner had received a leaflet printed with photographs of Amy and Tommy.

The killer had a seat toward the back and watched as, one by one, people came to the podium to deliver their memories of the young couple. When Meg McGregor began to talk, the killer stiffened, knowing what was going to have to be done when the memorial service was over.

# CHAPTER 118

AS PEOPLE FILED INTO the theater, Meg spotted Caroline with the KEY News crew. She went over to her stepmother and held out her tote bag. "Would you mind holding this for me, Caroline, until after the service?"

But after the memorial, Caroline and her colleagues stationed themselves in a corner of the lobby. Lamar and Boomer recorded B-roll of the mourners and the interviews that Caroline was able to conduct with people willing to talk about Belinda Winthrop's disappearance. Most had heard nothing about Remington Peters's arrest for marijuana possession and were shocked at the news.

Spotting Keith, Langley, and Victoria talking near the doors, Caroline approached. The director, actress, and playwright all seemed tense.

"It was a moving service, didn't you think?" asked Caroline.

"Yes," said Victoria. "I thought Meg, in particular, did a lovely job."

"That's nice of you to say, Victoria," said Caroline. "Meg has been very upset about all this."

"That's understandable," Langley interjected. "I used to see Meg and Amy hanging out together all the time."

"Let's hope we don't find ourselves having to plan a memorial service for Belinda," said Keith. "Victoria just told me that the police came to her with a shoe found in the woods. Victoria identified it as Belinda's. Has anybody heard what's going on with Remington, by the way?"

Caroline nodded. "He's been released on bail. Actually, I'm hoping one of you can help me. We're working on a story for tonight's *Evening Headlines*. We checked with the audiovisual department to get a copy of the tape of the opening night performance of *Devil in the Details* and were told that they can't find the only copy they made."

"That's because I have it," said Victoria. "I wanted to look at it, but I'd be glad to hand it over to you—or better yet, I should give it back to the AV department to make some copies."

"That's wonderful," said Caroline. "But we don't really have the time right now to make a copy. Could I have the original? You have my word, I'll deliver it myself to the audiovisual department when we're through so they can make the appropriate copies."

"Fine," said Victoria. "The tape is out at Curtains Up."

"Great," said Caroline. "We wanted to come out there anyway, to record a stand-up. If that's all right with you."

"I suppose I don't have a problem with that," said Victoria. She turned to look at the director. "Right, Keith? Any publicity is good for the play."

Keith didn't answer.

Caroline turned to Langley. "Yesterday, I said we would like to interview you, Langley. Would you still be willing?"

"Sure I would. When?"

"We have to feed in all our material to New York at about five-thirty. So it would definitely have to be before that. In fact, the sooner the better."

"I have a couple things I have to take care of right now," said Langley. "How 'bout we meet in my dressing room at around four o'clock?"

AS THEY FOLLOWED VICTORIA to Curtains Up, Caroline roughed out a script. She wasn't sure exactly what sound bites she would be using, but she had a general idea of the types of things she would be choosing from her interview subjects' comments. She left spaces in the script for sound from Langley Tate, representing the theater world, two of the mourners to give public reaction to everything that had been happening, and a spot for some sort of reaction from a law enforcement official or perhaps Remington's attorney if they could get that. New York had told Annabelle they were allotting two minutes for the story, a generous amount of time as *Evening Headlines* pieces went.

When they got to Belinda's estate, Victoria had already run inside the farmhouse and retrieved the videotape. She handed it to Caroline through the car's open window.

"All set then?" Victoria asked.

"Yes, this is great," said Caroline. "Thank you. Now, if we can just shoot that stand-up?"

"Sure, go ahead," said Victoria. "But you won't mind if I don't hang around, will you?"

"No, of course not," said Caroline. "We'll be fine."

"More than fine," said Annabelle as they watched Victoria get back into her car and drive away. "I prefer not having anyone breathing down our necks while we work."

"HOLY CRAP," SAID BOOMER. "Is that Remington Peters?"

All four sets of eyes looked in the direction of the carriage house.

"Yep. That's him all right," said Annabelle. "Hurry, Lamar, get some pictures."

The cameraman hadn't waited for the command. He was already recording images of Remington standing in his doorway.

"I'm going to see if he'll talk," said Caroline, starting up the hill.

"I'M NOT SUPPOSED TO talk to you or anybody else," said Remington.

"Is that what your lawyer told you?" asked Caroline.

Remington nodded.

"I can understand that," said Caroline. "But I want you to know that KEY News is doing a story about you tonight on the *Evening Headlines*. You might want to give your version of things."

"I don't watch television."

"Millions of other people do."

"I've long given up caring what other people think," said Remington in a low voice.

"Even if they think that you're responsible for Belinda's disappearance?"

The artist glared at Caroline. After a few moments of consideration, he made a decision. "All right. Have your cameraman come over here."

ANNABELLE SUGGESTED THEY GO inside the carriage house to conduct the interview, but Remington nixed that idea. "It's outside or nothing," he said. "I don't want people seeing my personal space. It's none of their business."

The newspeople agreed, both because they had no other choice and because they didn't want to risk having Remington change his mind about giving an interview at all. Lamar suggested a spot off to the side of the property, next to a pretty maple tree. Boomer wired Remington with a microphone while Lamar framed his shot.

Caroline began. "First of all, what do you say to the fact that the police found boxes of marijuana in your cellar?"

"I certainly had nothing to do with it."

"You have to admit it doesn't look good," said Caroline.

"Haven't you ever heard appearances can be deceiving?"

Caroline answered with another question. "Do you have any speculation about how the marijuana got there?"

"I don't know for sure, but I've seen things at night, things falling from the sky," said Remington. "Maybe that has something to do with it."

Caroline glanced at Annabelle. The producer rolled her eyes.

"What kinds of things?" asked Caroline.

"Boxes."

"Do you think they were the boxes the police found?"

"They could be."

"So these boxes fell from the sky and ended up in your cellar?"

"Someone had to put them there. I didn't," said Remington with decisiveness. "Now that's all I have to say on the matter."

Caroline switched subjects. "What about Belinda Winthrop's disappearance?"

"What about it?"

"Do you have any idea what happened to her?"

Remington's eyes began to water. "I wouldn't want to live in a world without Belinda in it."

"That doesn't really answer the question," said Caroline.

"No, I don't have any idea what has happened to Belinda," said Remington as he began to take off his microphone.

Caroline hurried with her final questions. "What about the new portrait of Belinda Winthrop you're working on? How is that coming?"

"It's incomplete."

"Do you think it will ultimately be a tribute to Belinda? Will it express your feelings about her?"

"My portraits of Belinda are meant to capture her in her roles in Warrenstown each summer, so in that respect, I suppose you could say they're almost historical," said Remington. "And of course, an artist's feelings for his subject influence his work."

Caroline felt uncomfortable, knowing she had video of Remington's disturbing painting of Belinda as Valerie and planned on using it with his last statement in the piece tonight. It wasn't going to make him look good.

But what exactly did Remington's troubling rendition mean?

• • •

"EUREKA!" EXCLAIMED ANNABELLE. "WE have an exclusive with our perp."

"*Alleged* perpetrator," said Caroline. "And, at this
point, Remington is only allegedly connected with the
marijuana in his cellar."

"All right, *alleged*," said Annabelle. "But whatever you
call him, the *Evening Headlines* producers will be
thrilled."

"And Linus is going to be royally ticked off," said
Caroline.

"Don't remind me." Annabelle glanced at her watch.
"Come on. We better get going and record that stand-up.
We still have to interview Langley. Why don't you and
Lamar and Boomer do that, while I go back to the truck
and have the operator bulk-feed the rest of your video to
New York so they can get this thing edited in time?"

# CHAPTER 119

AFTER THE MEMORIAL SERVICE, Meg accepted compliments from several people who were moved, they said, by her words. A group of apprentices approached her, too, and asked if she wanted to go out with them for a beer.

It was the first time any of her Playhouse peer group had sought her out. Instead of begging off and going back to her room, as she instinctively wanted to, Meg forced herself to accept their invitation. If she wanted to have a better social life, she knew she had to make an effort.

She left the theater, forgetting all about the tote she'd given Caroline to hold.

# CHAPTER 120

THIS WAS ANOTHER TYPE of noise, thought Belinda as she strained to listen in the darkness. It wasn't the low growling she'd heard just before she'd so mercifully blacked out. This was a scratching sound coming from above.

The sound was repetitive and persistent. Belinda tried to imagine what it could be. The only thing that came to mind was the image of a dog digging a hole to bury a bone.

She called out, and the scratching sound stopped, only to resume a few minutes later. If it had been a human being up there, a voice would have called back. That meant it was an animal, desperate to get in.

Tears of hopelessness and utter fright trickled from the corners of Belinda's eyes. She was buried alive, and nobody was going to find her. A wild animal was trying to get at her. Belinda groaned as she weighed which way would be better to die.

Belowground, she prayed as the female bobcat above tried to claw her way down to her cubs.

# CHAPTER 121

CAROLINE HOPED THAT MEG would be in the dressing room with Langley Tate when she arrived to interview Belinda's understudy, but she wasn't. Ever aware of the ticking clock, as soon as the crew signaled they were ready to record, Caroline got right to her questions.

"How are you feeling about filling in for Belinda Winthrop again tonight?"

"Of course, I would never want to get a role this way. These are difficult times, and I'm trying to do justice to Belinda and the role of Valerie."

"When was the last time you saw Belinda, and how did she seem?"

"The last time I saw her was at the cast party at Curtains Up on opening night." Langley shook her blond head with disbelief. "My, that was less than forty-eight hours ago. It seems like an eternity. Anyway, she seemed up and happy, for the most part."

"What do you mean 'for the most part'?" asked Caroline.

"At one point, I did see Belinda get pretty angry at her caretaker."

"Gus Oberon?" asked Caroline.

"Um-hmm."

"Do you know why?"

"I think it was because he was coming on to me."

"Why would Belinda be angry about that?"

Langley shrugged. "Maybe she was a little jealous. Maybe Belinda wanted Gus to only pay attention to her."

"Belinda didn't seem to be running short on attention that night, Langley."

Langley shrugged again. "You never know. Some people are never satisfied. They always want more."

Caroline was surprised by how unself-conscious Langley was as she not-so-indirectly maligned Belinda. Wanting to wrap up the interview, she got back to the subject of Belinda's disappearance.

"Do you have any thoughts on what could have happened to Belinda?" she asked.

"Not a one," said Langley, her face serious.

"Okay then, a final question, Langley. What do you envision this unexpected turn of events will do for your own career?"

"Of course, it isn't going to hurt it," said Langley. "It wouldn't be honest to say otherwise. But as I said at the beginning of the interview, I didn't want to get the role this way." Langley stood up. "Now, if we're through, I have some things I have to take care of before tonight's performance."

As she and the crew left to get to the satellite truck, Caroline considered leaving Meg's tote bag so it would be waiting for her when she arrived at the dressing room. But she thought better of it. Meg had entrusted the bag to her, and she would hand it back to Meg herself.

"What did you think of the interview?" asked Caroline as they got in the car.

"I'd hate to have that one breathing down *my* neck," said Boomer. "Langley Tate has ambition written all over her."

# CHAPTER 122

MEG JOINED IN WITH the other apprentices as they toasted Amy and Tommy. She nursed a single beer, conscious of the time and of her responsibilities. She should be clearheaded when she assisted Langley in the dressing room tonight.

As she came out of the dim bar, Meg's eyes adjusted to the brightness of the late-afternoon summer sun. There was still plenty of time before she had to report to the theater. Meg considered going back to the dorm and taking a nap. The anxiety about speaking at the memorial service had left her drained, and just that one beer had made her feel sleepy. But knowing someone had been in her room to steal from her made Meg feel uncomfortable about going back there right now. Plus, her room key was in the tote bag she had forgotten to take from Caroline.

*The greenroom*, thought Meg as she began to walk toward the theater. She could take a nap on the cot in the greenroom.

# CHAPTER 123

THE SATELLITE TRUCK HAD set up in the sprawling parking lot of an enterprising gas station owner. The KEY News team arrived to find that trucks devoted to *Entertainment Tonight*, ABC, NBC, and CBS were parked there as well. Caroline recognized several on-air talents standing outside their respective rigs, some of them talking on cell phones, others checking their BlackBerrys and pacing as they practiced their lines for live transmission at airtime.

"Having the field to ourselves couldn't last forever," said Annabelle.

Inside the truck, Lamar fed almost a half hour of raw video to the KEY News Broadcast Center in New York City while Caroline sent her script to the Fishbowl for approval via computer. She felt relief and satisfaction that the senior producers sitting in the glass-walled *Evening Headlines* nerve center suggested only minor tweaking.

"All set, Caroline?" Boomer held out a lip mike.

Caroline nodded and cleared her throat. "Belinda Winthrop, Remington Peters track for *Evening Headlines* in three, two, one."

Even as she heard herself say the words, Caroline couldn't quite believe she was reporting for the network's flagship broadcast. She, who had no experience in hard news, would be telling millions of people what was going on up here.

*"The Berkshires are known for two things: nature and culture. People who live here year-round, or come to vacation, value beauty and serenity. But in Warrenstown, Massachusetts, home of the legendary Warrenstown Summer Playhouse, loveliness and tranquillity have been shattered this summer. Two young theater apprentices were killed in a car accident last weekend, a town librarian was found murdered Thursday morning, and the Academy, Emmy, and Tony Award winner Belinda Winthrop has been missing for two days.*

"Insert sound bite of woman in theater lobby: *'I can't even let myself think about something happening to Belinda Winthrop. She's been bringing me, and so many other people, happiness for years. She's an extraordinary talent.'"*

Caroline paused to give further editing instructions. "Okay, this is the place to bring up some sound from the video we just fed in of Belinda onstage opening night."

After clearing her throat again, she continued her narration. *"Winthrop has been coming to Warrenstown every summer for the last twenty years. This season, she was starring in the premiere of* Devil in the Details, *a new play that is expected to be headed for literary awards and Hollywood glory.*

"Insert sound bite from interview done with Belinda Winthrop on opening night: *'Imagine being associated with someone who has no conscience. Victoria Sterling has given us a staggering view of the true terror it must be to be joined to a sociopath. I count myself fortunate to be able to interpret this rich and fabulous material.'*

"Back to track: *But after an opening-night performance which was hailed as a triumph, Belinda Winthrop disappeared following a cast party at her home. Today, police and volunteers combed her one-hundred-fifty-acre country estate. One of the actress's shoes was found in the woods. Police also found eighty pounds of marijuana stored in the cellar of a carriage house on Winthrop's property. The carriage house is the home and studio of ac-*

*claimed Berkshire landscape artist and Winthrop portraitist, Remington Peters. He was taken into custody and then released on bail.*

"Edit in my question and his answer," Caroline instructed into the microphone. "I ask: *'Do you have any speculation about how the marijuana got there?'* He answers: *'I don't know for sure, but I've seen things at night, things falling from the sky. Maybe that has something to do with it.'*

"More track: *The artist is known for being reclusive and somewhat eccentric. He came to live on the Winthrop estate after a fire destroyed his previous studio, incinerating all of his portraits of Belinda Winthrop in seventeen successive roles on the Warrenstown Summer Playhouse stage. Peters's latest portrait, of Winthrop as Valerie in* Devil in the Details, *was scheduled to be unveiled this week, but at the last minute, Peters refused to show the work, claiming it wasn't ready. KEY News has obtained exclusive video of the current portrait.*

"Okay," said Caroline. "Cover that last sentence with the video taken with the camcorder of the painting on the easel in Remington's studio, and let it run over the next sentences as well.

"*These alarming images show a character in direct opposition to the role Belinda Winthrop is playing onstage. Valerie is a fear-tortured character as she comes to realize her husband is a sociopath. In Peters's portrait, Valerie looks like the one who is doing the torturing. Remington Peters has never made any secret of the fact that he fell in love with Belinda Winthrop twenty years ago, when they were working together at the Summer Playhouse. The actress rejected him.*

"Now put in the Remington sound bite; pick it up at: *'An artist's feelings for his subject influence his work.'*

"And finally, edit in the stand-up close shot in front of Winthrop's farmhouse with the carriage house in the background.

"*Still, a disturbing painting and some marijuana do not prove anything. It will be up to the police to unravel this case as the search for Belinda Winthrop continues. Caroline Enright, KEY News, Warrenstown.*"

# CHAPTER 124

CHIP MUELLER ALWAYS HAD his breakfast at other people's dinnertime. His job as the night watchman at the storage facility meant that he slept most of the day. When he got out of bed, Chip showered, dressed in his dark blue uniform, then headed to the kitchen to fry up some eggs and sausage. He sat at the kitchen table by himself and watched the *KEY Evening Headlines* as he ate.

This evening Chip watched intently as the reporter told the story of the artist fella in Warrenstown who had the pot stored in his cellar and lived on Belinda Winthrop's property. The story said the man was famous for painting pictures of Belinda Winthrop but most of his work had been destroyed in a fire a few years back.

Chip was pretty certain that the man shown on the television screen was the same guy who had made two trips to the storage facility last night. And those large, flat packages he'd been unloading sure could have been paintings. If they were, why was he putting so many in storage in the middle of the night?

# CHAPTER 125

*KNOWING THAT MEG WOULD* eventually have to come back to the theater, it made sense to check the dressing room first. It was empty.

Considering what to do next, the killer walked down the hallway, glancing into the rest area. The killer silently approached a figure lying on the cot in the greenroom.

There was Meg, sound asleep.

# CHAPTER 126

MEG'S EYES SPRANG OPEN as she felt the hand clamp
down on her mouth. It took her a second to orient herself.
She didn't understand what was going on.

But it quickly dawned on her as she looked into piercing eyes and felt hot breath on her face. Meg struggled to
push her attacker away.

"Don't even try to resist. Do as I say and you won't get
hurt, Meg."

# CHAPTER 127

AFTER THE KEY NEWS people received a good-night from the Broadcast Center, Caroline called Meg but got only her outgoing voice-mail message.

"Meg, it's me. Caroline. I'm sorry I couldn't connect with you after the memorial service to tell you what a good job you did. You were so moving, Meg. I was so proud of you, and I know your dad would have been, too. Let's talk. I still have your tote bag and want to get it back to you. Call me."

Caroline hoped Meg wasn't hurt or annoyed by the lapse. But as she thought more about it, she decided that Meg would just have to understand. While Caroline would hate to think her improving relationship with Meg might be jeopardized, she couldn't allow herself to be intimidated, either. She had a job to do, and she shouldn't have to make apologies for it.

She put away her cell phone and returned to Annabelle, Lamar, and Boomer, who were deep in conversation outside the satellite truck.

"We've got to return the tape of the play to the audiovisual department. After that, we're going to dinner," said Annabelle. "Want to come with us?"

"All right, great," answered Caroline, knowing that Meg would be occupied with her dressing duties for Langley Tate for the next few hours. "Where are we going?"

• • •

IN THE THEATER'S SUBBASEMENT there were many storage areas. Meg found herself in one of them. She was tied up and shaking.

"Tell me where it is," demanded her captor. "Tell me where that script is."

Meg knew exactly where the script was, but if she gave up the information, she would be putting Caroline in danger. She looked into the cold, determined eyes boring into hers. The pupils were dilated, the corneas glassy.

"Don't think I'm fooling around, Meg, because I'm not."

"I don't know what you're talking about." Meg's voice quivered.

"Don't play dumb with me. I know you have it. I can tell from your journal."

"How did you read my journal?" As Meg finished asking the question, it dawned on her. "You stole my computer." The enormity of the realization overwhelmed her. She was face-to-face with the thief who had sneaked into the dorm and come into her room, invading her privacy. Knowing the thief was not just some kid who shared the dorm with her but an adult with an agenda—prepared to abduct Meg just to get a script—was both confusing and terrifying.

"Smart girl, Meg. I guess they don't call you Brightlights for nothing. So be intelligent, and tell me where the script is."

Meg's mind raced, suspecting the script was the thing that was going to keep her alive. If that was turned over, she'd have no leverage.

"I don't have it," she said, trying unsuccessfully to keep the fear out of her voice.

"Maybe you need some time to think it over," said the killer, stuffing a gag into Meg's mouth. "I'm going to leave for a while, but you can sit down here in the dark and reconsider."

# CHAPTER 128

SOMETHING WASN'T LINING UP right, thought Howard Stanley as he sat at his desk in the police station. He'd have thought for sure that, if anyone was working a drug-dealing operation, it would be Gus Oberon, not Remington Peters. With Oberon's history, it would have made a helluva lot more sense if they'd found the marijuana at his place instead of the artist's.

"It's Gus Oberon's parole officer on the line, Chief."

Chief Stanley snatched up the phone. "Thanks for returning my call," he said.

Filling the parole officer in on what had been happening in Warrenstown, and about the cartons of marijuana they'd found in the carriage house at Belinda Winthrop's estate, Chief Stanley shared his uncertainty about the arrest of Remington Peters. "I'm thinking there's a possibility Gus Oberon might have planted that pot in the cellar," he said.

"Well, Gus has seemed to be on the straight and narrow," said the parole officer. "He's been coming for all his appointments and passing his periodic drug tests, but I don't delude myself. A parole officer can be fooled. And Gus Oberon is a very manipulative person who can charm the bark right off a tree."

# CHAPTER 129

AFTER SURVEYING THE PACKED house, Keith and Victoria conferred in the wings before the curtain went up. Belinda's disappearance was not hurting attendance at all.

"I heard one person say that he bought his ticket *because* of all the fuss," said the director. "Maybe things are going to work out after all."

"That's a pretty callous thing to say, Keith, considering all that's happened."

"I know tact isn't my strong suit, Victoria, but you know what I meant. What would you think about Langley in the movie version?"

"You're getting a bit ahead of yourself, aren't you, Keith?"

"Unlike Belinda, at least Langley would jump at the chance to star in *Devil in the Details* on-screen."

"What about financial backing?" asked Victoria. "Langley isn't going to bring in the investors the way Belinda could."

"Yeah, but Langley isn't going to demand the salary Belinda would, either."

"Stop living in la-la land, Keith. Belinda means so much more than Langley. We both know that."

# CHAPTER 130

AFTER DINNER, ANNABELLE ANNOUNCED she was going back to the inn to get some sleep.

"Don't forget, you guys, Constance will be here in the morning. Our host will be expecting us to be bright-eyed and bushy-tailed very, very early tomorrow."

Lamar and Boomer said they still wanted to stop for a drink at the local pub. "Caroline, are you ready to go back now?" Annabelle asked.

"You go ahead, Annabelle. I'm just going to make a short stop at the theater to see Meg before I turn in for the night."

THERE WAS NO ONE in the dressing room when Caroline arrived. She could see on the television monitor that the actors were nearing the end of the first act. She sat down to wait, resting Meg's tote bag on the floor next to the chair.

As she watched Langley on the monitor, she had to admit that the young woman was talented. Not in Belinda Winthrop's league, of course, but with the right opportunities and seasoning, Langley would likely have quite a career in front of her.

The script stuck up from the top of Meg's tote bag. Caroline pulled it out and flipped through the pages, catching up to the spot where the actors were onstage above her. She read along but was confused. Langley's Valerie was reciting the lines of her husband. He was reciting hers.

It must be a misprint, thought Caroline with impatience, slipping the script back in the bag. Where was Meg, anyway? She was supposed to be waiting in the dressing room when Langley arrived at intermission for her costume change.

LANGLEY TORE INTO THE dressing room. Her expression darkened further when she saw that Caroline, not Meg, was the only one waiting.

"She's still not here?" Langley demanded. "Bad enough I had to dress myself for the first act. I damn well expected Meg to be here to help me at intermission."

"What do you mean Meg wasn't here? That isn't like her at all. I hope nothing has happened to her."

Langley shrugged. "Well, if it has, her problem has become my problem. And while we're at it, why did you bother to interview me if you weren't even going to use any of it in your story tonight?"

"Look, Langley. I'm sorry if you're disappointed by not being included in the piece. That's just how it works out sometimes. But I'm more concerned about Meg. I've called her a couple of times and there's been no answer." Caroline scribbled down her own cell phone number. "I'm going over to check her dorm. If she turns up, please call me right away."

ANOTHER APPRENTICE LET HER into the dormitory, but there was no answer when Caroline repeatedly knocked on Meg's door. Caroline canvassed other hall residents. No one had seen Meg since the memorial service that afternoon.

The uneasiness Caroline felt was turning to panic.

# CHAPTER 131

LANGLEY WAS GIVING A better performance tonight than last night, thought Keith as the final scene began. Though the director thoroughly knew the lines, he consulted his script from time to time, marking the passages he wanted to discuss with Langley.

### ACT TWO, SCENE FOUR

*When the lights come up,* DAVIS *has followed* VALERIE *onto the balcony. The sky is riddled with stars, and the moon is bright.* DAVIS *admires the view and then turns his attention to* VALERIE, *who is standing in the center of the balcony.* DAVIS *is frighteningly calm.*

DAVIS:      Why shouldn't these narrow balconies ever be called "widowers' walks"? Do architects not imagine that men who have suddenly found themselves alone in life need a breath of fresh air? (*He looks up at the night sky.*) Are not the stars meant to bring solace to grieving husbands, too?

VALERIE:     I have already told you. I am not going to commit suicide for you, Davis. (*She brings her hand up to her head, teeters dizzily for a mo-*

*ment, and finding the railing with her other hand, steadies herself.*) I've got such an awful head. I had better get to the medicine cabinet.

DAVIS: For what? This? (*He holds up a small paper envelope.*) I don't think I can let you have your medicine, my dear Valerie. I prefer you dizzy and unsteady. Alas, suicides are far too messy. (DAVIS *walks toward* VALERIE *until he is next to her, blocking her exit.*) It will have to be an accident.

VALERIE: (*Holding on to the railing with both hands*) Keep away from me, Davis. I have looked into your eyes lately and seen something horrible, something inhuman and evil. I beg you, if there is a shred of decency left in you, let me pass. And if you refuse me my medicine, at least let me go back inside and lie down.

DAVIS: The night is too beautiful to spend indoors. (*He whispers in her ear.*) Look at how high up we are. Imagine how quickly the end would come if the railing were to give way. What blessed relief it would be to finally have these headaches behind you. (*He begins slowly to shake the railing, loosening it from its moorings.*) Marriage to me has been a living hell, has it not? You want peace, don't you?

VALERIE: Stop it, Davis. Stop it. (*She steps away from the railing and in two steps has her back against the wall.*) I cannot fight you any longer. I surrender, do you hear? I surrender!

DAVIS: (*He finally loosens the railing completely, and it crashes to earth, leaving them both just steps away from the edge. He pulls the revolver from the pocket of his smoking jacket and aims it at his wife.*) Surrender is all I needed to hear, darling. (*He reaches out to*

*her, putting his free hand on her shoulder.)*
Now come. Two small steps and it will be
over. Your surrender will be complete.

*(VALERIE resists DAVIS, pinned to the wall as if by nails. DAVIS
pulls harder while VALERIE fights to stay where she is. DAVIS
finally yanks VALERIE away from the wall, and the two of
them stand tottering on the edge. In a flash, VALERIE rips the
gun from DAVIS's grip, and DAVIS falls, silently, off the balcony. VALERIE stands stricken for a moment and then, tri-
umphant, she EXITS.)*

*LIGHTS OUT. FINAL CURTAIN.*

Yes, Langley was certainly inspiring, thought Keith as
he watched the actors take their bows.

# CHAPTER 132

MEG HEARD HER CELL phone ringing again. The calls
had been coming more and more frequently, and she was
all but certain that it was Caroline, trying to find her.
When she thought of all the times she had ignored or
avoided Caroline's calls in the past months, Meg felt tears
come to her eyes. She tried to get ahold of herself. If she
let herself really cry, the gag would make her choke.

In the darkness, Meg heard the door opening. A shaft
of light seeped into the storeroom. She watched the silhouette approach and reach over to pull the gag out of her
mouth.

"Are you ready to talk yet?"

"I don't have anything to tell you," Meg said.

"I think you should reconsider, Meg. Your friends Amy
and Tommy found out the hard way what happens when
someone crosses me."

Meg finally broke down and began sobbing.

"ALL RIGHT, THAT'S A good girl. Now take your cell
phone and call your stepmother and tell her to bring the
script. Tell her you'll meet her in the laundry room."

Meg hated herself for revealing that she'd left the
script in her tote bag and given it to Caroline. She wasn't

going to compound things by luring Caroline into a trap.

"No," she said. "I'm not calling her."

The killer laughed, snatching the cell phone. "All right, Meg. Have it your way."

# CHAPTER 133

IT WAS DARK, BUT the outdoor lights provided illumination as Caroline watched the *Devil in the Details* audience leaving the theater. She studied the faces in the crowd, hoping that, by some chance, Meg's would be among them. It wasn't.

Caroline knew she should be on her way back to the inn for some sleep, but she also knew she wouldn't be able to rest. Where was Meg?

She took out her cell phone and dialed Nick's number. Disappointed at getting his recorded message, she left one of her own. "Nick, it's Caroline. Will you please call me, honey? It's important."

NOT RELISHING THE IDEA of coming face-to-face with Langley again, but thinking it was worth one more trip to the dressing room, Caroline went back into the building. The halls were quiet, and she passed only an occasional person on the way out for the night.

Langley, her face scrubbed clean, was still in the dressing room.

"Did Meg show up?" asked Caroline.

"No," said Langley, clearly annoyed. "And I hope she has a good excuse, otherwise, I'm going to be requesting someone more responsible to help me tomorrow."

"I'm sure there is going to be a reasonable explanation," said Caroline. "This isn't like Meg."

"I better not find out that she's been out there somewhere, stoned, at my expense," said Langley.

Caroline didn't say anything.

"Yeah, I know she smokes pot," said Langley. "I recognize the signs. I've been there myself."

"Well then, I hope you'll give Meg a break," said Caroline. "She's been through a lot recently." *I should be on top of this,* thought Caroline. *Pay attention, get some professional advice on how to handle this with Meg, find out about getting her some help before the problem gets bigger.* She wanted to be there for her stepdaughter, and now, it seemed, Meg might finally be letting her in a little bit. But where was she?

Langley shrugged and rose from behind the dressing table, turning to leave the room. "Oh, I almost forgot." She opened the drawer and took out the golden chain. "I found this outside the door. I've seen Meg wearing it. You can give it to her when she turns up."

Caroline took the bracelet from Langley, thinking it must have fallen off Meg's wrist just as it had at Belinda's party. But as she studied it, Caroline realized that the faulty clasp was still holding the bracelet together. Instead, the chain had been severed in the middle, as if it had been yanked off.

CAROLINE CALLED THE POLICE and explained her concerns. She felt her chest tighten, sensing she was being politely dismissed.

"Sorry, ma'am. We can't go charging out looking for every college kid who's been missing for a couple of hours."

Trying not to panic, but with a feeling of dread, Caroline started to walk toward the inn. She was at the threshold of the building when her cell phone rang.

"Thank God, it's you," she said.

"What is it? What's wrong?" asked Nick.

"It's Meg. I'm worried something has happened to her." Caroline explained how Meg hadn't shown up for her play duties and told him about the torn bracelet.

"I don't think we should get hysterical, Sunshine."

"I'm not hysterical, Nick. I'm telling you. I really think something is wrong. I just feel it."

The sound on the phone dropped out, and Caroline heard the familiar noise that signaled her battery was running low. Then the connection went dead.


NICK HUNG UP THE phone and paced the room. What if Caroline was right in her suspicions? What if Meg was in danger? Or worse yet, what if something had already happened?

If his daughter was really in trouble, he had a duty to do anything it took to protect her. Should he tell Caroline his secret and risk ruining their marriage?

This was what they meant, he thought, about being caught between the devil and the deep blue sea.


CAROLINE TURNED ON THE television in her room and connected her cell phone to the charger. Not wanting to undress, she went into the bathroom to splash some water on her face. Then she heard her phone beep twice instead of ringing. Caroline held up the screen, which confirmed she was getting a text message from Meg.

IM OK. NEED U @ COSTUME SHOP. BRING TOTE.

*That's doable,* thought Caroline with relief at finally hearing from her stepdaughter. She grabbed Meg's tote bag and headed back to the theater.

As she walked briskly down the deserted sidewalk, she thought of calling Nick to tell him that Meg was all right, but she remembered she had left her phone in the charger.

Besides, he hadn't seemed all that concerned. That had annoyed Caroline, though now it appeared that he'd been right.

No, the call to Nick could wait until she and Meg were together. His daughter could call him herself.


"PLEASE, DON'T PULL MY stepmother into this," Meg pleaded. "She's no threat to you. She doesn't suspect you of anything. There's no reason to get her involved. You just want the script. You don't want her."

The killer considered the young woman's words. Meg could be right. At this point, Caroline Enright wasn't really a danger. And though, as a personal matter, it was inconsequential if Caroline lived or died, from a practical point of view, it would be better to avoid another murder. There had been too many this week, none of them planned in advance. All of them were decided on in minutes; all of them were executed with the instruments available. A car, a letter opener, a silk tie. The killer was proud of the ability to act on impulse and to do, decisively, what needed to be done.

Of course, Daniel's death two years ago was a different matter altogether. That one had taken real deceit and manipulation. The exhilaration of getting away with that had lasted a long, long time.

But Meg must have realized that she herself was going to have to be eliminated because she knew too much. That meant she might try something desperate.

"Tell you what," said the killer. "We'll both go to meet Caroline. You get the script from her and then send her packing. I'm going to be right there listening to both of you. If you don't do exactly as I tell you, Caroline is going to die."


"MEG?" CALLED CAROLINE AS she came to the door of the darkened costume shop. She felt for the switch on the wall. The light revealed mannequins, professional irons, and cutting tables, but no Meg.

Caroline placed Meg's tote bag on top of one of the tables. In the few moments she waited for her stepdaughter, she looked at the script again.

THE KILLER STOOD AT the back of the partially opened closet, holding a pair of scissors grabbed from the sewing supplies, listening to every word.

"There you are." Caroline walked over to Meg and put her arms around her stepdaughter as she entered the room. "Where have you been?"

"I was with a friend," Meg answered dully, pulling herself from Caroline's embrace.

"But you didn't show up for your job tonight, Meg."

"That's not the end of the world," said Meg.

"That's not how Langley sees it. She's pretty irate."

"That's not the end of the world, either," said Meg.

Caroline studied Meg's face. Something wasn't right. Was she stoned? "Langley thinks you might have been getting high."

"I wasn't."

"You don't want to ruin your apprenticeship, Meg."

"I know, Caroline. I know." Meg sighed with exasperation. "I'm tired now. Just give me my bag and I'll talk to you tomorrow, all right?"

As she handed over the tote bag, Caroline felt hurt and disappointed by Meg's attitude. They were right back where they'd started from.

"Well, will you please call your father and let him know you're okay?" she asked.

"I'll call Dad later, Caroline. When I get back to my room."

"I'll walk you back," Caroline offered.

"No, thanks. I'm going to see if I can at least clean up the dressing room before I leave."

"All right, Meg, if that's the way you want it." Caroline

began to walk away. She stopped and turned at the door. "Oh, did you realize your bracelet was missing again? Langley found it lying in the hallway outside the dressing room."

"No big deal," said Meg. "It's just a bracelet."

Caroline walked out, shaking her head.

THE CELL PHONE RANG in Caroline's room at the inn, finally switching to voice mail.

"Hi. It's me. Maybe it's better I'm not getting you, so you can listen to this message and have some time to digest what I'm going to tell you, Sunshine. I might be making a big mistake telling you this, because the mistake I made was two years ago. I'm not proud of it, and I've kept quiet about it for many reasons."

Nick's voice trembled. "But if Meg could be in danger, I have to tell you what I know, what I saw.

"You've been asking me about the party the night that Daniel Sterling died. I've evaded your questions, telling you it was because I didn't want to be reminded of the summer before Maggie died. That was true. But there was more to it, Sunshine. I knew more than I ever told the police. I never told them because I didn't want to hurt anyone—not Maggie, then, or you or Meg, now."

His voice broke.

"The night Daniel Sterling died, I was at Curtains Up, not just at the party but later, after everyone went to bed. I was leaving in the middle of the night when I saw Victoria walking up from the road, back to the house. Obviously, she hadn't been in bed all night, alone, while Daniel went for that ride to cool off that she told the police about.

"I've always suspected that she had something to do with Daniel's death, but I couldn't say anything because then I would have had to explain what I was doing leaving Belinda's in the middle of the night.

"I know it's a lot to digest, Caroline. And I promise I'll try to explain it to you.

"But now, with all that's been happening, I just can't keep this to myself anymore, especially if Victoria Sterling could have something to do with Belinda's disappearance and now that you tell me Meg is missing, too."


NICK HUNG UP THE phone, knowing there was no going back now. In a way, it was a relief, unburdening himself of the shameful secret he had lived with for the past two years.

He'd held himself back from confessing to Maggie before she died, knowing that, while it might have made him feel lighter, he'd only have been hurting her. He'd strayed. Just once. But the effect of that one night was far-reaching.

He could have explained that he'd been celebrating how well the reading of his screenplay had gone, that he'd ended up drinking too much, how radiant Belinda was that night. But Maggie didn't need to hear all that. She was already experiencing searing physical pain and dealing with the knowledge that she wasn't going to get better. How could he add the emotional pain of betrayal and infidelity to that?

As he went to his computer to check airline schedules for a possible flight back to the East Coast, Nick was well aware he had made a mistake. He wished he could take it back, but he couldn't change what had happened with Belinda. Still, if having been at Belinda's that night, and having seen Victoria, enabled him to save his daughter tonight, maybe some good would have come out of something bad.

He prayed that would be the case, and that his future with Caroline wouldn't be ruined by his past.

# CHAPTER 134

IT WAS ELEVEN O'CLOCK when Caroline walked back into the lobby of the Warrenstown Inn. With disappointment, she saw Constance Young standing at the front desk. *Well, that takes care of that,* thought Caroline. She knew she was losing her chance to report the story—her story—now that Constance was here.

"How was your ride up?" asked Caroline.

"I'm exhausted." Constance frowned. "I should have been in bed, asleep, three hours ago."

Caroline waited while Constance finished signing in and then walked with the *KEY to America* cohost to the elevator.

"So what's going on up here?" Constance asked. "Any news on Belinda Winthrop?"

Caroline shook her head. "They still haven't found her, but I heard they're bringing in a canine unit tomorrow."

BELINDA STRAINED TO READ the luminescent numbers on the face of her watch. Was it eleven o'clock in the morning or night?

*It must be night,* she thought. The mother bobcat was still scratching somewhere above her.

• • •

CAROLINE TOOK HER CELL phone from the charger to call Meg again. She didn't care if her stepdaughter was going to be exasperated with her. She just wanted to know that Meg was safely in her dorm room.

As she glanced at the tiny screen, Caroline could see that she had a message waiting. She called her voice mail and played it back, concerned at first, as she listened to the upset in Nick's voice. Then, as she digested what his words meant, she closed her eyes as if that would shut out the pain as they played back in her mind.

"The mistake I made was two years ago. . . .

"I've evaded your questions. . . .

"I couldn't say anything because then I would have had to explain what I was doing leaving Belinda's in the middle of the night."

Caroline thought back to two nights before, and Nick's crestfallen look when Belinda had said she hadn't connected Meg as his daughter despite the McGregor name. Later, at the party, Belinda had been momentarily flustered when Nick had commented that he was having almost as much fun as the last time he'd been at Curtains Up—two years before.

The night he'd slept with Belinda Winthrop.

Caroline sat on the edge of the bed, trying to focus her thoughts. Nick had been unfaithful to Maggie. He could be unfaithful to her. He had lied to his first wife. He could be lying to her. But even as disillusionment, hurt, and anger gripped her, Caroline knew this wasn't the time to analyze their relationship or even begin to decide what she was going to do with this gut-wrenching information. Unless Nick actually wanted to try to destroy their marriage, he would have no reason to make up this story about Victoria Sterling.

Nick had seen Victoria walking up the driveway at Curtains Up on the night Daniel Sterling was thought to have been by himself when he suffered a fatal accident. Victoria had lied to the police about that.

The two apprentices had died in another car accident. At least, it *looked* like an accident. What if it wasn't?

Could Victoria Sterling actually have had something to do with that? She was a renowned playwright at the top of her game. She was a likely candidate for a Pulitzer Prize.

Caroline's thoughts turned to the script she'd been looking at in the costume shop just a little while ago. Everything had been reversed. Valerie's lines were marked for Davis, Davis's lines for Valerie. Caroline had written the confusion off to typographical errors. But what if it wasn't? What if there had been another version of *Devil in the Details*? What if the play that was being acted out on the Warrenstown Summer Playhouse stage was not the one that had been written originally?

Caroline's mind sped back to the night of the party at Curtains Up, when Belinda had asked Meg to take the script from her. She had just come from Remington's carriage house. Was that why Remington's portrait of Belinda was so disturbing and so different from the role she seemed to be playing on the stage? Had he worked from the wrong copy of the play? An earlier version perhaps, a version in which the wife was the sociopath and the husband the victim? A version that Victoria Sterling had not written?

If Belinda had figured out that there was another version of the play, would Victoria have felt she had to get rid of her?

And why would Meg have just said that losing her bracelet was no big deal? She treasured that bracelet. Was she saying something so outrageous as a way of signaling something was wrong?

Suddenly, it was crucial that she get in touch with Meg. Caroline pushed the buttons, but no one answered Meg's cell phone.

• • •

HER MOUTH WAS COTTON-dry; the gag pushed against the back of her throat. As she tried not to cough, Meg wished she had shouted out in the costume shop. She should have called to Caroline. They could have taken their chances against the deranged, chain-smoking woman who stared at her now. Meg could feel a bead of perspiration dripping down her side as she listened to the latest declaration.

"We're going to wait until we're good and sure that everyone is sound asleep for the night, and then we're going to take a little ride."


THE PHONE RANG IN Annabelle's room.

"Hello," she answered groggily.

"It's me. Caroline. I need your help."

Annabelle sat up and turned on the light. "What's wrong?"

"I think Victoria Sterling might have had something to do with Belinda's disappearance. It's too long to go into now, but can you please get over to Meg's dorm and see if she's there? Bang on the doors and wake the whole place up if you have to. I'm going back to the theater to see if I can find Meg there."


CAROLINE SHOOK THE HANDLES, desperate to get inside. The front doors of the theater were locked. She banged on the glass, but no one came.

She looked around for help. The grounds were completely deserted. Trying to think clearly, she decided to try the back doors. As she came around the corner, her worst fears were realized when she saw the two figures coming out of the rear of the building.


MEG FELT THE POINT of the scissors pressed against her back as she was escorted down the ramp that sloped from the rear of the theater to the entrance of the parking deck.

*"Meg!"*

She had never been happier to hear a voice in her whole life. Meg turned to see Caroline running toward her. Victoria turned to look as well.

In that instant, Meg broke away, running just three or four feet before Victoria realized what was happening. The older woman propelled herself forward and lunged at Meg, pinning her to the ground. Victoria poised the scissors at Meg's neck, the sharp points pressed against her jugular. Victoria struggled to her feet, forcing Meg to stand up with her.

"Get over here," Victoria called to Caroline, "or I'll slice her throat right now. And don't try anything funny, because you'll be amazed how fast I can move."

"Like you did with that poor librarian." Caroline felt her pulse pounding.

"What happened to her was her fault. She should have minded her own business."

"I guess those poor kids deserved what they got, too?" asked Caroline, stalling for time as she tried to figure out what to do.

"Again. Their fault, not mine. They shot themselves in the foot with technology, taking a picture that could have made me look bad," said Victoria. "How would it look to the Pulitzer Prize committee? When you're aiming at a world-class award, you don't need any adverse publicity."

Caroline was stunned at the lack of emotion in Victoria's voice. It was as if she was attaching no value to her victims' lives. "It must be nice when nothing is ever your fault," she said. "When you're able to justify anything you do, even murder. How does it feel, never having to worry about right and wrong?"

"Quit stalling and get over here," commanded Victoria, pressing the scissors more tightly against Meg's neck. "Don't think I'm kidding."

Seeing the stricken look on Meg's face, and with no other choice, Caroline did as she was told.

ANNABELLE JOGGED FROM THE dorm to the theater. She hoped that Caroline had found Meg, because the young woman wasn't in her room.

As she ran up the path that led to the main entrance of the Playhouse, she noticed a Volvo pull out of the driveway from the parking deck.

# CHAPTER 135

INSIDE THE CAR TRUNK, Caroline and Meg were pressed together, barely able to move. Caroline could hear her stepdaughter whimpering in the darkness.

"Meg," she whispered, "try to get ahold of yourself, honey, please. There must be a way we can get out of this."

"How?" Meg cried. "When we get to wherever she's taking us, she's going to kill us. Maybe she'll get a gun. . . . Maybe she'll just leave us in here to suffocate."

"Stop it, Meg," hissed Caroline. "Stop it right now. We've got to figure out what we're going to do to get away from her."

The car took a curve in the road. Caroline and Meg were pushed closer together. It was then that Caroline spotted the thing that could lead them to safety.

FIRST CAROLINE ENRIGHT, THE girl's stepmother; then Nick McGregor, the girl's father; and now Annabelle Murphy, a producer for KEY News. That made three callers worried about Meg McGregor, a Warrenstown Summer Playhouse apprentice. Nick McGregor and the KEY News producer both claimed that Victoria Sterling might have something to do with the girl's disappearance, as well as Belinda Winthrop's. That was enough to convince the night officer to call Chief Stanley at home.

• • •

"WHEN THE CAR STOPS, we should be able to hear her walking around to the trunk. Just as she gets here, we'll surprise her."

"What if she doesn't come back here?" whispered Meg. "What if she goes off to get something better than a pair of scissors to kill us with?"

"Sooner or later, she'll come to us," Caroline whispered with more conviction than she felt.

WITH ONE HAND ON the steering wheel, Victoria leaned over and unlocked the glove box, fumbling through its contents. Underneath the driver's manual she'd never bothered to read, she felt the cool metal handle of her gun.

When you had two troublemakers to deal with, a pair of scissors just wouldn't do it.

THEY COULD HEAR THE difference in sound as the car turned off the smooth macadam of the roadway onto the crushed stone.

"I think she's taken us to Curtains Up. We're on the driveway," whispered Caroline. She told Meg her plan and then insisted, "Now, no matter what happens, Meg, I want you to stay here in the trunk."

The Volvo pulled to a stop. The driver's door opened and then closed.

Caroline's hand gripped the fluorescent safety release handle on the inside of the trunk lid.

CHIEF STANLEY LISTENED TO his night officer's report.

"Only time will tell if that kid is really missing," Stanley concluded, "but if Victoria Sterling has had something to do with Belinda Winthrop's disappearance, we can't afford to wait until morning."

• • •

THE SOUND OF THE footsteps stopped outside the trunk.

*"Now,"* whispered Caroline. She pushed upward on the trunk lid with the only arm she could move, while Meg was able use her foot to kick outward. It was enough to catch Victoria off guard, and she fell back, hitting her head on the ground.

Caroline and Meg struggled to untangle themselves while Victoria faltered, trying to clear her head. As she came to a sitting position, Caroline spotted the gun still clutched in Victoria's hand.


THERE WAS NO ANSWER on either Caroline's cell or hotel room phone, and Annabelle was worried.

Maybe the cops were going to follow up on her call and maybe they weren't, but Annabelle wasn't going to wait around any longer.

Still, she didn't want to go to Curtains Up by herself. She called Lamar and Boomer, waking them up, and told them to get dressed.


CAROLINE'S STRUGGLE TO GET her balance as she climbed out of the trunk gave Victoria enough time to get to her own feet. The two women found themselves standing face-to-face, just a few yards apart. Victoria took aim at Caroline.

"You can shoot if you want, but that would be awfully stupid of you," Caroline shouted. "I've already told KEY News about my suspicions that you had something to do with Belinda's disappearance."

Victoria shook her head. "Suspicions aren't proof. Nobody was ever convicted on suspicions."

"The police will be interested, Victoria, when KEY News tells them I thought you were linked to Belinda—and a witness tells them that he saw you walking up from the road in the middle of the night that your husband died—at the time you said you were sleeping alone in your bed."

"I don't believe you. If there was a witness, why didn't he come forward then? Who's this witness of yours?"

Caroline was conscious that Meg could hear her. She wanted to shield her stepdaughter, but no matter what happened tonight, it was all going to come out eventually. Nick would go to the police, and people would learn that he'd been unfaithful to his wife. There would be nasty gossip about it, but ultimately, only Caroline and Meg would be truly hurt. They'd only be hurt, though, if they survived. If the information might help save them, then it had to be used.

"Nick saw you."

"Nick McGregor?"

"Yes," said Caroline. "You killed your husband that night. It wasn't an accident, was it?"

Victoria shifted her weight from one foot to the other before she spoke. "I was tired of sharing the limelight, tired of everyone thinking that *he* was the talent and I was just hanging on. Once I read the play that he'd been working on alone, I knew I wanted it to be mine."

"So you killed him."

"Some might view it that way." Victoria shrugged. "But Daniel hadn't been taking care of himself all summer. He wasn't getting enough rest or eating the right things, and he was drinking way too much. He couldn't get away with that because of his diabetes. After the party that night, he felt very weak, and when he went to get his insulin, there wasn't any left. He hadn't been keeping track."

"I would think you would have. An observant wife would have," said Caroline.

"Actually, I did know he was running low. I'd been waiting for just that opportunity." A smile came to Victoria's face. "It takes a while to die from low blood sugar, though, and time was the one thing I didn't have. Someone could have come to Daniel's rescue. So I . . ." She seemed to relish the next words. "So I just helped things along."

Despite the danger she was in, Caroline found herself fascinated as Victoria matter-of-factly recounted her story, showing no sorrow whatsoever.

"I told him I'd drive him to the hospital, and along the way, he got drowsy and then fell asleep. When we got to a nice, dark, deserted stretch of road, it was so easy to pull over and quietly open the car door. Once outside, all I had to do was reach in, put the car back in drive, and shove it over the edge."

"But it looked like Daniel had been the driver when they found him, didn't it?" Caroline coaxed.

"Yes, and that was the beauty of it. I climbed down into the gully to make sure he was dead and try to drag him over to the driver's side of the front seat, but the car had toppled in such a way that Daniel's body had shifted and he was already behind the steering wheel. After that, all I had to do was get home without anyone seeing me," Victoria stated with pride.

Dr. Margo Gonzalez's *KTA* segment flashed into Caroline's mind. Victoria had shown no emotion as she described destroying four lives. She was taking an enormous risk recounting what she had done, but she did so, defiantly. She'd lied, manipulated, stolen, and murdered. Still, Victoria stood before her, bragging about it all, showing absolutely no remorse.

Victoria Sterling was a sociopath. She had no conscience.

The realization terrified Caroline, but she used all her determination not to show it. "So, it was as easy as that," she said mockingly.

Victoria's finger tightened on the trigger. "You are too smart for your own good, Caroline. Just like Belinda was. I still don't know where the script that gave me away came from."

"Belinda got it from Remington Peters."

Victoria seemed to be digesting the information. "Daniel must have given Remington an early version," she said.

*And Remington was working off that,* thought Caroline as she recalled the murderous expression on the face of his painting of Belinda's Valerie.

"Where is she, Victoria?" asked Caroline. "What did you do to Belinda?"

Victoria didn't answer. She had turned her head in the direction of the sound coming from the distance. Sirens were growing closer.

Caroline took advantage of the distraction. She lunged for the gun, grabbing it by the barrel with both hands and forcing Victoria's arm into the air. As the two women wrestled for control of the weapon, Victoria pulled the trigger, and Meg screamed from inside the trunk when the bullet hit the back window of the Volvo.

With the sirens wailing louder and louder, Caroline forced Victoria to loosen her grip on the gun. It flew wildly out of Victoria's hand, skittering across the gray stones and settling beneath the car.

Knowing there wasn't enough time to retrieve it, Victoria pushed Caroline to the ground.

"Get out, Meg. *Now!*" screamed Caroline as she landed hard on the sharp stones.

Meg scrambled out of the trunk, tumbling onto the ground just as Victoria ran to the front of the Volvo, got in, and sped down the driveway.

# SUNDAY

*August 6*

# CHAPTER 136

CAROLINE AND ANNABELLE STOOD by while the satellite truck operator fed the video to New York.

"Great stuff, great stuff," Linus roared with enthusiasm from the Broadcast Center as he watched the images of red lights flashing against the night sky, milling law enforcement officers, and a late-model Volvo nose-down in a ditch, having been forced off the road by pursuing police cars. Victoria Sterling was seen being taken from the car and, able to walk on her own, being escorted to the backseat of a police vehicle.

"Nice work," said the executive producer. "Do we know if she's told the police anything about Belinda Winthrop?"

"If she has, the cops aren't telling us," said Annabelle. "But why would Victoria Sterling incriminate herself? Maybe her lawyer will swap information on the whereabouts of Belinda's body for a plea bargain or something, but at this point Victoria wouldn't be acknowledging her participation in anything."

"All right," said Linus. "But keep on top of it with the police."

"Of course," said Annabelle. "And, Linus, I think Caroline should be the one on air to report this story."

"No go," Linus answered. "Constance is up there. It's got to be hers. But let's use Caroline as an eyewitness."

• • •

POLICE SEARCHED VICTORIA STERLING'S bedroom at Curtains Up. A computer owned by Meg McGregor was found at the back of the closet.

Chief Stanley waited while the German shepherd's handler prepared the dog, making her familiar with Belinda's scent.

"How that dog is gonna be able to home in on Belinda Winthrop is a mystery to me," said the chief. "People have been all over this property."

"Sure. It definitely would have been better if you'd had Daisy in here first," replied the handler. "But she's a busy lady, and she can't be in two places at one time. She found a little boy who'd wandered away from home in Lenox yesterday."

"Let's hope she can find Belinda Winthrop today," said Chief Stanley as he bent down to pet the tracking dog. "If she's out there, we have to find her, and if she's alive, she'll need medical attention."

"Sir, if there's a chance in hell a dog can find her, Daisy will."

THE SUNDAY MORNING EDITION of *KEY to America* opened with an exclusive KEY News shot of Victoria Sterling in handcuffs as she was ushered into the Warrenstown Police Station, while Constance Young's voice narrated.

"Is Belinda Winthrop alive? And will this woman reveal where the actress is? Police are trying to find out this morning, Sunday, August sixth."

Lamar's camera transmitted the images to the satellite truck, which in turn sent them to the Broadcast Center and on to viewers all around the world. Constance stood in front of the Warrenstown theater. Reporters from the other news networks and syndicated entertainment shows were scattered in various positions on the lawn. Most of them had already approached Annabelle to see if KEY News would share the video shot by Lamar and Boomer the night before, video the others had missed. The answer was a firm no. *KEY to America* was keeping the exclusive for itself.

While Constance recapped the events of the last days, Caroline waited for her cue to join the cohost.

"With us this morning is KEY News film and theater critic Caroline Enright, who has been up here this week covering the Warrenstown Summer Playhouse, where her stepdaughter is apprenticing this summer. Caroline, you found yourself right in the middle of this thing. Tell us about it."

Caroline summarized the pertinent points.

"So, Victoria Sterling admitted to you that she killed her husband two years ago, ran those two apprentices off the road, murdered the town librarian, and was responsible for Belinda Winthrop's disappearance?" Constance asked.

Caroline nodded. "Of course, everyone is innocent until proven otherwise, but yes, Victoria Sterling admitted all that to me. My stepdaughter heard it as well."

"And what was her reason?" asked Constance. "What could her motive have been?"

"I'd say ego and greed," said Caroline. "She wanted to take credit for writing *Devil in the Details,* the play her husband had actually written. She wanted the praise, attention, and money that writing a Pulitzer Prize–winning play warrants. Nothing was going to get in her way."

AS SOON AS CAROLINE walked out of camera range, her cell phone sounded.

"Hi, Sunshine."

"Hi, Nick."

"You did a great job just now."

"Thanks. Almost as good a performance as you and Belinda Winthrop in her dressing room and at her party the other night. No one would ever have suspected a thing."

"Caroline, I want to explain."

"It's not something I really want to talk about on the phone," said Caroline. "This should be done face-to-face."

"I'm wrapping it up out here," said Nick. "I think I can be back in New York tomorrow morning."

"You know, Nick, even though what happened was before we were together, I'm scared. I'm afraid I won't be able to trust you. If you were unfaithful to Maggie, you could be unfaithful to me." She carefully considered her next words. "Yet, if you hadn't come clean, if you hadn't spoken up about Victoria when you did . . ." Her voice trailed off.

"Please, Caroline. Let's not go there. All that matters is that you and Meg are safe. But I hope we'll be able to work things out between us. I love you, Caroline."

"I hope we'll be able to work it out, too, Nick. But in the meantime, you better think about what you're going to say to Meg."


"IN RELATED NEWS, ALBANY police confiscated seventeen oil paintings from a storage facility there. The paintings are reported to be the bulk of the Belinda Winthrop portrait collection, thought to have been destroyed by a fire at artist Remington Peters's studio three years ago."

Constance shifted positions. "Police were tipped off by a viewer who saw a KEY News story last night about the artist, who was arrested yesterday after eighty pounds of marijuana were found in his cellar. The viewer, a night watchman, recognized Peters as the man who had moved the paintings into the storage facility in the middle of the night.

"Peters collected nearly four million dollars in insurance payments for those paintings."

# CHAPTER 137

DAISY CAME OUT OF the farmhouse, put her long nose to the ground, and traveled directly to the garage. She went to the parked golf cart and gave a heads-up reaction.

"What is she trying to tell us?" asked Chief Stanley.

"Not sure. It could just mean that Belinda had driven the cart," said the handler.

Chief Stanley clenched his jaw. "Or it could mean that she was transported in it against her will."

HELICOPTERS, LEASED BY NEWS stations and entertainment shows, circled the skies over Belinda Winthrop's property. Inside, photographers aimed their cameras, getting aerial shots of the farmhouse, the carriage house, the garage, and the meadow.

The photographers saw the men coming out of the garage. They trained their cameras on the tiny figures and watched as the even smaller creature led them across the meadow, toward the woods.

THERE WERE MANY FOOTPRINTS on the mossy floor of the woods, but only one scent belonged to the person the German shepherd was looking for. Starting at the spot where Belinda Winthrop's shoe had been found by searchers the day before, Daisy's long nose skimmed the ground.

"If Belinda wasn't traveling by foot, how will the dog be able to find her?" called Chief Stanley as he followed a few feet behind.

"Even if she was carried or driven or whatever out here, eventually she would have to be deposited somewhere," said the handler as he kept his eyes on the dog. "If she was dragged at all, it will have caused ground disruption and chemical breakdowns, creating scent patterns. In other words, it's possible for Daisy to find her. Not easy, but possible."

BELINDA'S PULSE QUICKENED AS she thought she heard a noise from above. At first, she was terrified, thinking it was the mother bobcat scratching to get in again. But the sound was different this time. It was similar, but different.

She tried to call out, but her voice was only a croak.

DAISY'S HEAD SHOT UP, and her moist nose flared.

"Got something, girl?" asked her handler.

The dog walked round and round on the spot, the nails of her paws scratching against what was left of the dirt and leaves that disguised the plywood covering the opening to the underground cave.

"Hey, Chief, look at this."

AFTER HER DAYS IN the blackness, the shaft of light slicing into the darkness forced Belinda to close her eyes. She heard a male voice calling from above.

"Hello. Ms. Winthrop? Are you all right?"

Slowly, Belinda permitted herself to open her eyes just a bit. Through the slits, she could see the blurred outlines of heads looking down at her.

"It's all right now, Ms. Winthrop. It's all right. We're gonna get you out of there."


CHIEF STANLEY NOTICED THE cigarette butt that lay on the ground next to the cave opening. He pulled a pair of latex gloves from his pocket and put them on. Then he picked up the cigarette and slid it into an envelope.

If the butt had Victoria Sterling's DNA on it, prosecutors would have a nice little piece of evidence that could place her at the crime scene.

# CHAPTER 138

TEN MINUTES BEFORE THE broadcast was scheduled to end, the Warrenstown police announced that Belinda Winthrop had been found in an uncharted underground cave on her property. Constance Young was able to report on *KEY to America* that the actress was alive.

# EPILOGUE

WHEN BELINDA WOKE UP, Keith Fallows was sitting beside her hospital bed.

"Thank you for coming, Keith."

"Langley wanted to come, too, Belinda, but you know, she has the matinee."

"It's nice that you came, though," Belinda said softly. There were scratches on her face, and her bottom lip was split. Her blond hair lay limply on the pillow. An IV line fed into her arm. "I know you hate to miss a performance."

"They don't really need me now. The company knows what it's doing."

"How did Langley perform?" asked Belinda.

"Better than you might expect," said Keith. "She's not you, of course."

Belinda smiled.

AFTER LUNCH, AS THE crew car traveled south to the Berkshire Medical Center, Caroline was conflicted about interviewing Belinda Winthrop. Her professional side was delighted that the actress had agreed to give her an exclusive interview, but knowing that Belinda had been with Nick was exceedingly discomfiting.

The parking lot and sidewalk in front of the hospital were jammed with reporters, camera crews, and live-shot trucks. The crowd of newspeople groaned in protest as Caroline, Annabelle, Lamar, and Boomer were waved on, allowed to walk straight into the lobby, up to the front desk, and on to Belinda's room.

"My doctors don't think this is a good idea," said the actress as Boomer took special care in clipping a microphone to her hospital gown. "But I insisted. From what everyone's been telling me, I have a lot to thank you for, Caroline."

"The dog found you, not me," said Caroline.

"But because of you, Victoria Sterling is going to get what she deserves. You stopped her."

"Nick's daughter, Meg, had a lot to do with it, Belinda."

The two women looked directly into each other's eyes.

"It didn't mean anything, Caroline. Believe me, it didn't. And we both regretted it afterwards."

BELINDA TALKED ABOUT HER time in the cave, about coming in and out of consciousness, about the bobcat cubs and her fear that she would never be found. She had already been instructed by the police that, because of pending legal proceedings, she should not give any details of Victoria Sterling's attack on her.

"What do you think about the seventeen Remington Peters portraits of you being found?" asked Caroline.

"I'm glad they weren't destroyed, but it makes me sad to think Remington could have deceived everyone and collected all that insurance money." Belinda's expression grew solemn. "He called a little while ago, and he says he did it because he couldn't stand the whole world gaping at me. God help him. He told me he'd given all the money to charity. And to tell you the truth, I'd be willing to compensate the insurance company with my own funds if they don't press charges."

"And what about the marijuana the police found in his cellar? Did you ever think that he was dealing in drugs right on your property?" asked Caroline.

"No," said Belinda firmly. "But I do have my suspicions about someone else, and I've shared them with the police."

ANNABELLE TOOK THE INTERVIEW tape to the satellite truck to feed it to New York while Caroline went back to the Warrenstown Inn to try to get some rest. The evening broadcast wanted her to do a live two-way, and having had no sleep at all overnight, she needed a nap to be able to function.

No sooner had she put her head on the pillow than her phone rang.

"It's me. Meg. Can I come up?"

"Sure, honey."

Caroline had time to splash some water on her face and run a brush through her hair before Meg knocked on the door.

"Come on in." Caroline held the door open wide.

Meg stepped across the threshold and threw her arms around her stepmother. "I just wanted to thank you," she said. "If you hadn't come looking for me when you did, I think Victoria really would have killed me."

"Let's not even think about that, Meg," whispered Caroline, hugging her stepdaughter back.

"It's like a bad dream," said Meg as she and Caroline took seats on the edge of the bed.

"I know," said Caroline. "But it's over now."

Meg looked down and wrung her hands in her lap. "Part of it's not," she said.

"You mean about your father?"

She nodded. "I guess I shouldn't be talking about this to you, of all people, but I just can't believe that Dad would have cheated on Mom with Belinda. I just can't believe that. I idolized her." Meg paused. "I idolized him," she said softly.

"Even the best of us make mistakes, Meg," Caroline said softly.

"So you're all right with it? You can forgive him?"

"I'm not sure, Meg. I hope so, but it's going to take some time to be able to put things in perspective. I do know that making a decision one way or the other right now wouldn't be fair to anyone."

Meg looked up. "I really hope that you and Dad *can* work it out, Caroline."

"I do, too, honey."

AFTER MEG LEFT, CAROLINE lay down again. She was exhausted. All the tension and worry and lack of sleep had caught up with her.

*I've got to get some rest,* she thought, rubbing her burning eyes. But she found herself staring at the ceiling, thinking of Nick and what their future was going to be. There were things that had to be ironed out between them, but Caroline wanted to try to be optimistic. They had so much that was good in their relationship. Nick had made a mistake, and he had admitted it. He was sorry for it. What more could he really do now? It was going to be up to her to get past this. In her heart, she wanted to.

Caroline closed her eyes, trying to relax, but the events of the last days sped through her mind. What would they mean for her future at KEY News? If Linus was going to continue to give her a hard time, so be it. She had to tell the truth as she saw it, even if it didn't always please her boss. But these days in Warrenstown had given her a different view of things. Maybe there were other opportunities for her. If she really wanted to, it wouldn't be too late to switch directions and try reporting.

Caroline turned over on her side and fluffed the pillow, knowing, if she wanted to fall asleep, she'd have to turn off the dialogue in her head and try to think of something pleasant, something positive.

*Meg.* In the midst of everything, she and Meg had been able to work things out. Their breakthrough meant Caroline could look forward to having the kind of relationship she had hoped for with her stepdaughter. She couldn't, and didn't want to, take the place of Meg's mother, but she could be a good friend. Caroline knew what it was like to feel alone, and she didn't want that for Meg. She hoped she'd be able to support Meg as she straightened herself out, finished school, and went on to find her way in life.

Caroline hadn't slept in thirty-two hours. Now, she finally could.

# Acknowledgments

THERE WOULD BE NO *Lights Out Tonight* without Eliza-beth, my daughter. Her summer apprenticeship at the Williamstown Theatre Festival led to recurring trips to the Berkshires. Each visit left me more convinced that I wanted to tell a story set in this unique and memorable area. Throughout the research for and writing of this book, Elizabeth was a source of much enthusiasm and in-sight.

For this production, many who worked behind the scenes now deserve a hand. A round of applause to the cast at St. Martin's Press. Jen Enderlin, my thoughtful and creative editor, offered so many good suggestions. I am grateful for Jen's expert direction. To Sally Richard-son, Matthew Shear, Ed Gabrielli, John Karle, John Mur-phy, Kim Cardascia, Jerry Todd, who designed the cover, and Tom Hallman, who illustrated it, my sincere thanks. Once again, I was truly fortunate to have the benefit of Susan M. S. Brown's fine copyediting.

Joni Evans and Jennifer Rudolph Walsh should take their bows for their unflagging support. They are good critics and keen mentors. I know I am lucky to have them guiding my writing career.

As ever, Father Paul Holmes was waiting in the wings, ready to assist in so many, many ways. Sounding board, wise man, and loyal friend, Paul never misses a cue. For this story in particular, he contributed his theatrical knowledge, talent, and flair.

Stephanie LaRiviere shared her experiences as an apprentice dresser with me, explaining how actors are readied for the stage. Stephanie's recollections helped me quite a bit.

Ann Ames and Joan Andriani were forthcoming and generous with their time as they assisted me with research. Their positive spirits are contagious.

Beth Tindall gets strong reviews for keeping maryjaneclark.com running. Thanks to Beth it's current as well as inventive. Thumbs up to Colleen Kenny for adapting *Lights Out Tonight* into the Web site's mini-movie.

*The Sociopath Next Door,* by Martha Stout, Ph.D., aided me in my research on people with no conscience.

Finally, a standing ovation for Peggy Gould. She communicated with me almost every single day, giving me the peace of mind I needed to be able to write this story. I will always be grateful, Peggy.

So now the curtain comes down on *Lights Out Tonight*. To the friends and family I've neglected, thank you for your patience with me. Now we can go to the show.

CPSIA information can be obtained at www.ICGtesting.com
Printed in the USA
LVOW11s1018090214

372939LV00001B/1/P

9 781250 057761